The Way Back to You

James Bailey was born in Bristol, and currently lives and works in his home city. A graduate of King's College London, James has previously carried the Olympic Torch, made a speech at the House of Commons, and worked as a red-carpet reporter. *The Way Back to You* is his second novel. His debut, *The Flip Side*, has been published in eleven languages. Find out more about James on www.JamesBaileyWrites.com, or on Instagram @JamesBaileyWrites.

By the same author

The Flip Side

The Way Back to You

JAMES BAILEY

PENGUIN BOOKS

PENGUIN BOOKS

UK | USA | Canada | Ireland | Australia
India | New Zealand | South Africa

Penguin Books is part of the Penguin Random House group of companies
whose addresses can be found at global.penguinrandomhouse.com.

Penguin
Random House
UK

First published 2022
001
Copyright © James Bailey, 2022
The moral right of the author has been asserted

Set in 12.5/14.75pt Garamond MT Std
Typeset by Jouve (UK), Milton Keynes
Printed and bound in Great Britain by Clays Ltd, Elcograf S.p.A.

The authorized representative in the EEA is Penguin Random House Ireland,
Morrison Chambers, 32 Nassau Street, Dublin D02 YH68

A CIP catalogue record for this book is available from the British Library

ISBN: 978–1–405–94573–8

www.greenpenguin.co.uk

For Mum, Dad, and Rebecca

I

I sometimes wonder if all the difficult guests secretly conspire to stay on the same night.

In our small B&B, in a sleepy Dorset village – or 'quaint', as the travel guide would say – we can go for weeks without having a single nuisance customer, but then, like London buses, they all arrive together.

And I mean together.

They are free to check in at any time between 3 p.m. and 7 p.m., but no, the five separate couples all choose 6.55 p.m. precisely to descend on the reception, giving the last couple a reason to start huffing and puffing as soon as they join the back of the queue.

Clearly it's all part of their plan.

Today has just been one of those days.

It didn't start very well. Mrs Cook (our cook) had one of her usual tantrums during breakfast. Her name made me believe she would be well-suited to the role, but it seems she doesn't actually like cooking. In her own words, she 'doesn't have time' for people with dietary requirements. So when she plonked an egg on the plate of one of our vegan guests, I had to scurry into the kitchen and create an alternative dish myself.

And then Daisy, our housekeeper, didn't show up to work. Again.

Although, truthfully, that is often advantageous. When she cleans she seems to leave the rooms in a messier state than the guests. I only gave her the job because she's Sue in the Post Office's daughter and she needs to earn some money before she goes to university.

My daughter, Anna, who I run the place with, has got the weekend off. Her wedding is in a few months' time, and she and her fiancé, Ollie, have gone into town to visit the florists so I could hardly disturb them for help.

Once I'd sorted out the breakfasts and cleaned the rooms – the couple in Room 2 kindly left me whipped cream and oil stains as a parting gift – a coach-load of tourists turned up wanting afternoon tea in the gardens, swearing that they'd booked. I didn't have anything written down, so maybe my memory is starting to go, or they'd booked through one of these new-fangled websites that Anna signed us up to. I'd already let Mrs Cook go home for the day, so I had to cater for all twenty-four of them – and then do all the washing up.

Which brings me to now and I realize that I've not had the chance to sit down all day. No wonder I'm fast going grey.

'Welcome to Castle Cottage B&B,' the welcome spiel rolls off my tongue without any thought, having said those very words every day for the past thirty years. 'Just give me a second, and then I'll get you all checked in. Did you have a good journey here?' I say, as I frantically try to wake the computer and load the reservation system. The PC breathes heavily, overheating with all the programmes running, and the old mahogany grandfather clock chimes the hour a few minutes early.

I look up and smile, but no one replies, they just stare expectantly at me. None of them look very happy to be on holiday. It's been over a decade since I last went away but I swear holidays used to be a cause for enjoyment.

'Oh, not now,' I mutter under my breath as, from the corner of my eye, I see one of our regulars coming down the stairs. Mrs Leigh is charming, but deaf as a post, and really not the person who I want coming for a chat at this very second.

'My toilet isn't flushing,' she shouts to everyone, as if she's delivering the official welcome speech from the staircase.

'I'm sorry about that, Mrs Leigh, I will come and take a look at it just as soon as I've checked these guests in.' I give a strained smile, trying to convey that now isn't the best time.

She doesn't get the message.

'Well, I wouldn't hang about . . .'

The guests waiting don't look amused. I can tell that Mr Huff and Mrs Puff at the back are already planning their scathing TripAdvisor reviews.

'OK, Mrs Leigh, I understand. I'll be up shortly, and I'll bring your sandwich too.'

We don't strictly do evening meals, but as she's a regular, and can't stomach a large plateful of scampi and chips at the pub round the corner, I normally make an exception and rustle her up a cheese sandwich in the evening.

'Sorry, where were we,' I turn to the couple at the front of the queue, trying to muster my most cheerful face and voice to combat their frowns, hoping that we're not interrupted any further. 'Can I take your names please?'

'It's Mrs Jolly,' she replies curtly.

I accidentally snort.

'I thought you were a four-star establishment?' Mr Jolly says bluntly, pointing at the three-star sign hanging on the wall behind me.

'I'm the fourth star,' I grin, rather than explain the nuances of the different rating systems.

He doesn't find that funny. His furrowed brows deepen even further.

Clearly not the time for humour.

'I'm Simon, and you might meet my daughter, Anna, during your stay. Should you need anything please just let one of us kn—'

'Can we get a room service menu?' He barks. His frame hunched over, looking out of place, with the low, dark wooden beams only inches above his head.

'Sorry, we don't do evening meals. But there is a pub just round the corner which serves very nice food.'

4

'But you just said that you'd take a sandwich to that lady?'

'She's a . . .' I decide there's no point in trying to explain. *Thanks a lot, Mrs Leigh.* 'OK, I can probably make you a sandwich but it won't be much. Cheese, OK?'

'That will be fine.'

Thank you.

'So you're in Room 5, which is on the top floor, just up these stairs,' I hand over the key.

'Is there a lift?'

A lift? We're in a nineteenth-century cottage.

'No, there's no lift.'

'Is there a porter then?'

A porter?! This isn't The Ritz.

'No, sorry it's just me.'

'Can you carry our bags up then?'

I have to stop myself sighing.

'I'll bring them up with the sandwiches, once I've checked in these other guests if that's OK?'

The couple look unimpressed, but nod, before stomping their feet loudly up the wooden stairs.

'Enjoy your stay!' I call after them, knowing that they're bound to have a problem with the room.

After I finish checking in the other guests, I bring in the chalkboard from the front of the cottage, and stop to admire the bright pink flowers in the garden, the green undulating countryside which surrounds the cottage, and the sliver of blue sea which pokes out between the hills. The landscape which inspired Hardy and later McEwan now distracts me from my series of tasks.

During the peak summer months, the old castle ruins on the hill are busy with tourists clambering up for photo opportunities, looking across the majestic views of the Jurassic Coast and Chesil Beach. However, this evening there doesn't appear to be anyone in sight. I look to the empty bench atop the hill, which used to be mine and Caroline's spot. That was the bench from where we'd watch sunsets when we first moved from Cheltenham to Dorset. Looking down at the building work, planning our new life – our moment of tranquillity away from the construction work on the cottage. And then shortly afterwards – sooner than we had really planned – Anna joined us on the bench. In those early years, I'd carry her up the hill on my back, and twirl her around in the air as if she was flying. Until she got too heavy, and then she'd pick up a twig and use it as a walking stick, having seen my father use his. As Anna grew up we'd regularly have picnics up there, the three of us, all together. A happy family. Then three became two again, when Caroline passed. And, as I look out at the landscape, there's part of me which selfishly fears soon, after Anna's wedding, it will be down to just one.

As I walk back inside to make the sandwiches, I catch sight of the framed newspaper cutting which hangs beside the door, alongside the various certificates we've accumulated over the years. It features Caroline and me when we opened Castle Cottage, some thirty years ago, from the front page of the village *Gazette*. Admittedly it's not particularly difficult to appear in the *Gazette*. Last week's front page exclusive was about the potholes in the main street.

'I bet you're laughing at me, up there,' I think to myself.

This was all Caroline's dream. Her idea. Her passion project. The move, the area, the B&B. Everything.

Of course all the annoying guests, all the problems and the mishaps were funny when she was here, we could moan and laugh about them together.

But then a decade ago she went out and never returned, and now it's just me.

Alone in a house full of strangers.

2

'Can I just check if it's gluten-free bread?' Mr Jolly says as he opens the door, and looks down at the cheese sandwiches I've just conjured up for them.

I admit, for a split-second, I'm tempted to lie.

This is my third trip up the stairs, having already struggled with their heavy bags (God knows what they've got in there, they're only staying two nights!), and seen to Mrs Leigh's toilet troubles. A sight I wish I hadn't seen. Maybe she should consider going gluten-free herself.

'Sorry, you didn't say you were coeliac?' I ask.

'We just prefer gluten-free. Didn't we say?' Mr Jolly looks behind him at his wife.

'No, no you didn't,' I sigh.

I don't say anything further, hoping that they will just take these sandwiches out of my hands. But they don't. They just stare at me.

'Can we get two gluten-free sandwiches instead?'

A 'please' wouldn't go amiss.

'Sure.'

'Do you have any biscuits too?' Mrs Jolly calls out.

'I don't think we have any gluten-free ones, I'm afraid.'

'That's OK, whatever you have.'

I bite my lip as I walk away, and note that I'll have to prepare their breakfast tomorrow. Brilliant.

'And one last thing,' he calls out as I reach the staircase. I'm tempted to pretend I can't hear him. 'The Wi-Fi doesn't seem to be working.'

'I'll go and check it for you now,' I shout, clambering down the stairs before anyone else pops out of their room with an issue. Over the years I've heard them all. The man who complained that the view looked better on the photos, to whom I had to explain it was currently foggy. The family who asked me to repaint their walls because they didn't like the colour yellow. The woman who wanted a refund on behalf of her dog . . .

Admittedly Mr Jolly does have a point about the internet. The signal in our small B&B is patchy at best, and the guests – especially those who venture out of London – don't seem to realize that we're in an isolated, sleepy countryside village. Nor do they realize I don't run British Telecom.

I put the two plates on the reception desk, and try the only method I know of fixing the Wi-Fi – turning the router off and on again. As I wait for the green lights to start flashing, I start nibbling at the rejected sandwiches. My doctor will be despairing. He's already prescribed me statins to lower my cholesterol, and today I've eaten a series of discarded sausages, scones, and now a cheese sandwich.

As I chew, I flick on the table lamp, and look down

through my glasses at the brightly coloured Post-it notes threatening to submerge the reception desk.

- Fix Mrs Leigh's toilet
- Make cheese sandwiches x 3
- Take bags to Room 5
- Bring cream tea chalkboard in from garden
- Read the newspaper!

Nearly there, I think to myself as I scrunch up the completed tasks and throw them into the bin. The scrunched-up orange ball bounces off the rim and falls on to the floor. Doesn't that just sum up my day?

Finally the lights turn green, and the computer pings loudly with a series of email notifications proving the Wi-Fi is working. Thank God. At last, something is going right.

Before I let Mr Jolly know and go to make him his next set of sandwiches, I quickly scan through my emails. There is the usual spam, amidst a flurry of notifications from Booking.com and a few direct enquiries. Ryanair are having another sale – when don't they? – the energy company want another meter reading, and Facebook are notifying me about, well, everything.

I only signed up so I could see Anna's photos and posts.

'*Wish Genny a Happy Birthday.*'

I don't even know who Genny is.

'*Buy, Sell, Swap Dorset: Second-hand swivel chair for sale.*'

No, I don't want a swivel chair. Thank you very much.

'*New post in QAB School Alumni.*'

Before I delete this, I catch sight of a name I've not seen in a very long time.

But one which means so much to me.

My heart stops.

I read the post over and over again, until it sinks in.

'*Raj Sharma (1970–75) passed away unexpectedly on Friday 26th April aged 60 years. A memorial service will be held at the family home on Monday 6th May. All welcome. Please wear white. For more details click here.*'

Raj.

Dead.

I can't believe it.

3

THEN

July 1975

'How long do we have?' Raj shouts to Simon and Ian across the blare of the traffic, as they try to pedal up yet another of Bristol's steep hills. Their legs aching, their bodies sore.

People say that the return trip always feels shorter, but not in this case. The boys' ill-thought-out bike ride back from Bordeaux has seemed to last an eternity, not helped by a cancelled ferry, a punctured tyre, and many wrong turns along the way. The impractical glam-rock outfits in which they started their cycle ride to France, three weeks ago, are now far less glam. Their bright, striped trousers are mud-splattered, and smelly. In fact, the wet and miserable British summer weather, which now pelts into their faces, is providing them with their first wash in days. As they continue back to school, up Park Street, pedestrians hide in red telephone boxes and women push prams into stores. Everyone is in a hurry to escape the downpour.

'We've still got a few minutes. We're not going to get caught if we hurry up! Come on!' Simon's rallying cry is drowned out by the sound of a loud moped overtaking them. The city centre is a vast contrast to the quiet of rural France.

'We can't get caught . . .' Raj says, trying to keep up with Simon, his voice trembling as a green double-decker bus splashes the ever-growing puddles over them. Given the conditions, Raj's usually neatly side-parted jet-black hair is as wild as Simon and Ian's large barnets. He is short, thin, and looks the youngest of the trio despite being the eldest.

Ian Pratt – ginger haired, and large in every sense of the word – follows at the back. He dwarfs the bike that they've 'borrowed' from school. Bikes which are barely suitable to ride around the city, let alone the hundreds of miles they've just endured.

Their parents believe they have all been on the school summer camp to Wales. Their boarding school believes they went home for the holidays three weeks ago. Meanwhile, they've actually cycled all the way to Bordeaux to visit Simon's French pen pal.

Thanks to the boys spending the last couple of months intercepting and deviating correspondences, they've somehow managed to get away with their elaborate ruse until this point.

They can't fall at the final hurdle.

The culmination of their grand plan relies on them arriving back to school by midday, giving them time to discreetly drop off their bikes and get cleaned up. They told their parents to collect them at 3 p.m., and they'd meet them outside the gates pretending that they'd just been dropped off by the school coach. The coach is due back at 4 p.m., by which point they'll be long gone and neither the school nor their parents will ever be the wiser.

Simple.

If it wasn't now 2.50 p.m.

'We're cutting this very fine!' Raj shouts out, checking his watch, as they eventually reach the top of the hill and stop at the set of traffic lights.

The school – the finish line – is only minutes away.

'We're almost there now. We're going to be fine!' Ian celebrates, as he joins them, breathing heavily. 'We just have to quickly hide our stuff, and no one's ever going to know.'

He starts humming David Bowie's 'Rebel, Rebel', which has become the unofficial anthem of their journey, prompting all three boys to smile at each other, proud that they've completed their crazy trip. Quite an achievement for three non-sporty, sixteen-year-old music obsessives who have never left the country before.

'Come on, lights.' Simon stares at the red light which is taking an age to turn green. He fidgets with his large thick-rimmed glasses, and rubs his hands across his chin, where he has sprouted his first few strands of facial hair.

As they wait, they hear the sound of a loud exhaust chugging and struggling to get up the hill too. The dirty fumes filling their lungs.

Simon turns to his right to see the vehicle pulling up

alongside them, presuming it must be another one of the lorries that they've had to contend with over the past few weeks on the roads.

'Shit,' his smile is immediately wiped from his face. 'You've got to be joking.'

It can't be.

It is.

Simon stares up at his classmate Mark Thompson who smirks knowingly at them through the back window of the school coach.

As the lights turn green, the coach continues, but the boys are rooted firmly to the spot.

'Was that . . . ?' Raj looks at the coach which bumps and rattles into the distance.

'What's the coach doing back early?' Ian looks perplexed.

Simon holds his hands to his head. He looks up to the skies, and then across at the other two.

'We. Are. Fucked.'

By time the boys make it to the school gates, all the other pupils are bundling out of the coach and into their parents' cars.

Simon, Raj and Ian look at each other, knowing that they've been caught out. That their ruse is over.

As they get off their bikes and creep forward, waiting for the inevitable bad news to come, Simon looks across to Raj, expecting him to be hyperventilating with worry about getting into trouble, but he appears calm.

'Can I just say, whatever happens, it was all worth it. I know it's not been easy, and we had a few fallings out, but thank you for the best few weeks. I think I had the best time, probably, of my life, so yeah, thanks a lot,' Raj turns to look at Simon and Ian.

'Yeah, I agree. I hope we can do it again one day!' Ian says hurriedly, his eyes flicking around, wary of being spotted.

'I still had a great time too. Thank you both for coming with me. There's no way I'd have been able to do it on my own,' Simon manages a smile, despite knowing what is about to happen.

As they go to turn the corner on to the school drive, Simon, bravely leading the way, peeks his head around the gates and catches sight of his and Raj's parents and the school staff huddled together.

'Shhh! Wait!!' He quietly calls out to the others, forcing the trio to stop in their tracks, as they perch on their bikes outside the front wall of the school, eavesdropping on the loud voices.

'How have you lost our sons?' Raj's dad asks worriedly.

'We haven't lost your sons, Mr Sharma. Right now, I'm not exactly certain where they are, but I'm quite sure there's a reasonable explanation and we'll find out where the boys are very soon.' Mr Jones, the school headmaster, tries to diffuse the situation.

'Have you left them in Wales?'

'No, no, I can assure you we haven't left them in Wales. They definitely didn't come on the trip.'

'But if they weren't on the trip . . . then they've been missing for three weeks?'

'I appreciate your concern but I'm sure this will all be resolved swiftly. If you could please wait a second, I'm just going to ask our school secretary for our records.'

Simon sneaks another glance around the corner, as the headmaster scurries up the stairs. He wonders whether they should reveal themselves now, whether they should just come clean.

'Your parents aren't here yet,' Simon whispers back to Ian.

'No surprises there!' Ian rolls his eyes, unsure if he should feel relieved or disappointed. 'So I can go around the back and dump my stuff there?'

'What, and leave us two to take all the blame? That's not fair.'

'Come on Ian, we were all in this together. One for all, and all for one . . .' Raj quotes.

Ian looks back dubiously.

Before they can hand themselves in, they hear Mr Jones rushing down the stone steps.

'We were informed that the boys were going home at the end of term after their exams –' Mr Jones attempts to explain but he is cut off before he can finish his sentence.

'– No, they definitely went on the camp. I've got the letters about it.' Simon's father responds angrily.

'Look here, Mr Brown, they signed out to go home at the end of term.'

'So if they didn't come home, where did they go?'

Simon scrunches up his face.

'Time to face the music?'

The boys hesitantly creep around the front gateway, leaving their bikes by the road.

'Brown! Sharma!'

The group of faces immediately turns to glare at them as the headmaster's voice booms out.

Simon wonders why the headmaster only called out two names. As he looks back, he realizes that Ian has deserted them.

'Bloody Pratt,' Simon whispers under his breath.

'Gentlemen, where have you been?' The headmaster immediately asks as they approach.

Simon and Raj look at each other, hoping one of them has a way of explaining it, but they are speechless. There's no way of talking themselves out of this one.

The silence is more uncomfortable than sitting on the jagged bike seats for the last three weeks.

'We went to France,' Simon eventually murmurs, after looking at Raj for permission to come clean to the headmaster.

It is not the headmaster that Simon is scared of. It is his own dad, Reginald. He is wearing his trademark suit and is red in the face. Worse than furious, he looks absolutely mortified.

'You've been where?'

'In France?'

'What the bloody hell have you been in France for?' Reginald looks down at Simon.

'We went to see Sylvie.'

'Who's Sylvie?' Mr Sharma asks.

'Your pen pal?' Reginald's face is turning purple. 'I thought I'd explicitly told you that you weren't allowed on the exchange. I spoke to your teacher Mr Sullivan about it. How has he taken you without my permission?'

'The French exchange trip returned last week,' the headmaster interjects, looking as confused as the parents.

'We . . . we went on our own,' Raj stutters.

'What do you mean you went on your own to France?' Mr Sharma asks.

'We cycled,' Simon replies, looking at the ground.

For the past few weeks the teenagers have felt like adults – experiencing their first taste of independence, exploring the world – but as they stand on the driveway, their clothes soaked through, they're back with a bang to feeling like naughty children.

'Just you two?' Mr Jones asks suspiciously.

The boys look at each other.

'Yes,' they reply simultaneously.

'I might have expected such antics from other boys in your year, but not you two.'

'How did you let these boys go to France on their own? What are you teaching them?' Reginald now turns on the headmaster, who until this point has stayed calm, but now provoked turns a shade of red himself.

'Mr Brown, I might ask you the same question. Your son has lied to us. He has clearly lied to you. He has breached too many school rules to even list. I am afraid there's no place for dishonest pupils at this school.'

'I am very sorry, Mr Jones, for Raj's behaviour. He will be punished, and he will make up for it in September,' Mr Sharma apologizes.

'I think it's too late for that. I don't think either boy is welcome back here in September.'

'What? No!' Simon gasps as he suddenly takes his eyes off his shoes, looks up, and across at Raj, who simply looks stunned.

Mr and Mrs Sharma continue shaking their heads in total shock, while Reginald stares at Simon, clearly humiliated by his behaviour. 'Grab all your stuff, and be in the car in five minutes. Don't make me wait,' he says sternly.

As Simon solemnly trudges back into school, and into his dorm room to get the suitcase he'd hidden under his bed, he doesn't have time to check his pigeon-hole for post. He doesn't even have a chance to say a proper goodbye to Raj, or to Ian wherever he may be hiding.

He walks out of school, for the very last time, wondering how things could have gone so disastrously wrong.

4

I barely sleep all night. Those words whirling around my head constantly.

Raj. Dead.

I wake up groggy, and I immediately reach to put my glasses on so I can check the bedside clock. It's only 6 a.m. As my mind automatically rewinds to the years Raj and I spent together, I'm not entirely sure whether I am awake or still dreaming.

I replay memories I haven't watched for decades, over and over again on loop. I see his smile. I hear the laughter. The real laughter we had. The laughter you only have at that age.

It was a friendship formed over five years of boarding school, spending twenty-four hours a day, seven days a week in each other's company. We were more like brothers than friends.

As I get dressed, I start to question if I'm even allowed to mourn. I mean, I haven't seen or spoken to Raj since we were forced to lose contact, yet I can't help the sadness that washes over me.

I think back to *that* trip. And those embarrassing school discos where we stood together awkwardly shuffling from side to side. All the discussions, the arguments, the debates about music, about bands, about artists. All my memories playing to a soundtrack of Glam Rock. The lyrics of T. Rex's 'Teenage Dream' seeming more relevant than ever.

Passed away aged 60 years.

In my head, I can only picture the teenage Raj I knew.

I contemplate calling Anna but I know she won't be awake yet, and anyway I don't want to disturb her exciting weekend of wedding planning. Instead I decide I want to find something to make the memories more vivid.

I get out of bed, pull on some clothes, and wander down to reception where I leave Mrs Cook a note about Room 5's gluten-free breakfast, hoping that she will manage not to offend them.

I pass Daisy – who has miraculously recovered from her mystery illness overnight – setting up the breakfast room. I try to tell her I'm going up into the attic but she has her headphones on and can't hear me.

When I reach the top floor of the cottage, I pull down the white trapdoor from the ceiling and unfold the silver metallic staircase which descends into the narrow corridor. The steps are steep and unsteady, and I wobble as I begin to climb up, having to hold on to the wall for support. I know full well that Anna will tell me off for going up into the attic alone. We've reached that age when the dynamics of our relationship are quickly changing.

The attic has always been my realm, but my trips up

have become markedly less frequent over the years. When we moved to Dorset, we chucked our old lives in the attic, and we never got them out again. The boxes of memories stayed put, but I would be up and down like clockwork for the suitcase, or to bring down the masses of Christmas decorations which helped us transform the cottage into a winter wonderland.

Now the suitcase has long been retired, seeing out its life in the dark, gloomy space, rather than some sunny, far-flung destination. And, much to Anna's disappointment, I only get a small selection of the decorations down these days at Christmas. In fact, I now only really venture up to the attic to check for the dreaded mice.

As I reach the top step I turn to my right, flip the light switch on and peer across. I almost jump as I'm immediately stared down by a variety of Santa Clauses — all of different shapes and sizes, enough to stock a shopping mall's Christmas grotto. Beyond the Christmas decorations, the single, hanging, shadeless bulb casts a dim light across an array of cardboard and plastic boxes.

I remember, as a boy, an attic always seemed to be such a mysterious place full of secrets. As an adult, it's equally mysterious as even those boxes inscribed with felt-tipped inscriptions may or may not correctly correspond to what is inside. It's a game of chance.

I should have sorted everything out years ago.

I swing my legs around and hoist myself up from the steps.

Ouch. I yelp, as I clatter my knee, and then almost catch my fingers in one of the mousetraps.

I'm certainly not as agile as I used to be, and I tread deliberately carefully across the wooden planks. Whilst concentrating on the delicate floor, I forget to crouch and bang my head on one of the low-hanging beams.

'Damn.'

Maybe this wasn't such a good idea.

Above me, I hear the irritating seagulls scampering around on the roof, and below, a couple of guests heading downstairs for an early breakfast.

I pull open the first box, brushing off the cobwebs and mice droppings.

Inside are some of Caroline's possessions which I kept after her death, and I still can't face throwing away. I prise open the box fully and run my hands through her clothes. I pick out a navy cardigan, one of her favourites, and hold it up. Even after all these years it doesn't stop bringing a tear to my eye. I move it towards my nose, hoping it may still carry some of Caroline's scent, but any aroma has long since faded.

I suddenly wonder if Raj was married and if so, I think of the pain his wife must now be experiencing.

A pain which lasts a lifetime.

The next box is full of Anna's school items. I smile as I pull out an old photo of her in her netball kit. It still seems unfathomable that she is getting married. I swear it was only yesterday we were dropping her off at nursery. I take out her secondary school sketch books and marvel at her talent, flicking through pages and pages of detailed drawings of buildings and houses. She inherited my maths ability, and Caroline's artistic talent, and wanted to be an architect until Caroline's death changed everything.

With every box I open I am transported back in time to a specific place and moment, conjured by an image, a smell, an object. It is like browsing a nostalgia shop dedicated to our lives. I realize I could spend all day in here at this rate, but I can't be sidetracked.

Given how low the beams are, I switch to crawling on all fours, my knees hurting as I drag them over the rough wood. The further I crawl towards the back of the attic, the further back the memories go. I try and reach the boxes right at the back, those that we shoved there when we first moved in.

I uncover a whole box full of my old *Melody Maker* magazines that I forgot I still had. I wonder if I should try and sell them to some collector before the moths and the mice completely ruin them. I'm tempted to leaf through the pages, to reminisce about the glory days of music, but as I pull out a copy I finally catch sight of the box I've been looking for. I manoeuvre myself, uncomfortably and inelegantly, across the wooden boards to reach it right in the very depths of the attic, underneath all the cobwebs. 'Simon School Stuff' is scrawled across the side, and this time the inscription doesn't lie.

'Got you,' I say to myself.

I rip the tape from the top and prise it open. A treasure trove of memories from my youth. I pull out my old school tie, but the dim light makes it difficult to see into the box so I decide to take it all downstairs before the breakfast rush begins.

As I go to close the lid, I notice a loose photo tucked into the side. I bring it closer to my eyes. It is a photo of me, Raj and Ian on our bikes in Bordeaux.

I stare at Raj.

That's the Raj I remember.

5

'And next up we have the brand-new single from the hottest new singer who rose to fame on ITV's reality show . . .'

'Alexa,' I call across the kitchen to my Amazon device, trying to interrupt the radio. Since when did Radio 2 start playing modern music all the time? Why can't they play proper music? Don't they realize their demographic?

I walk past the box I brought down from the loft which still sits untouched on one side of the room. By the time I came down from the attic, the daily onslaught of tasks had begun – worsened by a guest spilling a bottle of red wine in their room and deciding not to inform us until after they'd checked out – and now I'm running behind preparing for dinner.

It's become a weekly tradition that Anna and Ollie come every Sunday evening. It's the quietest night of the week for the B&B so we can usually enjoy ourselves without too many disturbances. It's nice to eat dinner with someone other than the TV for company, and it will be especially nice to see Anna after the weekend I've had.

My back creaks as I bend down to check on the progress of the cottage pie cooking away in the oven – I'm still blaming the guests who made me lug their ten-ton suitcases up the stairs – and the music continues to blare from the small black speaker.

'Alexa! . . . Alexa! . . . Alexa!' I shout again as I slowly stand up. Ouch. When did simply standing up become so painful? I raise my voice each time, getting more and more frustrated.

I notice that the tinned tomatoes have splashed on to my grey wool jumper. I should have changed. Or at least put on Caroline's old apron which still hangs in the cupboard. Now I'll have to wash this. And it's hand wash only.

'Oh sh . . . sugar,' I say, stopping myself from swearing as I notice Anna and Ollie walking into the kitchen. I know she says a lot worse, but it's one of the throwbacks to parenting. I still remember when she overheard me say *bugger* when she was a kid and then wouldn't stop saying it for a week. Caroline found it funny at first, but wasn't so impressed after we got a call from her teacher.

'You all right, Dad?' She asks, laughing at me talking to myself. Every time she smiles I see Caroline again. She has her dark hair tied back in a ponytail, and is dressed in jeans and a white t-shirt. I may be biased, but she always looks beautiful.

'I don't think Alexa likes me,' I say, exasperated, shrugging my shoulders to Ollie, who smiles back sympathetically. He has a rugby player's physique but is a gentle giant, and something of a genius. He works in AI, or coding, or something along those lines. All I know is his company seems to have offices around the world. He's tried to explain his role to me a million times, but I normally get lost at the point where he talks about programming languages. I'm not sure if Anna fully understands his work either.

'I'm not surprised if you shout at her all the time!' Anna jokes.

'Alexa, turn off the radio,' I try again.

'Sorry, I don't know that one,' the digital voice replies. The blue ring flashes from the top of machine.

I look pleadingly at Anna.

'Alexa, please turn off the radio,' Anna says calmly and clearly.

The room goes silent, and I can finally hear myself think.

'Thank you,' I say to Anna. 'I don't know why you got me this Alexa thing; it never seems to work.'

I do know why she got it for me. She thought it would give me someone to talk to.

'Sorry, anyway, how are you both? I'd give you a hug but I don't want to get tinned tomatoes on you too! Tell me, how has all the wedding prep gone this weekend?'

'Yes, I think it's going well, we got everything sorted that we needed to, didn't we?' Ollie looks across to Anna, who seems slightly subdued. 'I must admit I didn't realize there would be so many decisions to make. I've learnt more this weekend about flowers than I have done in my whole life!'

The pair of them have been together for five years

now, and as such he's become something of a surrogate son. I know fathers aren't typically meant to approve of their sons-in-law, but Ollie has been a rock for Anna.

'Would you both like a glass of red?'

'Please. Do you need any help?' Ollie offers, as Anna simply nods. She's only normally this quiet if she's got something to tell me.

I check on the green beans before reaching up to the cupboard to take out three glasses.

'Has everything been OK here?' Anna asks.

'Just the usual array of interesting guests. You didn't miss anything too exciting,' I reply, not boring her with the details. 'I'm sure you must have something more interesting to tell me. What else did you do apart from go to the florist's?'

She's too busy nosing at my calendar hanging next to the fridge, to which I've added the details of Raj's memorial. It is my only scheduled event this month bar an overdue optician's appointment. Despite her not having lived here for years, I still have a column for Anna and jot down what she's up to. Her column is a lot fuller than mine.

'Actually, Anna and I did have something we wanted to talk about —'

'Who is Raj?' Anna interrupts Ollie mid-sentence, looking like she's trying to recall Raj's name, before shooting Ollie a scathing look.

'Raj was one of my best friends at school,' I uncork

the bottle and pour us each a glass. 'Unfortunately I found out yesterday that he passed away.'

'Oh, why didn't you say anything? I'm sorry to hear that, Dad. Where's the service?'

'It's in Chepstow, where he was from. I mean, I haven't seen him for years, but we were very close when we were kids. We shared a dorm room together for five years. You know, he was the friend who I cycled to Bordeaux with.'

'What? When did you cycle to Bordeaux?' Anna scrunches up her face in bemusement.

'Come on Anna, I've definitely told you this story before.'

'No, you definitely haven't. I think I've heard you mention Raj before but you've never told me anything about going to Bordeaux. Have you ever heard about this?' She turns to Ollie.

'No, I don't think so,' he says, before taking a sip of wine.

'I remember telling you about it when I was teaching you to ride a bike,' I say to Anna.

'I would have only been about four, Dad, I can't remember that! That's twenty-four years ago!' She replies animatedly.

How was that twenty-four years ago?

'Well anyway, Raj and I, and another friend, Ian, we all cycled to France together when we were fifteen or sixteen,' I explain.

'That was very adventurous of you,' Ollie looks impressed.

'You wouldn't let me go out on my own at fifteen, let alone to France! I wish I'd known this as I could have used that as leverage against you,' Anna jokes.

'To be fair, your grandparents wouldn't have let me go if they'd known, and they certainly weren't impressed when they found out.'

'You went without telling them?' Anna laughs. 'Why did you even cycle to France?'

The timer on the oven sounds.

'It's a long story,' I say as I silence the beeping noise and put on the oven gloves to carefully take out the steaming hot cottage pie.

'We've got all evening!'

6

THEN

July 1975
(Ten days earlier)

'Is this it?'

'Yes! We've found it!' Simon looks up at the street sign, and then down at the scrawled address on his torn scrap of paper, double checking that this is indeed the right place. The three boys have spent the last hour cycling around the centre of Bordeaux – passing the Opera House and Cathedral three times – trying to find this back street. The city is more grubby, more polluted than Simon had imagined, but then again he really had no idea what any of France would look like. He's never been abroad before.

'Thank God,' Ian jumps off his bike, and starts walking it along the narrow alleyway. No wonder it took them so long to find. The quiet road is set back behind a main street, and there are just a few stone houses on both sides.

'We're looking for number twelve,' Simon consults his piece of paper again, which he holds tightly. His moist fingers, sweaty with nerves, threaten to destroy the page.

The boys' heads flick from side to side, like they're watching a tennis match, as they check the numbers on the fronts of the properties.

'That's five . . . that's six,' Ian says aloud.

Simon's heart beats faster and faster with excitement and trepidation as they get closer, walking past an attractive house with a light-blue door, white shutters, and flowers in the window.

'It's all odds on that side, so evens this. Eight . . . ten . . . twelve! It's that one! That's her house. We've made it,' Raj exclaims excitedly as he stands in front of a house with a dark-grey door.

Despite the incredible achievement of making it to Bordeaux, and to Sylvie's house, in one piece, Simon remains quiet. For him, the biggest challenge is still to come.

Ian and Raj's gaze now falls upon him, waiting for him to approach the door.

He stands there motionless, trying to slow his heavy breathing. But if anything, his breathing gets faster. His heart beating more rapidly than when they were cycling.

'What are you going to say?' Raj asks, prompting him.

'I'm not sure, I haven't really thought about it,' Simon lies, having thought of nothing else for the past few months, but now he's here in this position, his mind has gone blank.

What is he actually going to say? He worries.

Sylvie doesn't even know he's coming.

What happens if she's not happy to see him?

'I'm sure she will just be pleased to see you,' Raj says, as if reading Simon's mind.

'Yeah . . . I hope so. This is it then . . . I suppose,' Simon says reluctantly as he lays his bike down.

He was so keen to arrive, but now he's here he wishes they could cycle around the city one more time to give him a chance to calm down.

'Good luck, you'll be fine,' Raj says supportively.

'Don't mess it up!' Ian calls out, as they stand back, waiting on the other side of the narrow street, looking on proudly at Simon's first-ever real interaction with a girl.

Simon slowly walks towards the door. His mouth has gone dry. He starts thinking through a series of endless scenarios, all ending with rejection.

As they've sent letters back and forth for the past seven months, his feelings have grown, and he thinks Sylvie's have too.

Surely she'll be pleased to see him. Surely he hasn't misread all the signals over their growing connection. No?

His heart stops as he knocks on the door.

There is silence for a few moments. Simon looks nervously back to Ian and Raj, fearing nobody is home. And then suddenly he hears footsteps.

Simon starts breathing rapidly, his body almost overwhelmed by oxygen.

The door swings open.

The man in the doorframe is bald, large, imposing,

and dressed in a mechanic's navy-blue boiler suit which is well worn and stained with oil. He looks at Simon suspiciously, reluctant to open the door any wider than is absolutely necessary.

Simon takes a step back, wondering if this is Sylvie's dad.

'Bon, qu'est-ce que vous voulez?' The man says brusquely.

'Ummm bonjour . . . monsieur . . . Je cherche Sylvie?' Simon nervously stumbles over his words and delivers them quietly.

The man stares at Simon, visibly trying to decipher what he said.

'Vous êtes anglais?'

'Yes . . . sorry . . . oui, nous sommes anglais. Ummm, je suis ami avec Sylvie . . . Nous nous écrivons des lettres,' Simon hurriedly mimes writing.

'Il n'y a personne qui s'appelle Sylvie ici,' the man says angrily waving and crossing his arms. 'Non, non, non.'

He slams the door shut.

'What did he say? Is this the wrong house?' Ian asks Raj.

'He said there's no one called Sylvie in the house,' Simon explains frantically as he stares at the door, which has been closed in his face, before turning back to face Ian and Raj, thoroughly confused.

'Is this definitely the right street?' Raj looks at Simon.

'Yes, this is the street. Unless there's another street

with the same name?' Simon stares at the piece of paper, the ink now blotting.

'And it's definitely number twelve?'

'Yes,' Simon shouldn't need to check, he's written out Sylvie's address enough times over the last six months in their correspondence, but doubting himself, his memory, his sanity, he looks at the piece of paper again.

'Why don't you try one of the neighbours?' Ian suggests.

Simon, shyly, goes door to door but no one answers. A suited man glances out the window at them, but doesn't come out. Given the state of their dress it is unsurprising.

'This is hopeless,' Simon despairs, as Raj takes the scrap of paper off him.

'Look, it's definitely this house. Just try again.'

Of all the scenarios Simon had conjured in his mind, this was not one of them. He reluctantly returns to knock on the grey door of number twelve again. The footsteps from inside are louder as they approach the door this time.

'Can you ask him where she is?' Simon asks Raj to take over, losing faith in his French as well as his search for Sylvie.

'Oui?' The man says aggressively, clearly wanting the boys to leave him alone.

'Pardon monsieur, nous cherchons cette adresse – je crois qu'une fille qui s'appelle Sylvie habite là. C'est bonne, cette adresse?' Raj directs his question almost fluently, if not entirely accurately, to the man's surprise, and he peers at the scrap of paper Raj holds out.

'Oui, c'est la bonne adresse mais j'ai emménagé dans cette maison hier. Votre amie n'habite plus ici.'

Simon looks at Raj, picking up the gist if not every word. The man's accent is strong, and he speaks quickly. It is harder understanding a real life Frenchman than Mr Sullivan in class.

Ian stands behind them, completely confused, not understanding anything. He looks across, hoping someone will translate for him, but Raj continues talking to the man who seems to be growing more reluctant by the second.

'Savez-vous où elle et sa famille sont allés?'

'Non, je n'en ai aucune idée, je ne peux pas vous aider, désolé.'

Simon goes white.

'I'm sorry, Si. It sounds like Sylvie's family moved house yesterday, but he doesn't know where they've gone to. I can't believe it.'

The man shrugs his shoulders, and then shuts the door, leaving Simon, once again, staring at a closed door.

'He honestly has no idea where she's moved to?' Ian calls out. 'You made us come all this way for nothing? Are you kidding?'

'Leave it, Ian,' Raj turns around, giving Ian a stern look.

Simon's heart plummets.

How could this be? How could it have happened?

He doesn't understand how Sylvie could not have told him she was moving.

He stands motionless.

'Yesterday? She only moved yesterday? We'd have been here yesterday if it wasn't for your stupid detour!' Simon turns to argue with Ian. 'It's not my fault, it's yours!'

'Come on, both of you. Stop it.' Raj places his hand on Simon's arm to get his attention, trying to de-escalate the situation. 'We could go to her school?'

'But I don't even know where it is. I didn't bring the address for the school. And anyway it's going to be closed for summer so that's not going to help unless we wait there for the next two months! I just don't get it. Why didn't she tell me she was moving?'

'I'm sure there's got to be an explanation. How else can we find her?'

The boys stand in the street looking at each other, and contemplate another 600 miles back to Bristol.

'I don't think we can,' Simon's optimism is fully deflated.

Despite Raj's best attempts, Simon knows there is nothing anyone can say to cheer him up. And as annoyed as he is with Ian, he knows that an argument now isn't going to change anything.

He isn't thinking about the trip back, the arduous ride, or more nights stuck sleeping in their damaged tent.

He's just confused. Confused and distraught.

He climbs back on to his bike, his dreams and heart shattered.

He didn't even get to meet the girl who has now broken his heart.

7

'So, sorry, let me get this straight . . . You cycled all the way to France to meet your pen pal who you had a crush on, all without your parents or school knowing? And she wasn't even there?' Anna looks at me, completely baffled by this revelation.

'Yes, in short, that's about right,' I reply as I take my last mouthful of cottage pie. It's stone cold, given I've been talking for the last twenty minutes whilst Anna and Ollie, sitting opposite at the dining table, have been listening intently. It is the first time I've told the story in years, and I can't help but feel a huge pang of nostalgia.

'That's just heartbreaking, I can't believe that you cycled all that way and she wasn't there. How have you never told me about this before! I think this is the most exciting thing I've ever heard about you.'

'Thanks Anna,' I shake my head, unsure how to take that.

'What happened when you got back? You said Nana and Gramps found out?'

'Yes, I don't think our plan was exactly the best thought through. We got caught as soon as we arrived back, or at least Raj and I did. We were expelled from school, and let's just say I didn't do too well in my O Levels either. Gramps was furious, but I moved back home to Stroud and he got me a job working with him in the bank.'

'What about Ian?' Ollie looks across, seemingly as intrigued by the whole affair as Anna.

'He snuck off before we got caught, and stayed on for Sixth Form.' I shake my head, still unable to believe he got away with it.

'And you never saw either of them again after the trip?'

'No, that was the last time I saw them. To be honest, I wasn't that keen to see Ian again after he abandoned us, and anyway Gramps thought they were a bad influence on me and banned me from seeing either of them. After how much I disappointed him with getting expelled, I didn't dare disobey him. I think I might have written to or called Raj a few times, I know he moved to another school. But by the time they'd both finished school, I'd been working for two years, and I think I just presumed they'd moved on and made new friends. You have to remember it was different back then. You don't know what it was like pre-internet, or pre-mobile phones. We just ended up losing contact, sadly.'

'It's sad, isn't it, that you were so close, and you never saw them again?' Anna asks.

'Of course, and I wish now that I'd reconnected with Raj. I wish I hadn't left it too late.' I pause, feeling emotional. 'I was meant to go to a school reunion, about fifteen years ago I think, but it clashed with taking you to a netball game if I remember correctly. But even that's so different now. Back then you'd go to a school reunion and it would be the first time you'd seen or heard of your classmates since school. If you two both went to a school reunion, what with social media, you'd go along and know everything about your old classmates already. You could probably tell them what they've had for breakfast every day since!'

'That's definitely true,' Ollie laughs.

'As it is, I hadn't heard anything of Raj until yesterday. And I know even less about Ian.'

'But what about Sylvie? Did you carry on writing? Did you ever get to meet her? Did you find out why she wasn't there?' Anna asks rapidly. I didn't realize she would be so interested in my teenage years.

'No, I never heard from Sylvie again after that.'

'She ghosted you?'

'Ghosted me? What does that mean?' I reply confused.

'It doesn't matter, carry on.'

'To be honest, I still don't know what happened. I presumed she'd gone off me. All I know is she never wrote again, and I didn't have any other address for her so there wasn't anything I could do. It sounds a bit daft thinking about it now, but I was absolutely devastated for weeks, months after that.'

I pause, thinking about it all. How crazy it was for us to just run away from school to France, back when hardly anyone even holidayed abroad. Back when we knew nothing about France, apart from the stereotypes that pervaded that era.

'Do you still have any of the letters from her?' Anna jumps up excitedly.

'Probably. Why?'

'I want to see them!'

'I'm not sure about that!'

'Oh, come on Dad!'

'I don't know. I got a box of my school stuff down from the attic earlier,' I point to the box sitting the other side of the room. 'I haven't had a chance to look through all of it properly yet. They might be in there. Do you know what I also found? Loads of your old sketchbooks. I was flicking through them. They were so good. I still don't know why you don't try and do something with your talent.'

'She really should, shouldn't she,' Ollie jumps in, raising his eyebrows at Anna.

I feel someone accidentally kicking me under the table before Anna jumps up from her seat to collect the box.

'You know we'd help you if you want something from the attic,' she exclaims, ignoring Ollie, as she starts rummaging through the ephemera of my youth. 'Oh God, look at these.'

She brings the box over to the dining table and passes a few of the photos across to me and Ollie, giving him an irritated look.

'Look at my hair in this one!' I try to change the subject, worrying that I've said something I shouldn't have. 'Wow. I love these photos. It's not just your hair, look at your clothes . . .' Ollie admires the photos of me with long hair, big sunglasses, a very exposing V-neck shirt, and platform heels.

I smile, looking at me from another life. As I cringe at my haircut, I notice Anna pulling out a metal tin from inside the box and trying to remove the stiff lid.

'Do you want a hand?' I ask, realizing it's not been opened in decades.

'No, I've got it.'

She empties out a stash of letters. The letters that meant so much to me as a teenager. As I watch them cascade on to the table, my mind flashes back to the excitement of receiving them, and how I'd scurry them away in my bedside drawer so I could read them over and over again.

'Are these them? Can I read them?'

'Go on then,' I reply reluctantly, knowing that nothing will stop her.

She goes silent, her face smiling as she reads.

I reach across and pick up one of the letters. The envelope decorated with Sylvie's swirly handwriting, and a series of grey commemorative stamps of President Georges Pompidou lined along the top of the envelope.

I hesitantly unfold the seal and pull out the letter inside.

It is the first time I've opened these in years. Certainly since we moved here. Probably since school.

I skim through the correspondence, picking out lines.

'It very nice that you say I that I look pretty in the photo. I don't very much like the photo. It is for my passport. You look very handsome in your picture. I always blink in photos also! It looks like I always sleeping!'

'I love T. Rex also! I think they are probably my group most preferred in the world. This is very bizarre. What is your song favourite? I think mine is "Hot Love", but I love all their songs. I listen to a lot of music from UK. I like also David Bowie, The Rolling Stones, and The Sweet.'

'In Bordeaux, there is very good record store, which has lots and lots of English records. I can listen to them before I buy them. I think you very much like it. I look to see when the new T. Rex album is there. I want it too. I hope you can save your money.'

Reading her words again transports me back all those years. I remember how jealous Raj was that I had a pen pal who shared our love of music. I remember the months when I was desperately trying to save up for the new T. Rex record. I remember the excitement of receiving all of Sylvie's updates, of sharing about her life in France, of imagining the record store she talked at length about.

I chuckle to myself, thankful we're only seeing her

notes. I imagine how cringeworthy my teenage letters were.

'Aw, these are so cute, Dad,' Anna hands across another letter. 'Wow, you've kept a mixtape too.'

'Is that in there?' I lean across excitedly.

'Oh, there's actually a couple,' she pulls out two tapes from the tin, and starts admiring the handmade cover art.

'Yes, so this is the one Sylvie made me, I listened to this over and over again. And actually this is one I made her.' I point to the respective tapes. 'But I took it on our trip to give to her, and obviously never got to give it to her.'

'10cc. Mott the Hoople. Slade. Sweet. Elton. Bowie. T. Rex . . .' Anna recites the track listing handwritten on the back.

'You probably wouldn't appreciate the time that was spent on creating these . . . We'd take hours curating the songs, waiting for them to play on the radio, and then you'd normally end up having the presenter talking over the end of the song. It's not like now when you can listen to whatever song you want at the touch of a button.'

'Can we listen to them?'

'I don't even know if I've still got a tape player, but we'll have to try and find one.'

She reaches into the bottom of the tin to check if there's anything else hiding. She pulls out the black-and-white passport photo of Sylvie, the only photo I ever had of her.

She pauses, and then smiles.

'I can see why you cycled to see her now. She was beautiful.'

She hands the small, square photo across to me – its edges worn – and I look at the face I haven't seen for years.

Teenage Sylvie poses in front of the wrinkled curtain of a photo booth. Her hair, parted down the middle, is long, straight and dark, flowing past her shoulders beyond the bottom of the photo, as if it's endless. She smiles widely, as if she's been snapped mid-laugh. She has a dimple on her right cheek. Her dark eyes glisten, framed by thin eyebrows. She stares directly at the camera, and now at me.

She is still smiling sweetly.

'From these letters, it sounds like you got on so well,' Anna pours herself another half glass of wine and offers to pour another for me, but I cover my glass with my hand.

'Yes, we really did. That's why it was so sad to lose touch with her, for whatever reason. But as I said, there wasn't really anything I could have done. You have to remember we didn't have Facebook or the like back then.'

'But we do now.'

Anna launches herself off the chair excitedly.

'Where are you going?'

'To look her up!'

8

'Anna? What do you mean?' I call out, as I follow her.

She is already on her feet, walking out of the dining room, through the lounge, into the reception area towards the computer.

'I reckon we can find Sylvie on Facebook!' she calls back.

Ollie looks across at me sympathetically as we try and catch up with her.

With all my time swallowed up by the B&B, over the last few months Anna has suddenly taken it upon herself to find me new friends. Her obsession started with actively encouraging me to get involved with more of the groups in the village – I still haven't forgiven her for the tedious evenings spent at the Neighbourhood Watch meetings. And then things got even worse when she forced me to sign up for online dating websites, and – given the tiny village population – the only person I matched with was Sue from the Post Office. Now it seems she has her next idea . . .

By the time Ollie and I join her in reception, she has already opened up Facebook and is typing in my email address.

'What's your password, Dad?'

'I don't know. The usual?'

'With a capital, or lower case?'

'Lower case, I think.'

'Nope, that's not it.'

'It'll probably be in the book.'

'You've got to stop keeping all your passwords written in this book! Or at least don't leave the book on the desk!' She rolls her eyes.

'How else am I meant to remember them all? Especially now you have to have so many letters, or special symbols, or whatever.' I look at Ollie for sympathy but as a computer programmer there's not much forthcoming.

'Look at you, Mr Popular. Thirty-seven friends!' Anna says as she eventually manages to log into my account, before hiding my book of passwords in the bottom drawer.

'Thirty-seven? They're all just people in the village. God knows why they add me when I see them every day anyway.'

Anna's not listening as she starts typing into the search box.

'What was her surname?'

'Perrin. P-E-R-R-I-N,' I spell it out to her but she's already typed it out and pressed search before I reach the last letter.

'I thought you were meant to be the tech whizz,' I look at Ollie, as Anna scours through hundreds of profiles.

'Programming, yes. But when it comes to online stalking, Anna has far more experience than me! Actually, it's slightly scary!' he whispers.

'I heard that!' she jokes, as she clicks the mouse.

I feel a strange tingling in my stomach as I wait for news.

'Hmm, there's a Sylvie Perrin living in Southampton ... A Sylvie Perrin living in French Guiana ...' Anna talks to herself, as much as to me. 'It looks like it's quite a popular name.'

'Maybe you've met your match,' Ollie goads, placing his hand on her shoulder.

'Shhh, let me concentrate,' she utters.

I wonder if this is my fault for letting her stay up late on Sunday evenings as a child watching episodes of *Poirot* with me and Caroline.

I tap my hand against the desk, nervously fidgeting, as we're all hunched over, watching her work.

'OK, we can narrow down the search. I'll try listing Bordeaux as her city. Maybe she has it listed as her city of birth, or maybe she still lives there.'

As I watch her quickly type, tap and scroll, I question whether I want to know what's happened to Sylvie. I'm only starting to process the news about Raj.

She clicks on one of the Sylvie Perrins' profiles.

'God, she's aged incredibly well if that's her,' I joke, looking at the profile picture.

'No, it's not her, she's the wrong age ... maybe this one though,' she clicks on the next option in the list.

'From her number of friends, I'd guess that she was around your age . . .'

'What does that mean?' I ask.

'What year would she have been born?' she continues, ignoring my question.

'The same year as me . . . 1959.'

The profile which appears on the screen seems to be fairly bare. The profile picture is of a cat, and I quickly note the other details, before Anna clicks on to another page.

Lives in Bordeaux, France
From Bordeaux, France

'I think I've found her!'

'Really? Just like that?'

'I told you she was good!' Ollie smiles.

'Well, there's not much information. Her profile is fairly private and there's just a photo of a cat. There's no relationship info. No work info. But this Sylvie Perrin does live in Bordeaux and was born there in 1959. I can't be certain, but it seems like it might be her?'

I suddenly feel a strange sensation as my stomach turns and flips.

'I can probably find out more . . .' Anna's voice trails off as she starts scouring through this Sylvie Perrin's friends.

'What other private investigation services do you offer?' I joke.

'We might get some more clues from her friends, and obviously we could then use Google, and other social media. But I think you should send her a friend request, and hope she accepts.'

Anna hovers the mouse over the button.

Do you know Sylvie?

To see what she shares with friends, send her a friend request.

'Do you want me to add her?' Anna asks, as she turns around.

She and Ollie both stare at me.

I look at the screen, wondering – after all these years, after she totally disappeared off the face of the planet – if Anna really has found Sylvie in the space of a few minutes.

Just as Anna is about to click, the front door opens, and a guest – who's clearly had one too many – staggers back in from the pub.

'Thank you very much for trying to track Sylvie down for me, but I think we should leave the past where it belongs,' I respond, turning the screen off, watching Sylvie Perrin from Bordeaux fade to black.

9

THEN

December 1974
(Seven months earlier)

'Can I look at your homework? Please? I completely forgot to do it,' Simon asks worriedly as he dumps his bag on the floor and takes a seat next to Raj at the front of the French classroom. The faded white walls are decorated with maps, posters of famous landmarks, and pennants of French football clubs.

'I swear you never do your French homework!'

'What's the point? When am I ever going to need to speak French?'

Raj rolls his eyes but relents, sliding his exercise book across the gnarled wooden desk.

'Just make sure you change it slightly, OK? You know what Mr Sullivan's like.'

'Yeah, of course.'

As Simon frantically copies down the answers, he occasionally peeks up to check if their teacher is approaching. However, the only person he sees through the door is Ian, who peers through the glass and sticks out his tongue, before he heads to his German class.

'Bonjour messieurs,' Mr Sullivan bellows as he bursts into the classroom, appearing out of nowhere. He is dressed, as ever, in a shirt, tie, jumper, and his trade-mark beige corduroy blazer. His hair is so firmly combed over that it wouldn't budge even in a tornado.

All the boys, who have been larking around, fall silent and rise to their feet, standing to attention; their chairs screech as they are pushed backwards across the wooden floorboards. Simon quickly drops his pen on to the table, despite only being halfway through copying the homework, and discreetly nudges Raj's book back across the desk. His only hope is to keep his head down and pray he doesn't get picked on for the answers.

'Bonjour, Monsieur Sullivan,' the class respond in unison, although their Bristolian accents are a far cry from sounding French.

Simon tries to stop his stomach from rumbling as Mr Sullivan keeps the class in silence. However, it sounds like he has swallowed a philharmonic orchestra, rather than the miserly kippers he had for his boarder's breakfast.

'Asseyez-vous.'

Simon and Raj take their seats first, and then the rest of the class slowly fall like a pack of dominoes.

'I have some exciting news to start with today,' Mr Sullivan announces, his voice always a decibel louder than necessary. 'The educated ones amongst you will know that Bordeaux is Bristol's twin city, and every year we run an exchange programme with a school there. I will be giving out more information about the trip next term.'

Simon sneaks a risky glance upwards as Mr Sullivan walks through the scattering of desks to switch on the overhead projector, the bulb always taking an age to heat up.

'In the meantime, I'm delighted to say that for the rest of the year you're going to be partnered with a pen pal from the same school.'

As he points to Bordeaux on the large map of France, the room erupts into groans.

'Oh, great,' Simon mutters under his breath, not the least bit interested in having a pen pal or going on the summer exchange.

'I don't want to write to some Frenchie,' Mark Thompson, wearing his school tie as short as is possible, yells out from the back of the room to laughter from his mates around him.

Mr Sullivan picks the blackboard rubber off his wooden desk and chucks it full pelt at him. It skims precariously close to his left ear, missing by an inch. Mark sensibly opts not to smirk at the missed shot, and instead shuts up.

'You're lucky, Thompson. As I was saying before I was rudely interrupted ... With your O Levels at the end of the year, it will be good practice for you to write to a native speaker.'

The boys all look around at each other, unsure and unconvinced.

'I've got twenty-five letters here, I want you to take one and pass on. These will be your pen pals for the rest of the academic year. They've each written a little bit of information about themselves.'

Raj takes two of the sealed envelopes from the pack, and hands one across to Simon before passing the rest to the desk behind. They both tear open the envelopes simultaneously, Simon accidentally ripping the edge of the letter as well as the envelope.

'Who have you got?' Simon asks, as a black and white passport photo falls out of his envelope and flutters to the floor behind him. He quickly skims through the letter.

Le 03–12–74

Hello!

How are you? My name is Sylvie Perrin. I am a girl. I am fifteen years old. I live in Bordeaux, France. It is a nice city near the sea. I live in a house with my parents. I am an only child, but I have two cousins. I don't have pets.

I love music. It is my passion. I listen to music every day, and I also practise the guitar since 10 years. Also, I love school, learning, and reading. I speak French, and a little bit of English, and German. My colour favourite is blue. My birthday is 9ᵗʰ September.

*And you? What do you like to do? I am very excite to learn
about you. Tell me everything.*

*I need to practise for my English so I hope you help me.
Sorry if I make the mistakes. I never visit England before but
I would love to visit in the future.*

You are my first pen pal. I'm impatient that you answer me!

Bye!
Sylvie

'Yours wrote loads. All mine says is he is sixteen, red is
his favourite colour . . . and les araignées . . . he loves
spiders.' Raj leans across, comparing his letter to
Simon's. 'Who loves spiders?!'

'Gentlemen, your homework for the Christmas holidays is going to be to write your first letter to send to
your pen pal. Everyone noted that down? Now put
your letters away, and let's get back to today's lesson.
We'll start by going through your homework from the
last class. Who can tell me what the answer to question
one is?'

As Mr Sullivan places a new slide on the OHP,
Simon picks up the black and white passport photo,
and sees Sylvie for the very first time.

The perfect tense and reflexive verbs can wait.

Simon is too distracted to listen to Mr Sullivan as he
stares at Sylvie's smile.

He can't help but smile back.

10

'Are you absolutely sure you're going to be OK on your own all day?' I ask Daisy, as she somehow manages to knock into the cabinet behind the desk, prompting all the room keys to fall off their hooks on to the floor.

'Yep, no worries,' she replies nonchalantly.

She might not be, but I'm certainly worried.

'OK, we should be back before any of this evening's guests arrive to check in, so it's only checking Rooms 2 and 4 out, and cleaning . . .'

I stop as I realize she's not listening. As she bends down to collect the fallen keys, I notice she still has one earphone in, while the other – which is missing its earbud – dangles loosely down by her side. Some modern hip-hop song, which I wouldn't personally call music, blasts out.

'Come on Dad, Daisy's going to be fine, aren't you? You've got our numbers if you need us, haven't you?' Daisy simply nods, as Anna turns to face me. 'It's much more important that you go to Raj's memorial, and it's quiet here today anyway.'

I've been wavering about attending since receiving the news last week. Not because I don't want to pay my respects to Raj, but because I feel like an imposter showing up to his memorial after all these years. Whether it is simply to ensure I go I'm not sure, but Anna has insisted that she comes with me to Chepstow, and that we take a detour through Bristol so I can show her my old school after all my reminiscing.

As kind as the offer is, I'm nervous about leaving Daisy to run the place. I can only hope that we have a business and a home to return to tonight.

'When was the last time you came to Bristol?' Anna asks, as we pass Ashton Court, approaching the city centre. The top tier of Bristol City's football stadium, Ashton Gate, stands high in the sky.

'I think the last time we came . . . it must have been for the balloon fiesta, probably. Do you remember watching the Night Glow? It was so busy, Mum spent about an hour queuing to use one of the Portaloos.'

As I say this, I realize how old all my memories are.

I realize how long it's been since I did anything other than run the bed and breakfast.

'Ollie and I have been to Bristol a few times since then, it's really nice down by the harbour. There are quite a few cool restaurants now. We had Korean last time.'

'There was nothing by the harbour when I was at school, it was still industrial.' I look around admiring the city's bright-coloured houses and Georgian crescents which welcome us. The Clifton Suspension Bridge was always dazzlingly impressive. 'Yes, just carry on along here, and then it's on your left at the roundabout.'

I'm shocked by all the new developments which have sprung up, the river now lined with modern apartment blocks on both sides. It's amazing how a city can change so quickly. Everything seems different as we drive along Hotwells.

'Here it is, the old school,' I announce as I look up at its facade. 'You can just pull over in the lay-by there.'

We step out of Anna's mint green Volkswagen Polo diagonally opposite the old Victorian building to our right. The building which was my home for five years.

Unlike all the other changes to the city I've noticed on the drive in, the school building still looks the same – externally, at least. As I look around, the memories come flooding back. I almost wish we had time to pop in.

'Has it changed much? It looks quite posh,' Anna says, seeing my school for the first time.

'Well, I think it probably is now. It definitely wasn't posh in my day. Most of us were from pretty working-class families. It used to be a Direct Grant school so the Government funded our places, but it changed just after I left.'

'Is it still a boarding school?'

'No, I think that stopped a few years ago. Presumably there's not the same demand any more. Parents like their kids these days,' I joke to Anna.

She looks up at me, smiling as a few pupils stroll out of the front gates.

'It must be lunchtime,' Anna comments as she checks her watch and confirms we're OK for time. It's not too far to Chepstow from here.

'We weren't allowed out during the day, but we were given an hour of free time after school, so we used to go to a cafe just up the road there. I can't remember what it was called, it was pretty dire, but they'd do these massive warm doughnuts with chocolate sauce and cream. Everyone would go, and Raj, Ian and I would spend our time chatting about music, and what records we were saving up for, whilst all the other boys would be throwing a football around and talking about Kevin Keegan.'

I look at her, realizing she has absolutely no idea who Kevin Keegan is, but the nostalgia makes me smile.

'Maybe things haven't changed that much!' She discreetly points to a pupil walking back into school carrying a box of Krispy Kreme doughnuts.

'Back in our day, though, there's no way we would have been able to walk around dressed like that. We had a school marshall, Mr Montgomery, who would have killed us if we'd had our shirts untucked, and ties skew-whiff! He looks a right scruff!' I realize, as soon as I say it, how old this makes me sound.

'Shhh. You said that so loudly!' she looks at me, embarrassed.

'Oh, he can't hear me . . . And look, that's obviously different as well now,' I point to the red Royal Mail van which swings into the school driveway, nearly hitting one of the boys chasing a stray football. 'The postman used to be on his bike back then. We'd get our post dropped off in pigeonholes. It was always so exciting to receive letters from Sylvie. I'd run down every day from my dorm room to see if she'd sent me anything. Obviously, I had Raj and Ian, but it was different talking to her, as someone outside school, writing about things I wasn't going to admit to those two. Your grandparents didn't write that much so it was lovely that I could talk to her about everything, about problems at home, about feeling lonely.'

I smile looking across at Anna, realizing how nice it is to be sharing my memories with her.

'Look at you smiling. That's why I still think you should have tried to connect with Sylvie on Facebook the other night. I don't understand why you won't!'

'That was a lifetime ago. I'm sure she probably doesn't even remember me.'

'Well, I still don't think there's any harm in messaging her to see. It's not too late!'

As the Royal Mail van comes back down the driveway, and I suddenly get butterflies in my stomach, I realize that maybe Anna is right.

'Hang on, I thought it was a boys' school?' Anna asks, as a group of teenage girls walk out together.

'Yes it was. Even that's changed now.'

'Maybe you wouldn't have needed to go all the way to France if there'd been girls here with you!'

I can't help but laugh out loud.

'I'm not sure about that. I certainly wouldn't say I had much luck with the opposite sex!'

'Oh, that sounds like there are some more stories there!' Anna says as she gets back in the car and starts the engine. 'We've got half an hour for you to tell me all about your teenage heartbreaks.'

'I'm not sure it will last that long,' I laugh, as I take one last look at the old place.

11

THEN

December 1974

'Are you sure you don't want anything, Si?' Raj asks, as he and Ian return to the metallic cafe table with their whipped-cream-covered doughnuts and bottles of Cherryade.

The Christmas tinsel, beads and paper chains do little to brighten up the dreary cafe, but the teenage boys don't come for the aesthetics. They come in their droves after school for the cheap prices and, mainly, to mix with the girls from the neighbouring all-girls school.

'No, I'm OK, thanks.' Simon replies, looking enviously at their desserts. 'I'm saving my pocket money up for the new T. Rex album so I can get it as soon as it comes out.'

Simon budges his chair over, as Ian sits next to him.

'You're not still looking at that letter, are you?' Raj notices Sylvie's letter peeking out of his blazer pocket. He has been reading it repeatedly since the French class this morning.

'I was just thinking what to write back, that's all,' Simon blushes.

'What's the point in writing to some girl who lives in France? It's not like you can dance with her at the disco!' Ian mumbles as he dives straight into his doughnut, managing to get most of the cream on his nose.

'Are we actually going to that thing?' Simon asks, creasing his forehead.

'Sorry, by that thing, you mean the legendary Fifth Form School Christmas Disco we've heard about for the last four years. Umm yes, we are. Or at least I am. I've already got my ticket! I don't know about you two losers.'

Simon and Raj exchange glances.

'Who are you going with?' Raj asks, cracking a smile.

'Still deciding.'

'Deciding on what? You have so many offers, right?'

'Shut up, I have more offers than either of you.'

'That's not hard,' Simon says, resigned to the fact that none of them will be getting a date to the disco on the last day of term. 'Who are we even meant to ask?'

Right on cue, the bell chimes as the front door opens, and a gaggle of girls parade into the cafe. All the boys' heads turn immediately, and the cafe goes silent.

'It's Katie Hughes,' Raj whispers excitedly.

Katie Hughes is the most popular girl in their year. Despite the wintry weather, her tartan school skirt is rolled up high, exposing her long legs, and resulting in a bulge around her stomach. Her shirt is unbuttoned at least one button too low, and she flouts the dress code further by wearing thick, dark eye liner, and golden bangles all up her arms. Her long strawberry-blonde hair flows down her back, almost reaching her waist.

'They're going to sit next to us,' Raj mouths, realizing there is only one spare table in the cafe.

'I don't know why you're getting so excited, I know them all. Me and Katie are like this,' Ian tries to cross his index and middle fingers but struggles to do so, and has to force his middle finger around with his other hand.

'Of course you are,' Simon rolls his eyes to Raj.

'Why do you think I do choir? Because we always sing with the girls' schools!' Ian explains.

'Maybe you should ask her to the disco then?' Raj smirks.

'As I said, I am still considering who I want to take.'

'Yeah, yeah. Just go and say hi at least if you're so close,' Simon pushes Ian playfully, as the girls return from ordering and take their seats at the neighbouring table.

To prove his point, Ian waves across at their table as the girls sit down, but none of them wave back.

'It's going well then.' Raj laughs. 'I thought you knew *all* of them.'

'They're probably just shy . . . Or, or . . . you two put them off.'

'Sure, Ian.'

'We'd better get back or we'll get in trouble again.' Ian looks at his watch, making an excuse to get out of the cafe quickly, knowing that Mr Montgomery will be waiting with his pocket watch.

'Race you back!' Ian says, as he kicks Simon's chair and blocks him from getting out.

As Ian and Raj rush out of the cafe, Simon – knowing he's already lost the race – takes a bite of Raj's leftover doughnut. As he reaches the door, he hears someone call out to him. He turns around and sees Katie standing in front of him.

'I just heard you talking about the disco. I wondered if you wanna go?' Katie asks, as she chews her gum casually, coolly, almost arrogantly. She towers above him in her high heels, her strong floral perfume intoxicating.

Simon looks around, double checking that she is actually talking to him, and then he stares back at her, gobsmacked that Katie Hughes is talking to *him*, let alone inviting him to the school Christmas disco.

He twitches anxiously, and he starts to feel his face turn red.

'Well, do you wanna go, or not?' She prompts him.

'Uhh . . . ummm, would I like to go to the disco? Yes, yes of course I'd like to go, yes please,' he stumbles and spits out his words, fidgeting with his glasses as he answers. The words don't come out quite how he hopes but that is not important. What is important is he is going to the school disco. With Katie Hughes. *The* Katie Hughes.

'Good, here you go, that will be 30p each. I presume you want both?' She hands over two tickets to Simon, and then visibly wipes her hands on her skirt after touching his sweaty palms.

Simon doesn't understand.

'You mean . . . but . . . sorry. You're not going?' He looks back, even more confused now.

'No. Of course I'm not going. That's why I'm trying to sell my tickets. I'm going to a gig with my boyfriend. The disco is a bit lame. Sorry.' She adds the apology as an afterthought, realizing she is meant to be selling these tickets, not putting people off.

'But, but . . . I thought . . .'

Her friends, who are sitting behind her eavesdropping, and who were already sniggering before, now burst into full-blown laughter.

'Well, have you got the money or not?' Katie still stands with her palm outstretched.

Simon reluctantly digs around inside his pockets, trying to find the pocket money his parents sent him in the post, whilst Katie continues to chew loudly. Needing both hands to raid his pockets, he lets go of the door and it slams shut, ringing the bell again, drawing even more attention to himself.

After pulling out a used hankie, causing Katie to look most disgusted, he reluctantly hands over the last of his coins, realizing he's going to have to start saving up all over again for that T. Rex album now.

'Thanks,' Katie says curtly, as she turns back to her friends.

Simon quickly runs out the cafe, unsure what is worse: the embarrassment of thinking Katie Hughes wanted to go to the disco with him; the fact he's just spent his pocket money on two tickets to a disco that he has no one to go to with; or that he's about to get bollocked by Mr Montgomery for being late for tea.

'Well, thank you for inviting me. I'm flattered.' Raj stands awkwardly beside Simon at the very periphery of the school gym which for tonight only has been converted into the venue for the Fifth-Form Christmas Disco – as the banner says which hangs awkwardly above the painted goalposts.

Both boys smell like an airport duty-free shop, with four different deodorants squirted all over them. They tap their feet to the beat of the music, managing the occasional shuffle as 'Let's Twist Again' by Chubby Checker plays through the gigantic box speakers. Their backs are so close to the wall that they are virtually standing outside.

'I know it's a bit lame, but in the end I thought it would be better than an evening in the dorm,' Simon says, having kept the real reason for his ticket purchase quiet.

He looks anxiously around the room, sceptical that this is the same legendary night they've been hearing stories about for years from older boys. It doesn't look quite as special or exciting as it was made out to be. The main overhead lights have been switched off, and a few cheap disco lights have taken their place, but even in the relative darkness, there's no mistaking they're still in the school gym. In fact, the coloured tape on the floor, which normally demarcates the football pitch, now marks the separate spaces in the stand-off.

The girls, who have been mini-bussed in for the occasion, are all congregated on one side. The boys, dressed casually in baggy jeans, are all standing along the edge of the opposite side, kicking around a spare tennis ball which they've found, and resting their drinks on the pommel horse which has been left out. Mr Montgomery, a short, stout man of Royal Navy pedigree, who is monitoring proceedings, strides over to the boys, barking at them to remove their drinks, before confiscating their tennis ball.

'Do you think he's going to play any good music tonight?' Raj asks Simon, nodding towards the DJ who has set up in the corner of the hall. He is surrounded by large crates of single EPs, and twin turntables, which have his name, Mike Weaver, scrawled across in blue felt tip pen. He is wearing a leather jacket and looks too old to be a DJ.

'It doesn't look like it. I don't think he actually has any new records. I reckon he's been playing this same set for the last ten years.'

'I swear all his records are warped too.'

'I'm only going on the dance floor if he plays Bowie or T. Rex,' Simon says, making an excuse for his reluctance to move away from the wall.

'It looks like we have all the cool kids in the house. Remember we're going to be partying until nine o'clock tonight. We're having a late one.' The DJ talks into his microphone in between songs, thinking he's Noel Edmonds on the Radio 1 Breakfast Show. 'Mr Montgomery has just notified me that the tuck shop is now open at the back of the hall. We've got sherbet tubes, we've got fizzy pop, we've got all your favourites tonight. And another musical favourite now. This is Bill Haley. Please do sing along if you know the words.'

Both sets of pupils finally move from the confines of their demarcated areas, with a line quickly forming and snaking around the hall for the snack table which is positioned in the cupboard containing all the gym equipment. Mrs Montgomery, the marshall's wife, has got her work cut out trying to cope with the demand for Curly Wurlies and sherbet fountains.

'All right boys?' Ian, who managed to get to the front of the line first, having been loitering by the cupboard, rejoins Simon and Raj, as he chews on his liquorice and downs all the sherbet in one go. For what seems like an eternity, they stand, simply shuffling their feet, deciding whether or not to dance.

'Is it just me or are those girls talking about us?' Raj, who has been staring at the ceiling for most of the evening, quickly glances across at the row of girls opposite who have taken to dancing around their handbags. 'Aren't they the ones from the cafe the other day?'

Simon looks across, and blushes as he realizes they are indeed the same group – minus Katie – and he has no doubt they'll be chatting about him.

'See, I told you they all knew me. They probably

want a dance,' Ian cuts in before Simon can explain. 'I better get on to that dance floor. See you later.'

Simon and Raj watch as Ian launches himself into the centre of the gym, and starts dancing on his own in front of the girls. Mr Montgomery comes and stands beside them, equally reluctant to be there, bouncing the tennis ball he confiscated.

'What does Pratt look like?' Mr Montgomery asks before realizing the answer is in the question. He looks on with bemused incredulity and shakes his head.

'It's that time of the night, everyone. It's time for a slow one. I want to see all you lovebirds on the dance floor. This is "Unchained Melody".' The DJ grooves his head to the beat.

The first few chords of the song prompt a mass exodus from the girls who seem to all need the toilet at the same time, but Ian, high on sugar, decides to make his move. Simon watches on as he awkwardly taps one of the girls on the shoulder and asks her to dance, tentatively placing his hands on her waist, as she puts her hands around his sweaty neck. They slowly sway from one side to another for about twenty seconds until Mark Thompson decides that he's going to cut in.

'We're going to end tonight with a brand-new record . . .' the DJ announces.

'Finally!' Simon says to Raj.

'This is a track to get you all on to the dance floor. Even those of you who have barely moved all night.'

He looks across at the boys as he says this. 'Remember this is your last chance to get that dance, or that kiss. It's a new Glam Rock classic . . . it's from your favourite TV show . . . it's 'Wombling Merry Christmas'!'

'Urgh,' Simon groans.

As everyone else finally floods to the middle of the gym, wishing they hadn't left it till the last three minutes to enjoy the evening, Simon and Raj continue tapping their feet on the sidelines, wishing they had someone to dance with. Wishing they could have their first kiss.

'Never mind, at least you got to dance with a girl for twenty seconds,' Simon says sympathetically as Ian rejoins them.

'And at least we've got each other, right?' Raj replies.

12

I stand on the doorstep to the Sharmas' house. My finger hovers over their doorbell, but all I can think about is whether I should be here.

When they said all welcome, surely they meant people who have been in touch with Raj over the last four decades?

I haven't spoken to him since we were teenagers. Surely I can't just turn up to his memorial service now?

Maybe I should just leave.

After all, by now, there could be chaos at the B&B with Daisy in charge.

As I turn around and start to chase Anna's car down the road, I hear the clicking sound of the front door opening.

I pause in my tracks.

'Hello, sorry, are you here for the memorial?' A voice calls out from behind me.

I twist around and take a step back immediately. It's almost uncanny.

I stare at the young man – probably in his twenties – who shares the same eyes, the same mouth as Raj.

'Hi . . . yes . . . I am . . . Sorry, it's just you look so much like . . .' I stop myself before I finish the sentence.

'My dad? Right? I know, everyone always tells me I look just like him when he was my age,' he responds.

I didn't even know Raj had a son.

If I didn't feel uncomfortable before, I feel even more of an imposter now, realizing how I know nothing of the man Raj became.

'I'm Jay,' he says, sticking out his hand for me to shake as I walk back to the front door.

'I'm so sorry for your loss, Jay. My name is Simon. Simon Brown. I went to –'

'Simon! Hang on . . . You went to school with Dad, right?'

'Yes, that's right. How did you know?' I ask, surprised.

'I've seen a photo of you when you were at school, and Dad always talked about you.'

'He did?'

He did? Really?

I feel a lump in my throat.

'Yes, I've heard all about your escapades at school together, all the things you got up to.'

I smile, suddenly feeling less tense, less awkward about being here.

'Have you heard about when we cycled –'

'– when you cycled to Bordeaux! Yep, I think my sisters and I must know that story off by heart!'

Raj has daughters too? And he's told them about me? I have so much to learn about him.

'He would always tell us about your trip when we

were growing up. We actually have a holiday home in the west of France which you passed on your trip, and when we were kids we went every summer, and hired bikes and cycled around places which were on your route.'

'I can't believe you holiday there,' I say, surprised that the trip had played such a big role in Raj's life, let alone his son's.

'Actually, we were all meant to be going on holiday there in a few weeks' time, the first time in ages that we'd all be together . . .' Jay pauses, looking like it's just hit him that they won't all be together. He trails off, blinking to stop the tear which is trying to escape.

I look at him, incredibly moved to hear all this, and I think about how Anna and I struggled after Caroline's death, and how we still do. I want to put my arms around his shoulders and comfort him. He gulps loudly, before smiling again, masking the inner sadness.

'You know Dad always said he wanted to get in touch and reconnect with you. I think he was always just so busy with work.'

'I wish he had done. That's all I've been thinking about, wishing I'd reached out to him before.'

I realize how sad it is that I'm only discovering details of Raj's life now he is dead. I wish it could have been Raj telling me about his family, about his life, about honouring our teenage cycle ride with his own family.

I suddenly lose myself in my thoughts, imagining a parallel world where we'd kept in contact, where we'd holidayed together, where Anna and Jay grew up together.

'Sorry, please do come in, otherwise we'll just be talking the whole time on the doorstep,' Jay beckons. His smile is warm, despite the pain he must be feeling inside.

I step inside, treading on the bristles of their door-mat, greeted by a hallway full of shoes.

'I hope everyone remembers which are theirs!' Jay comments as I bend down to take mine off.

'How was the funeral? It was last week?' I ask sympathetically, struggling with my laces.

'Yes, that's right. We have the funeral and cremation the day after someone dies, and then we hold the memorial service later, for people to come and pay their respects.'

'I'm sure you have already heard from everyone about what a wonderful man your dad was, but even back when was he a teenager he was . . . well, put it this way, I wouldn't have got through school without him.'

'He used to say the same about you.'

I'm glad I'm bending down, so Jay can't see the tear which forms in my eye.

'As I was saying, so this service is for people to pay their respects and then it's normally traditional to spread the ashes in water. Obviously in India people spread them in the Ganges. But we've had Dad's ashes separated into multiple urns so we can scatter them in various places which meant something to him. We think he'd prefer that.'

'That sounds a lovely idea.' I say as I stand up, before he leads me through their beautiful house, which looks like it could be straight out of a magazine. Wooden laminate floor, cream walls decorated with modern artwork, statues of Ganesh, green plants in every corner.

As we walk, I look around trying to take everything in. Every object a clue to Raj's life. I feel like I'm in an episode of *Through The Keyhole*, Loyd Grossman's mid-Atlantic twang echoing in my mind. *Who lives in a house like this?* If my trip into the attic was like a foray into my past, the walk through Raj's house is like a trip through his life. I learn more with every step I take.

I'm distracted by the large record collection displayed on white shelves to my right. I smile to myself, pleased that Raj never lost his interest in music.

'Yes, don't worry, he gave me a proper musical education,' Jay turns around and catches me admiring the hundreds of records stacked neatly in rows. 'We grew up listening to all his records from the seventies. He told us about how you would save up for them, and then tape the charts every week.'

'Yes, that's right. I'm very pleased to hear he forced his music on you! I remember when I was a kid, and my dad banged on about classical music – or proper music as he put it – and I was having none of it. Fortunately I think my daughter has inherited some of my taste!'

We continue through their large, sumptuous property, through the kitchen where I breathe in the aroma

79

of whatever they've been cooking, and I can hear the growing noise of chattering from where we're heading.

I pause again to look at a family portrait hanging on the wall. I realize Jay must think me nosy, but as I catch sight of it, I can't help but stop. It is the first time I've seen Raj in decades. The first time I've seen him grown up.

It's like watching Raj's life on fast-forward. I only remember seeing Raj's dad a few times, but just as Jay looks like Raj at his age, Raj morphed into his dad. His hair receded, his face grew thinner, but his smile remained the same. He looks more confident, more composed, more at ease than he ever did as a teenager, as if he's grown into his body. He looks fit, healthy and happy.

I look at the others in the picture. Raj is standing next to a woman who I presume is his wife, and in front of the couple are three children. Jay and his two sisters. Such a beautiful family.

'We had that taken last year. I think it's the last photo we had taken, all of us together,' Jay says softly.

'I'm sorry, I'm being so nosy. It's just all this . . . this is all new to me. I wasn't going to come today because it's been so many years, but it's lovely to see the man Raj became, and the family he had.'

'Dad would have been so happy you came. I'm really pleased you did, it's nice to meet the mythical Simon Brown. I thought Dad was just making up that he had friends at school!'

I continue staring at the family portrait, at how happy they all look. I smile, delighted that Raj had such a warm, loving family.

'Can you introduce me to your mum? I'd like to pay my respects to her.'

'Of course I can, but I think there's actually someone you might like to see first,' Jay says as he beckons me on through to the spacious lounge-diner, where a small group of people are gathered, and a buffet has been laid out.

I look at him, confused, wondering who he is talking about.

'The third musketeer,' Jay says, smiling.

Before Jay has led me across the room, I've already spotted him.

It's Ian.

13

You can't miss him.

Unlike everyone else dressed in white – or as close to white as they could find – Ian is wearing a scruffy electric blue suit, which notably doesn't fit.

He looks older, of course, and quite a bit rounder, but he is still clinging on to his hair, which is gelled back to conceal his bald spot. His eyebrows are bushy, his forehead is chiselled with deep lines, and his wispy beard is partially white and partially ginger.

He is standing alone, filling up his paper plate with as much food as possible, as if he's at a buffet restaurant and is trying to get his money's worth.

'You look like you're diving into Boarders' Tea,' I joke as I approach him. My first words to him in nearly half a century.

He looks up, confused. It takes him a few seconds to clock who I am. I'm sure I've changed more than him in the intervening decades.

'Simon?' He says, unsure, through a mouthful of food.

'Yes, it's been a while, hasn't it? How are you?' I extend my hand.

He immediately puts his plate down, and begins to

shake my hand firmly, before upgrading it, and going in for a bear hug.

As we embrace, Jay winks and backs away.

'Bloody hell, Brown. It's been a lifetime. How are you doing, my old friend?' Ian says far too loudly, patting me on the back as he speaks.

I glance around the room, aware that all the other mourners have now turned to look at the commotion, and that our loud embrace is not entirely appropriate given the setting.

How are you seems an unanswerable question with someone you haven't seen for so long, but no question would do justice to this moment.

'I'm doing OK, thank you, although obviously just absolutely shocked about Raj,' I reply, almost whispering, hoping Ian will take the hint.

He doesn't. He continues to bellow out his words, and he is also seemingly unable to stay still, circling around me as he speaks. I'm unsure if I should also move or stay still.

'I know, I know. No age is it. Apparently he just had a heart attack. Just like that. No warning. Makes you think, doesn't it.'

I query Ian's thought process as I look at his large plateful of snacks.

'It's really so sad. I was just looking at the photo of him in the kitchen, and he looked so vivacious.'

'I was thinking before you came over that Raj would have liked some music here. Don't you? I mean, surely you have to play some Elton John at his memorial? Remember how much he loved Elton? Maybe not "Funeral For A Friend" though,' Ian jokes, as I squirm with embarrassment, hoping that by now the people around us have tuned out of our conversation.

'Maybe it's not culturally appropriate?' I question, as I think back to Raj's music obsession. We all loved music, but were each partisan about our favourite artist. Elton was Raj's number one, Bowie was Ian's. Mine was always Marc Bolan and T. Rex.

'Hmm, maybe not.'

'And, I don't know, maybe Raj stopped liking Elton? Had you kept in contact with him over the years?' I ask, hoping that they'd managed to keep in touch, even if I hadn't.

'No, the last time I saw him was the last time I saw you. I was only thinking the other day about our schooldays . . . and then, then I saw . . .'

I wait for him to say something else but he doesn't, so for a few seconds we just look at each other, assessing the impact that age has had on both of us. I smile, thinking about how little he seems to have changed. It's almost like he's been stuck in a time-warp. His hair, dress sense and personality haven't aged at all, he's simply inhabiting the body of an older man.

'What must it be? Forty-odd years, right?' He eventually exclaims.

'Yes, forty-four years now.'

I pause, thinking how sad it is that we lost touch,

having been so close. How sad that none of us reached out over the years, that it took a death for us to reunite. From his expression, it looks as if he feels the same. But neither of us says this aloud, neither of us admits our feelings.

'I actually drove past the old place on my way here,' I say, as he continues to walk around me as he speaks. Can he not just stay still? I'm starting to feel dizzy.

'It's still there then?' Ian chuckles as some of the remnants of the food drip out his mouth. 'Can you believe they've got girls there now? Imagine that in our day! Have you ever been back in since we left?'

'No, I don't think after being expelled I was particularly welcome for a while.'

We both pause, neither of us mentioning him running off. I realize it's petty to still be annoyed with him after all these years.

'So what are you doing with yourself?' he asks, interrupting the silence.

'What have I been up to since 1975, you mean?'

'Yes, I suppose so!'

I fill Ian in on the summary of my life – Caroline, Anna, the bank, the B&B – before asking him the same question. I'm not sure how much of my story he digests as he continues to enjoy the food spread.

'I'm still gigging, still doing Bowie. Did you know? Maybe you wouldn't have known? I perform as a Bowie tribute act.'

'No, no, I didn't know that. Are you really?' I ask, hoping my incredulity doesn't come across as rude.

'Yes, I've been the Diamond Dog now for forty years. Still travelling all over the place. I do about a hundred and fifty gigs a year. So far this year, I've been in Germany, Spain and Dubai. Weirdly there's more demand for Bowie tribute acts now the man himself has gone. He's very popular with all the millennials now.'

'I still remember at school when you said you were going to become Bowie, and you actually did!' I look up and down at Ian's outfit, and suddenly the bright blue suit makes more sense.

'Yes, I've been living the dream. Can't really complain.'

'I'm really pleased for you,' I smile.

I have so much more I want to ask and to talk about, but I don't know where to begin. I didn't even contemplate that Ian may be here.

'Any significant other? Children?'

'No, it's just me. You know what life on the road is like, it's hard to sustain a relationship touring. But trust me Bowie is still popular . . . women in every port.' He winks.

Of course, Ian.

I smile wryly. He really hasn't changed.

'I'm actually performing in your neck of the woods next week.'

'Really? Whereabouts?'

'Oh it's just some private gig,' he replies coyly.

'Any chance you could sneak me in? I'd love to come and watch.'

'How many tickets?'

'Just the one.'

'I'll put your name on the door.'

He looks at his watch, uncouthly grabs a paper napkin and starts writing down the details and his number.

'I actually have to head off as I have a gig tonight up in Liverpool, but yeah, see you then, Simon Brown. How funny . . .'

He gives me another big bear hug, before he walks off to pay his respects to Raj's family before leaving.

And that was Ian, I think to myself.

I take a moment to digest everything.

As chitter chatter and laughter spread through the room, I look around at the people here, and I wonder how they each knew Raj. I wonder how he touched all of their lives. I wonder about the man he became.

I slowly walk over to the large framed photo of Raj, underneath which mourners have laid their offerings, and I look up at his face.

'Do you believe anything Ian says?' I say to the portrait, smiling, knowing that we would have been laughing and calling bullshit on all of Ian's stories.

14

THEN

January 1975

'*Chere Sylvie, merci pour votre lettre. Je m'appelle Simon. J'ai 15 ans.* I'm sorry but I'm not very good at French, so I hope you don't mind if I write in English instead? What? You've written all the rest of the letter in English?!'

Raj reads the letter aloud that he's snatched off Simon as the boys get dressed in the wash rooms. Everyone else is gossiping about what happened after the disco at the end of last term, with unfounded rumours of couples sneaking off behind the gym.

'Sullivan's not going to know if the envelopes are sealed . . . is he?' Simon suddenly worries. 'Anyway, it's private. Give it back.'

He looks embarrassed as Raj continues to read through his letter to Sylvie that he spent ages writing over Christmas. What with his parents spending most of the time either at work or entertaining guests, he enjoyed having someone to confide in for once. He might have taken Sylvie's request to *tell me everything* too literally.

'You've written way more than I have,' Raj hands

back the long letter, as they continue to get changed into their school uniforms.

After the three-week gap of the Christmas holidays, it is a shock to the system being back at boarding school. Especially to be woken at 7 a.m. by Mr Montgomery marching around the dormitories banging a saucepan.

'No way, you got it for Christmas?' Simon's eyes light up as he spots a tape recorder in Raj's locker. It is the very one he wanted and asterisked in the catalogue.

'Yes, my parents said it will be good for me to dictate and record my class notes.'

'Or more importantly, we can record the charts so we can listen to the music whenever we want. I'm so jealous.'

'What did you get?'

Simon miserably holds up a cumbersome calculator.

'I'm sorry, mate.'

'My dad said it will help me with my studies. In fact, that was pretty much all he spoke to me about, telling me I need to work harder, so I can get a good job after school.'

'Tell me about it. My parents have already decided what my future profession will be, whether I like it or not,' Raj moans as he buttons up his shirt.

'Have you had any more thoughts about what you want to do after school?' Simon asks Ian, who is hidden behind his cubby hole and is uncharacteristically quiet.

'Probably go to the record shop?' he mumbles.

Simon looks confused.

'No, I don't mean after school today, you idiot. I mean like when we leave school properly.'

'Oh, well, you should have made yourself clearer.' Simon and Raj laugh as Ian speaks. 'I want to be David Bowie.'

'You can't just be David Bowie.'

'Why not?'

Simon peers around at Ian, and can't help but burst into laughter again. No wonder Ian's been quiet.

'What on Earth do you look like?'

Ian has accessorized his uniform by tying a handkerchief around his neck and dangling a clip-on hoop earring from his left ear. His ginger mullet has grown longer over the holidays, and his hair now stretches down to his shoulders.

'This is what Bowie wears.'

'Bowie wears a silk scarf, not a handkerchief. And he IS Bowie. He is one of the greatest musicians in the world, unlike you. Please don't tell me you've got an eye patch to put on too?'

Ian rather sheepishly places something back in his cubby hole, without Simon seeing.

'You're seriously going to wear that?' Raj asks, walking around to see what's going on.

'Yep.'

'You do know you're going to get in trouble, right?'

'I don't care. I've decided I'm going to change my name too.'

Simon and Raj look at each other, bemused.

'To what?'

'I'm fed up of being Ian Pratt. I'm going to be Ian Jones, you know Jones was Bowie's real surname?'

'Yes, we all know that, Ian.' Raj rolls his eyes.

'It's going to be bloody Christmas again before you're all ready at this rate.' Mr Montgomery, still clanging his pan, walks through the changing rooms, having presumably woken up the whole of Bristol by now. He stops as soon as he clocks Ian's new appearance.

'Pratt. What the bloody hell is wrong with you? Take that bloody handkerchief off your neck before I use it to strangle you,' Montgomery yells at Ian.

'But, Sir . . .'

Simon and Raj grimace as Ian bravely, or rather foolishly, dares to speak.

'Are you answering back, Pratt?'

'I just . . . actually I wanted to tell you I've changed my name to Jones. So I'm Ian Jones now.'

'What did you say?'

'My name isn't Pratt any more.'

'Your name is whatever I want to call you, and it will be a lot worse than Pratt if you don't shut your gob right now, understood?'

Ian nods sheepishly.

Simon and Raj struggle to contain their smirks as Ian unclips his earring and unties his handkerchief, puts them back in his pocket, and returns instantaneously from being David Bowie to Ian Pratt.

15

'Good evening, are you here for the concert?'

'Yes, there should be a ticket put aside for me, Simon Brown,' I reply, as the man guarding the door to the auditorium looks at his list, which isn't really a list, as it only contains two names.

This is not exactly the London Palladium. It is not even the Weymouth Pavilion for that matter. When Ian described his gig, I didn't realize it was going to be at a retirement home.

'Oh yes, there you go. Mr Brown,' he says, ticking off my name. 'There is no reserved seating so take a seat wherever you can find one and enjoy the show.'

I push open the solid wooden door and turn the corner into the auditorium, where I am greeted by a sea of grey hair.

There's a pungent, musty smell, which immediately transports me back to visiting my parents towards the end of their lives when they were in a nursing home. Those Christmas Days spent with them in their small unaired box room, Caroline making sure they were comfortable, and Anna trying to discreetly hold her nose.

I look around the hall, with its high domed ceiling,

beige walls, dark mahogany wooden floor boards, period features, and two large portraits of noble-looking figures which hang from either side of the stage. Rather than rows of seats, the hall is packed with round wooden tables. I hover awkwardly, trying to decide where to sit, before eventually spotting an empty seat near the front of the auditorium.

'You the new inmate?' One of the elderly gentlemen at the table turns slowly to face me as I sit down. As he smiles, his false teeth slip slightly out of place.

I know it's a while since I've been out socializing, but has it been that long? Surely I don't look that old.

'Oh no, I'm actually just here to watch my friend,' I say.

'Sorry, son, you'll have to speak up. My hearing isn't the best you see.'

'I'm here to watch my friend,' I shout, although I'm still not convinced he can hear.

'It's nice to meet you. I'm Stanley. And that's Doris . . . you've got to watch her.' He winks as he points to the elderly woman in the other neighbouring seat.

'Hello Doris.'

'Oh, look at you. Aren't you good looking.' She grabs my thigh, which I certainly wasn't expecting. 'When did you move in?'

Honestly, how old do I look?

I go to explain again but our conversation is interrupted by the dark red curtains drawing open. On comes the man with the clipboard, who has switched from usher to compere.

'Tonight, we have three of the most loved entertainers of the seventies on one stage, for one night here in Weymouth! We have "Rod is God" as Rod Stewart, "The Rocket Man" as Elton John, and "The Diamond Dog" as David Bowie. So without further ado, ladies and gentlemen, let's get the show underway.'

Normally, being the last on the bill would be a compliment, saving the main act for the finale. However, in this instance it's not quite so prestigious considering that by the time Ian bounds on to the stage most of the audience have already dozed off.

'I thought David Bowie had died,' Doris, one of the few still awake, turns to me, as Ian opens with 'Changes'.

'Yes, this isn't the real David Bowie,' I try to explain.

Imagine the coup if this retirement home had managed to get Bowie, Elton and Rod to perform, all together on the same night.

'Maybe it was someone else who died,' she says almost apologetically.

'No, you're right, it –'

'He's piled on the pounds though, hasn't he? I remember he used to be really thin.'

'It's not –' I say loudly but she can't hear me.

'It's sad, isn't it?'

'What's sad?' I now shout into her ear.

'You know, that these big stars have to perform here to make their living now.'

I don't try to explain that Elton John doesn't have to

perform at the Weymouth Retirement Home to survive. Only Ian has to.

Whilst I may not be convinced that he is the real Bowie back from the dead, Ian is surprisingly really good. Simon Cowell would probably tell him to lose some of the cabaret tendencies he's picked up over the years, but his voice is fantastic. I feel a swell of pride as I watch him belt out all the classics that we used to listen to together in our dorm room – the LPs we'd saved up for, the tracks we'd recorded off the radio.

Unfortunately he has an impossible task to muster up any atmosphere in the hall – those who are still awake chat the whole way through the performance, noisily undoing sweet wrappers, and regularly needing toilet breaks. I clap as loudly as I can without waking up Stanley, who is snoring away.

I notice one woman across the hall turn off her hearing aid as Ian moves on to 'Fame', and his attempt to get everyone on their feet for 'Let's Dance' falls, literally, on deaf ears.

'Thank you Weymouth!' He finally exclaims as he finishes his set with 'Life on Mars'.

A deadly, awkward silence follows, and then a slow, very muted applause. I rise to my feet and give him a one-man standing ovation, but before Ian can walk off the stage the lights are immediately switched back on, waking up the residents who managed to sleep through all the noise. There is no call for an encore.

'Well, thank gracious that racket is over. I much

preferred the school choir we had in last week,' Stanley says as he wakes up and struggles to his feet. I try and help him by pulling out his chair, but he almost trips over it.

'Do you want to come back to my room?' Doris winks to me, as she shuffles past on her Zimmer frame.

'Sorry, I'm just waiting for my friend,' I smile politely back.

'Well, I'm in Room 117 if you want to join me after,' she laughs.

'Oh Doris, leave the gentleman alone. He doesn't want to join you.'

'Just because I haven't invited you to my room, Stanley, there's no need to be rude.'

I'm not sure if this is quite what Anna had in mind when she was trying to set me up with someone.

As the last of the audience members are wheeled out, I am left sitting in the hall alone. I take my phone out to see if Anna has messaged, given she's kindly covering for me at the B&B, but there are no new notifications, apart from another BBC News update about Brexit.

'So, what did you think?' Ian bursts into the room, still in costume.

'I loved –'

'You know, it's just something I'm doing to give back really. Obviously, I normally play bigger gigs, and festivals in Europe, and for younger audiences. It's just nice to do something different so we're touring this currently.'

'Of course, I thought you were fan—'

'And obviously I normally have a band but we're just using backing tracks for these shows.'

'Yeah, I really —'

'Anyway, enough about me, how are you?' Ian interrupts again, pulling out the chair next to me and sitting down. Not only has he shaved, but on closer inspection I notice that Ian's even wearing different coloured contact lenses. He doesn't give me a chance to tell him how much I enjoyed it, or how nice it feels to have a night off from the B&B.

'You know, OK overall, thanks. I'm just still trying to get my head around Raj dying. It's strange, isn't it? Obviously we've not been close for years, but it just feels wrong that he's gone. I'm just regretting not reconnecting with him before . . . it was too late.'

'I know, it makes you think, doesn't it. We haven't got all the time in the world.'

'We really don't.'

I find it hard to have a philosophical discussion opposite Ian dressed as a 1970s version of David Bowie.

'You know what, we have to live life, before we're in a place like this, or cremated like Raj. We're not getting any younger,' Ian shouts, banging his fists on the table, even though I'm only a matter of inches away.

Before Ian can continue his passionate speech, we're interrupted by the event organizer.

'I just wanted to say thank you, they all really enjoyed

it. I thought you might like a drink.' He hands over a carton of Ribena and a Penguin biscuit. It's not quite a diva's rider. 'Sorry, that's all we've got. Will you be OK to see yourselves out?'

'Sure.'

'And can you turn the lights out after you?'

'Yes, that's fine, thank you,' Ian says through gritted teeth. He waits for the man to leave the hall before continuing.

'What was I saying?'

'About us not getting any younger, needing to live life.'

'Oh yes, that's it. I was actually thinking after the memorial about something. I have a proposition for you . . .' He pauses, as if to build suspense.

'Go on, what is it?' I take the bait, replying slightly nervously.

'I was talking to Raj's wife and she was saying they are going to scatter Raj's ashes in various places which meant something to him. They had a few meaningful places in mind, and they also wanted his friends to take some to scatter as well.'

'Yes, Jay mentioned that to me too.'

'Well, remember that night we spent in Arcachon before we got to Bordeaux, and how much Raj said he loved it?'

'Yes, of course. It was Bastille Day, we watched the fireworks, and then slept on the beach. That always felt like the highlight of the trip, especially considering the disaster of Sylvie not being in Bordeaux.'

'Exactly. So I thought we could ask the family if they'd be happy for us to take some of his ashes to scatter there.'

I was not expecting that.

'That's a lovely idea. I'm not quite sure wh—'

'I thought so too, so I've already asked Priti about it, and she thought it was a lovely idea.'

'You've already —'

'And then I started thinking that we could recreate our trip in his honour?'

'Cycle to Bordeaux again? Us? At our age?'

'Yes, why not?'

I look across at him, unsure if he's joking.

'I'd love to do something for Raj, but couldn't we do something a bit more . . . normal?'

'We were saying the other day it's a shame we haven't seen each other since —'

'Yes, but —'

'This time around we can actually see some of France, do some cultural things too along the way, and stay in hotels rather than camping.'

'When were you thinking?' I ask quickly, trying to get a word in, not sure why I'm even entertaining his fantasy.

'As soon as possible really, I've got a few more gigs on this tour then have a few weeks off before the summer. Obviously, I'm happy to plan it this time,' he adds.

I'm not sure if this is meant to reassure me.

'You are actually being serious?'

'Of course I am. We just said we have to live life to the full, right?'

'That's not quite what I thought we meant.'

'If you think forty-four years went by quickly, then we need to make the most of the time we have left.'

I stare at Ian, who I've not spent more than five minutes with since we were at school, and contemplate his proposal.

'So what do you say? Are you in?' he asks as he unwraps his Penguin.

I lean across the table, and playfully grab part of his chocolate bar.

'I say, old friend, I think you've lost your bloody marbles!'

16

As Anna walks through reception to take the bin bags out, I deliberate whether now is the right time to tell her about Ian's wild proposal, but I decide to leave it.

'You really wouldn't know we provide bins in bedrooms!' She rolls her eyes as she returns.

'Was that Room 3?'

'Yes, they've literally just chucked stuff all over the floor, and I'm pretty sure they've been smoking in the room too.'

'It's OK, they've checked out now at least.'

'I saw Room 2 checked out too. She was totally flirting with you.'

'No, she wasn't,' I shake my head, smiling as I tidy up the reception space – straightening the leaflets and moving the guestbook back to its usual spot.

'OK, if you say so,' she smiles.

'Firstly, that would be very unprofessional. And secondly, I don't think she would be interested in an old man like me. I'm going grey!'

'I've told you, Dad, grey hair makes you look sophisticated. Like George Clooney. Or Philip Schofield!'

The truth is I don't think I would recognize what flirting is these days.

'Are you going to help me allocate these rooms?' I say, trying to change the subject, as Daisy walks through with the dirty laundry. Miraculously, the B&B survived her one day in charge.

'I've already done it,' Anna smiles.

'Perfect, thank you. I've just got to do this week's accounts and sort out the roster for next week. I'll make sure to give you an extra evening off as you covered for me going to Ian's concert.'

'It's fine, Dad, honestly. You haven't told me how it was.'

'It was good, he was great.'

'I'm glad. I think it was lovely for you to actually do something and have a break from here for once. Remember how sociable you and Mum always used to be.'

'Yes, I know. It's just you know what it's like . . .'

'Don't make excuses. I've told you so many times I'm happy to cover for you.'

Should I ask her?

'Thank you. I don't know what I'd do without you,' I simply smile to her.

'I'm sure you'd manage, Dad,' she says, looking away and quickly picking up the clean towels. 'I'll go and make the rooms up. Do you want me to put this stuff away?' She points to the box I got out of the attic, which is under the desk.

'No, actually I was going to try and scan some of the photos and send them to Raj's family. I thought they may like to see some of them,' I say, opening the box again.

'That's a really nice idea. I can give you a hand once you've picked them out.'

As Anna heads upstairs, I flick through the contents of the box in private, without the scrutiny of her and Ollie. As I read Sylvie's correspondence again, I can't help but smile. I remember how nice it was having someone to write to. Someone I could open up to.

I think about Raj's memorial. About not leaving things too late. And then I think about Ian's words after his concert.

I wait until I hear Anna's footsteps treading along the floorboards overhead, as she goes to make up one of the rooms, and then I wake up the computer. The screen immediately flashes up a guide to New York. I presume it's one of the places Daisy is looking to travel this summer before she goes to uni. I open a new tab, and replicate what Anna did the other day. Albeit it takes me at least double the time before I eventually manage to find Sylvie's Facebook profile again.

I look at the photo of the mysterious cat, wishing I could see more. Wishing I could see what Sylvie looks like now.

I hover the mouse over 'Add friend', and I click before I can change my mind.

As soon as I let go, I suddenly realize Sylvie may not even remember who I am. Or that it might not even be the right Sylvie Perrin.

Crap.

I panic and quickly hit the 'Send Message' button beside her name.

A blank message box appears.

What am I meant to write to her? We've not spoken since we were teenagers. Will she even remember me? Does she even speak English now?

Dear Sylvie, I type.

This is as far as I get. I tap the desk, and look around for inspiration as if I'm stuck trying to write a novel, not a quick message.

I look over at the bookcase and at the framed photo of Caroline, Anna and me at a National Trust property. We are all smiling, in front of a backdrop of beautiful gardens. The photo must be nearly twenty years old now. Anna is wearing the same glittery headband that she wore on the night of the millennium.

I always wish we'd taken more photos of the three of us together. So often Caroline was the photographer.

Of course, we didn't realize that we would run out of opportunities.

'What do you think, Caroline? What would you do?'

I stare at her gorgeous face. She was always more of a risk taker – gambling everything on opening this place for starters.

I turn back to the computer, aware that the guests walking back through the garden can probably see me talking to myself.

OK. *What do I write?*

I start typing.

My daughter found your profile.

Delete. Delete. Delete.

I need to keep it short and sweet.

I type and delete, type and delete, until I notice the time and realize I have to go and help Anna prepare the rest of the rooms.

I read back over what I've written.

From: Simon, To: Sylvie

Dear Sylvie,

I'm not sure if you will remember me, but I am Simon Brown, and we used to be pen pals back when we were teenagers. I was trawling through my attic recently and I found our old letters. Reading them transported me back to 1975! Where have all those years gone? It still feels like yesterday. Anyway, my daughter somehow managed to find you online, and so I thought I'd just drop you a note to see how you are. I'd love to hear from you, and hear how the years have been treating you. Hope you've been keeping well?

Best wishes,
Simon (Brown) – your old pen pal.
PS. If you're not this Sylvie Perrin, please ignore this message!

How has it taken me twenty minutes to write that?

I hover the mouse over the blue send button, deliberating.

Oh, what the heck.

I click send.

17

THEN

February 1975

'*It's six o'clock on Radios 1 and 2, my name's Tom Browne, and this is the Top Twenty, as compiled for the BBC by the British Market Research Bureau.*'

'It's on, it's on!' Ian excitedly calls out from beside the radio, as the jingle counts down from five to one, and then cuts straight into playing Love Unlimited. 'Are you two not going to come and listen?'

'Sorry, I need to carry on revising,' Raj says without lifting his head. His textbooks and notes cover the entirety of his single bed. 'You can record the songs if you want though.'

'But we've got ages 'til our exams!' Ian moans as he rushes across their dorm room to collect Raj's tape recorder.

'Not really, it's only a few months now until the most important exams of our lives.'

'A few months is ages! What about you, Si?'

'Sorry, I'm busy,' Simon says, without looking up, still scribbling away.

'Don't tell me you're being a swat too?'

'I just need to finish my letter to Sylvie.'

The pair have exchanged a few letters already since Christmas, and their letters are getting longer each time. What started as a few paragraphs has quickly evolved into a few pages, as they ask and answer each other's questions about their lives. They've now started decorating the envelopes too, and including gifts. This time Simon has bought a few postcards of Bristol so Sylvie can see what the city looks like.

'You've literally spent the last three hours writing it!' Ian sighs at the reluctance of his two friends.

'What did I tell you?' Raj now looks up from his textbooks, smiling at Ian.

'Yeah, I think you're right. Simon and Sylvie sitting in a tree, K-I-S-S-I-N-G. No, wait for it . . . Simon and Sylvie sitting in a tree, W-R-I-T-E-I-N-G,' Ian laughs mockingly, putting on a kid's voice.

'You spelt writing wrong!'

'Yeah, I was being self-depreciating!'

'It's self-deprecating!'

'What are you two on about?' Simon finally puts his pen down, as Queen's 'Now I'm Here' starts playing. 'Ah, Sylvie likes this song.'

'You're definitely right, Raj . . . Sylvie, Sylvie, Sylvie.' Ian mimics Simon's voice.

'What? I just said she likes that song. What's the problem with that?'

'You do know she is literally all you talk about these days. It's like she's more important than Marc Bolan now.'

'That's not true. I barely ever mention her. I'm just saying –'

'– You've totally got a crush on her.'

Simon goes bright red, not aiding his defence.

'You are constantly writing to her, and you suddenly seem to be into French and I can't think why else!' Raj now joins in.

'Because . . . Because as you just said we've got our exams coming up. And anyway, I'm not constantly writing to her.'

'How many letters have you sent then?' Raj turns to Simon.

'I don't know, a few.'

'And it's only been homework to send, what? Two? So you're spending extra time doing French homework?'

'He totally likes her,' Ian shouts out.

'It's just . . . nice to have someone mature to talk to for once,' Simon hits back.

'Ooooh, OK, Mr Mature,' Raj jests.

'Why don't we get pen pals? I want a German girl to write to,' Ian now talks to himself, as he has one ear next to the radio, waiting to record any new songs.

'I'm not sure you do want one. Jean-Luc is so boring. Honestly, all he writes about is his spider. Spider this, spider that. Why do I want to know how his spider is? What do I reply to that?'

'What do you write to Sylvie about?' Ian asks Simon.

'I don't know. Just things.'

Simon smiles, thinking about her letters. He didn't

realize how much they'd have in common or how nice it would be to have someone to talk to about school, about his family, about music, and about life. It's the first time he's really opened up to anybody other than Raj and Ian, and it's different than with them.

'Well, I think it's very cute. It's about time you got yourself a girlfriend. You and Sylvie, Raj and Jean-Luc.'

'Shut up!' Raj jokingly throws his pen across the room at Ian.

'Me and Katie Hughes.'

'Dream on!'

'*At . . . number nine . . . we have a big mover, climbing the charts from thirty-three. This is Steve Harley and Cockney Rebel with "Make Me Smile brackets Come Up And See Me".*'

'Quick, record this one!' Raj calls out, as Ian fumbles around trying to quickly press the red button, missing the first few seconds. They stay silent for the next couple of minutes until the song is over, and then start chatting again over the sound of the motoring bulletin.

'Do you think you're going to apply to go on the Bordeaux exchange trip then this summer, Si?'

'I'm thinking about it.' He replies coyly, having day-dreamed about going more and more with every letter which arrives.

'If Sylvie applies too, then you could go and see her for two weeks, and then she would come and stay here for two weeks too. You'd have a whole month together over the summer!'

Simon smiles just thinking about it.

'Are you thinking of applying too?'

'I don't want to see Jean-Luc, to be honest, and I don't think my parents would want him staying with us for two weeks. Especially as he'd bring his damn spider!'

'Oh yeah, I didn't think about my parents. I've got to somehow convince them to let Sylvie come and stay with us. They barely like me being at home, let alone having a stranger in the house!'

'Just tell them it will be good for your education, your dad will like it if he thinks it's going to help you get a job.'

'True. Although I'm not sure I want Sylvie to meet my parents either,' Simon contemplates.

'It's moved up from eight, to number two, but it just misses out on this week's number one spot . . . The Carpenters with "Please Mr Postman".'

As Karen Carpenter sings about waiting for her letter to be delivered, Simon rereads his own, before making the bold decision to end it with a kiss.

18

'Has it started yet?' Anna rushes in from reception to the lounge, having checked in the last of the guests for the evening. She kicks off her shoes as she goes, before jumping on to the fabric sofa, and spreading out across it.

'You're just in time,' I pick up the remote control and turn the volume up as Graham Norton introduces the Eurovision Song Contest. The camera pans across the strobe-lit crowd, as face-painted men and women, waving their countries' flags, jump up and down partying.

Since Anna was young, we've watched Eurovision together every year. It's always been our thing. I remember when she was little, she used to dress up, copy the dance routines and sing along, making up her own lyrics. She'd fall asleep long before the final performance, and I'd carry her up to bed, while Caroline and I laughed at the political point-scoring finale. As she grew older, it gave us something to talk about during her angsty teenage years, and her geography teacher was always remarkably impressed with her knowledge of Eastern European countries. And now we laugh together at the show's absurdity, and watch on in agony as the UK finish bottom again, and again, and again.

'Ollie better hurry up, do you know if he's on his way?'

'No, he's not coming tonight.'

'Oh, what's he up to?'

'I think he's ummm . . . playing football tonight. Oh my God, you've got all my favourites,' she changes the subject as she admires the array of snacks sitting on the oak coffee table, and pours herself a glass of wine.

'Is everything all good between you two? You seemed a bit tense the other night?'

'Yes, of course. We're all fine. Just means more food and wine for us, doesn't it,' she jokes. 'Look at this, you've got our scorecards ready too. Brilliant. I also printed off Eurovision bingo for us to play this year.'

'What's Eurovision bingo?'

She reaches into her pocket and pulls out two pieces of paper.

'I found it online. You have to tick off when any of these things happen,' Anna glances down at the printed sheets and reads a few of the boxes. 'Presenter outfit change . . . Fake rain . . . Glitter cannon . . . Singing out of tune.'

'We'll have ticked off all of those within the first five minutes,' I joke.

'Cheers!' Anna clinks her glass with mine.

'Now let's just pray none of the guests disturbs us.'

It doesn't take either of us very long to tick off our bingo cards. By the time the tenth act, Slovenia, takes to the stage I only need to tick off 'mid-song outfit change' and that surely can't be far off.

The song is dreary – I only give it a two on my scorecard – and I decide to take the lull in proceedings to speak.

'The other night after –'

'Dad, there was actually something –' Anna clearly has the same idea as we talk over each other. 'Oh sorry, you go first. What were you going to say?'

'I was just going to say after Ian's concert the other night, well, we were speaking, and he had an idea.' I pause, as I contemplate whether I should tell Anna. 'He thinks that we should take some of Raj's ashes to spread in Arcachon, which was one of the places we went on our trip together.'

'Aww,' Anna smiles. 'I think that sounds a lovely idea. Are you going to do it?' She turns around to face me now excitedly, swinging her legs round, and sitting up on the sofa.

'I don't know, obviously it's hard to go away with this place.'

'As I said to you the other day, you know I'm happy to cover for you. And I'm sure we can ask Daisy to do a few more shifts if necessary.'

'It was one thing trusting Daisy for a day . . .'

'It will be really nice for you to get away, and spend time with your friend. You've not had a holiday in years.'

I realize I've not been abroad since Caroline died.

'When was he suggesting you go?'

'Well, that's the other thing. We wanted to be in Archacon on the fourteenth of July, which was when we were there before. And that works for Ian as he's got a gap in his touring at the end of June before he's busy over the summer.'

'But you'd be back for the wedding?'

'Obviously, Anna, I'd be back for your wedding!'

Does she really think that I'd miss her wedding?

'Then that's sorted.'

'But I can't burden you with everything before your wedding. You have enough to think about.'

'It's honestly fine, everything is already sorted. I really don't mind looking after the place while you're gone.'

She smiles, but I look at her, unsure.

Deep down, I don't know if I wanted her to convince me to go or not.

'Come on Dad, I'm happy to help. And I think it would be good for you. Anyway, you're covering for me during our honeymoon so it's only fair!'

'Yes, maybe,' I say noncommittally.

'So would you fly from Bristol or Southampton?' Anna asks, ignoring the fact that the Slovenian act has been replaced on stage by a woman with cropped peroxide blonde hair and bold red lipstick, representing Cyprus.

'Well, that's the other thing,' I hesitate before I carry on. 'Ian thinks we should recreate our journey. Properly.'

'What does properly mean?'

'He wants us to cycle again.'

'Dad, are you serious? Cycle the whole way? You didn't mention that!'

'You just said it would be good for me to go away!' I joke, taking a sip of my lemonade. 'Look, you're missing Cyprus. Does that count as a mid-song outfit change?'

The four male backing dancers rip the singer's leather jacket off her, revealing a very skimpy and almost transparent outfit.

'Stop trying to change the subject. I thought it would be good for you to have a holiday as this place is giving you a slow heart attack but now . . . now you're going to give yourself a quick heart attack.'

'Is that better or worse?'

'Dad!'

'Sorry,' I respond, feeling scolded.

'I didn't even know until a couple of weeks ago that you'd ever cycled before. Can you actually still ride a bike?'

'You don't forget how to ride a bike, as they say.'

'But at your age?'

'Thanks, Anna.'

I try not to take offence.

'What's this Ian even like now? He sounded a bit of an idiot when you were telling me about your original trip.'

I look back at Anna, trying to conceal my smile.

'I'd call him, ummm, a character.'

'Oh great. Is he fit and healthy at least?'

'He probably doesn't look the fittest, but he tells me he is.'

She doesn't look convinced.

'*And next up is the Netherlands, who won the competition in 1975 with Teach-In singing "Ding-a-Dong". Could this be their year again?*'

'Sorry if I'm sounding sceptical. I'd love you to go, and I really think you should do it. You know how much I want you to meet new people and stuff, and for anything else I'd be pushing you out of the door, but it's just there's part of me that is worried about you going off on some massive cycling trip. I don't want anything to happen to you.'

'Nothing's going to happen to me, I promise.'

'It's just . . . after Mum . . . I can't lose you too.'

'I know, darling. I know. If we go, I'll make sure we're very careful. What were you going to say anyway?'

'Oh. I can't remember now. It wasn't anything important.'

19

THEN

March 1975

'Hopefully when we leave the EEC, we will leave this stupid contest too. I mean what is this ghastly music?' Reginald strides into the living room, where Simon is sitting in front of the television, cross-legged, on the brown and orange patterned carpet.

The BBC's coverage of the Eurovision Song Contest, live from Stockholm, has only just begun, and Simon bops his head to the catchy beat of the first song – Teach-In singing 'Ding-a-Dong' for the Netherlands. The best thing about being home for Easter means having access to a television, and Simon has agreed with Sylvie that they'd both watch Eurovision and report back in their next letters.

'I'm not watching this nonsense,' Reginald switches the channel before settling down. Despite it being his own sofa, Reginald doesn't look comfortable sitting on it, rigid in his shirt, tie and blazer.

'But I was watching that. I haven't seen The Shadows yet,' Simon moans, wanting to watch at least until the United Kingdom perform.

Reginald doesn't listen and continues to switch channels, as the audience, all suited and seated, clap politely as the first song comes to an end. The TV fades to black before reappearing on BBC2 for the *Man Alive Special.* An old, bespectacled man in a suit rambles on about education as Simon tries to calculate what time The Shadows will be on.

'But my friends will be watching Eurovision, and my French teacher Mr Sullivan recommended that we watch it to practise our French because the host speaks in French,' Simon continues to argue.

'I don't know why you'd want to waste your time watching that. This looks much more informative.'

'But . . . but I need to practise my French as I want to go on the Bordeaux exchange in the summer,' Simon has been biding his time waiting for the right moment to raise the trip with his parents. He had planned on waiting until the end of the holidays, just before going back to school, to ask, but now he's blurted it out he can't take it back.

His dad looks away from the TV, perplexed.

'Why do you want to go to Bordeaux when we're going to Bognor Regis in the summer?'

'It's a really good opportunity. I get to go to France for two weeks, and stay with a French family, and attend language classes, and then we'd host a French pupil here, so I'd be able to practise my French a lot. It would be really good for my education. Mr Sullivan accompanies us too.'

'When exactly is it?'

'After term finishes at the start of July, and then . . .'

'I thought there was that summer camp to Wales then?' Reginald interrupts.

'Yes, there is, but I'd prefer to go to France. I think it would be really good for my career too, you know I might be more likely to get a good job at a bank if I can speak another language.'

The bluff seems to work.

'How much is it?'

Simon takes out the sheet of paper he's been keeping in his pocket and he hands it over to his dad.

'I can use my pocket money to pay for some of it if you'd like? Or it could be my birthday present? Or my birthday and Christmas present?'

The last time his dad lent him some money he set up an interest scheme higher than the bank would offer, with penalty charges for late payments.

Reginald reads the letter slowly, rubbing his chin as he thinks, whilst Simon nervously watches, wondering how long it can take for someone to read a few paragraphs.

As he waits, Mr Sullivan's voice echoes in his mind. *'If you would like to take part, then you will need to return this consent form signed by one of your parents.'* A signature is all that stands between him and Sylvie.

Finally Reginald looks up.

'I am pleased to hear you're finally thinking of your career, but I do believe the camp in Wales would be better for your development. I'm happy to pay for you to go on that trip instead. Team building and leadership skills are essential, and it would do you good to toughen up a bit. By your age I'd lived through the war . . .'

'But, I could go to the camp next year?'

'And anyway, after we get back from Bognor Regis, Alexandra is coming to stay so she will be in the spare room. There won't be room for us to put someone else up.'

Simon had forgotten that his cousin was coming. He tries to think on his feet.

'I can sleep on the sofa, and Sylvie can stay in my room?'

'No, it's just not going to work out.'

'But, Dad . . .'

'No buts, Simon. That's my final decision. I would appreciate you saying thank you to me for paying for the trip to Wales. If you want me to sign that form, I can do it now.'

'Thank you,' Simon mutters, giving his dad the Welsh camp form to sign, before heading upstairs to his bedroom with both letters.

Much to his parents' disgust, his avocado-coloured walls are plastered with posters cut from the pages of *Melody Maker*.

'Not sure what you're smiling about, Marc,' Simon sighs, talking to the large poster of Marc Bolan which stares down at him.

He plonks himself on the bottom rung of his bunk

bed, reaches across to the wooden chest of drawers and digs out his radio. He tunes into Radio 1, making sure to keep the volume down, listening to Terry Wogan's commentary from underneath his duvet.

He has already missed the French performance that he wanted to talk to Sylvie about, and his mind is working overtime so he barely listens to the rest of the songs.

As Terry Wogan introduces the UK's entry, and The Shadows start singing about the time being right to move from friendship to something more, a thought comes to Simon.

He decides there and then that his dad isn't going to stop him from seeing Sylvie.

He stands up, unfolds the letters, grabs a pen and, after a few practice attempts, replicates his dad's signature from the Welsh camp letter on the dotted line of the French exchange consent form.

He'll worry about the other details later.

20

'If you can just sign on the dotted line, that would be great. Thank you very much.' I slide across the registration card and room key for the new guest checking in, before I head outside to the gardens with a trayful of food. I'm trying to juggle all our customers on this busy weekend.

The weather couldn't be better for it, and I have to unbutton and roll up the sleeves of my white shirt, as I stand in the garden talking to a couple of regulars, Julie and John, who have been coming for the best part of twenty years. They are a similar age to me, and they visit every few weeks for a drink and a toasted tea cake if they're behaving, or if they're off their diet it's usually a cream tea or a slice of carrot cake.

'You haven't met anyone new, then?' Julie asks as she takes a bite of her scone. The clotted cream is smothered thickly over the strawberry jam. Today is clearly a cheat day.

My regular customers, just like everyone in the village, always seem to be very invested in my love life. Whether it's Shirley who writes for the *Gazette*, who treats my relationship status like tabloid gossip fodder, or Julie who asks the same question every time she visits, I realize I'm lucky that they all care and look out for me.

'No, no one,' I give the stock answer, as John, looking slightly embarrassed, picks up his Panama hat to protect his bald head. 'We're all just concentrating on Anna's wedding currently. Let's get her hitched before we focus on me!'

'I still remember when she was just a little girl. Doesn't time fly,' Julie smiles.

'Tell me about it.'

As I stand and chat, I help them erect the umbrella over their white metallic table. The sun beats down on the gardens on this blissful spring day, highlighting the beauty of the gardens. The hanging baskets full of colourful pelargoniums look pretty, and ivy scales the brick walls of the cottage. A trail of white clouds floats through the blue sky, a few local kids in their swimsuits rush back along the cobbled road from the beach, and a tractor harvests hay in a nearby field, lining up bales on the horizon. You can hear the mooing of cows, and the baaing of sheep, such is the peace and quiet of the rural countryside.

I should have known the tranquillity wasn't going to last long.

As I look to my left, watching a couple browse the cake specials board, John nudges Julie, and discreetly points to something behind me. And then I notice another table's attention turn. I wonder what they're all staring at.

I swivel my head, and I do a double take as I see Ian forcefully push open the small picket fence gate, which he leaves unlocked to sway back and forth in the gentle breeze.

'Oh, no.' I don't mean to say this aloud, but it comes out.

What is he doing here?

'Look who it is!' Ian's deep voice bellows across the gardens as he strides over towards me. Those few customers who have not already turned around to stare at him, now do so too.

You can hardly miss him.

Not only is his voice loud, but so too are his clothes.

He is dressed in a full-on Ziggy Stardust outfit.

Does he not own any normal clothes?

'How are you doing, Brown?'

I don't know what to say.

The chitter chatter of the tables has gone silent, the customers all bewitched by the new visitor dressed in a bright striped suit and large red platform boots.

'This is your place then, very nice. Could do with a bit of tidying up here and there, but it looks nice, doesn't it?' Ian tries to include the table in the conversation, and Julie and John nod along, not really sure what is going on, and why a man dressed as Bowie has rocked up at the tea rooms.

'How did you even find me?' I ask, despairingly.

'I looked you up. You've got some good reviews,' he blares.

All the tables continue to listen, but it's hard not to.

'What have you got in there?' I ask, pointing to the bag he's carrying in his hands.

'Raj.'

'Raj?'

Ian takes a small urn out of the bag and passes it to me. I can't believe Priti actually trusted him with some of Raj's ashes.

'Maybe we should go inside.' I smile politely again to Julie and John, and try to steer Ian away from them before he scares them off, never to return. I decide to keep hold of the small urn.

'Are you just passing through again? Performing nearby?' I ask as I direct him towards the entrance to the cottage.

'No, no. Actually, our tour is over.'

'I thought you had a load more dates?'

'Well, I had a bit of a falling out with Elton, you see. Artistic differences, shall we say. So I thought I'd come and stay with you so we can prepare for our trip.'

What?

'I haven't even said yes to the trip yet!' I exclaim as we enter the reception. It takes a while for my eyes to adjust from the brightness of outdoors.

'Well, then, it's a good thing I've come to convince you.'

'You could have phoned ahead. I don't even know if I've got a spare room.'

'I'm sure you can fit me in somewhere. It looks like

you've got a few rooms here,' he says as he noses around, opening the door which says 'Private'.

I put the tray down on the top of the reception desk, hide Raj's ashes behind, and check the booking system, working out how much it's going to cost me to block one room out. Goodness knows what Anna is going to make of Ian staying.

'We only have one room available. It's not en suite but it's got a bathroom just down the corridor.'

'That sounds like being back at boarding school again! Next you'll tell me you're going to wake me up in the morning clattering a saucepan with a wooden spoon!'

I laugh, remembering how Mr Montgomery used to wake us up every morning.

'Seven every morning.'

'On the dot.'

'What was it he used to shout at us?' I ask, as I type.

'Hands off cocks, feet in socks,' Ian says, impersonating Montgomery's voice.

'That's right. You'd be locked up if you said that in a school now!'

I laugh as we reminisce. It's strange how the things we hated back then now make us smile.

'How long are you staying for?' I ask as I finish typing.

'I suppose I may as well stay the couple of weeks until we go now, hadn't I?'

It's not even if *now.*

'And if we don't go on the trip?'

'Come on, I've got Raj now. We have to.'

I shake my head in disbelief.

What have I got myself into?

'You're all booked in, but you're going to have to work for your room. Come and give me a hand with bringing the drinks out, OK?'

As I head back outside to serve afternoon tea in a quaint, British countryside B&B garden, Ziggy Stardust follows me with a tray of scones.

21

'Do you think Mr Montgomery and Mr Sullivan are still alive?'

I quickly learn that this is Ian's favourite topic of conversation. This afternoon we've already been through every pupil either of us can remember and debated what they'd have done with their lives, and now we're clearly moving on to the staff.

'Surely they can't be. They seemed pretty ancient even back then,' I reply, trying to work out how old they must be.

After his afternoon duties serving customers, Ian's earned the evening off, and we've retired to the lounge, where he sits on the sofa opposite me, looking up accommodation and routes for the proposed trip.

I've still not agreed to anything yet.

'Hmmm, what do you think about Nantes? It looks quite nice, we could stop there?' Ian asks, turning his laptop round to show me an aerial photo of the French city on the Lonely Planet website.

'You're right, it does look really nice. I don't think we went through the centre last time? I think we camped on the outskirts.'

It feels strange having Ian sitting in my front room.

It's almost like the old days when we'd sit in our dorm room together – reading our magazines, doing our homework and, of course, planning our trip. At least now we have the internet to help with the latter, meaning things should be a little simpler.

As he continues to scroll through the guide, I check Facebook on my iPad.

Considering I'd barely been on the site once in the past six months, I'm now checking it routinely, wondering if Sylvie will accept my friendship request, or reply. And if she will even remember me.

Rushing down to check my pigeonhole for post has been replaced by refreshing a webpage; however, every time I log on – rather than any messages – all I see are pictures of people's food, unflattering selfies, and rants about Brexit. I really don't understand the attraction of social media.

'Priti also said that we can stay with them at their holiday home if we wanted. She and the children are probably still going to go over there for a couple of weeks as they'd planned.' Ian turns the laptop around again to show me a photo, but I barely glance up as I notice a message in my inbox.

My stomach suddenly jumps.

It's from Sylvie.

I quickly click to open it, but the page takes an eternity to load.

'Come on,' I mutter under my breath.

Suddenly her words appear on my screen.

I frantically skim through the message, racing to see her response, before reading it again, slower this time, digesting the words.

I can't help but smile.

It's her.

And she remembers me.

'It looks like we should catch the ferry from Poole rather than Plymouth this time,' I hear Ian say, not that I'm really listening. I continue rereading Sylvie's message, processing every word. The first words I've heard from her since I was sixteen.

From: Sylvie, To: Simon

Simon. Of course, I remember you. It is a most unexpected, but lovely surprise to hear from you after all these years. Sorry for my slow response. I don't often use Facebook. My sons set up an account for me, but I don't really understand how it works. What would we do without our kids?

It has been so long. I'm not quite sure where to start. But yes, it's hard to believe that was forty-four years ago now. God. I'm suddenly feeling very old. I still live in Bordeaux, it's just me and Jacques now. You mentioned you have a daughter? How old is she? I have two sons, Romain (32) and Nicolas (29). I even have a grandson – Leo, who has just turned three. I'm now feeling even older as I write this! What are you doing with your life?

Bizarrely, I was actually only thinking about you recently, I heard T. Rex on the radio and it made me think about you.

That's nice you kept all our letters! What made you dig them out?

I see that you still haven't learnt any French? Bises, Sylvie x

'Earth to Simon? Hello? Are you there?' Ian calls out, startling me away from the iPad.

'Sorry. Sorry . . . It's just . . . you'll never guess who I just got a message from?'

'I don't know . . . judging by your reaction, the Queen?' Ian replies.

'Not quite. It's from Sylvie.' I can't help but smile as I say her name.

'Sylvie?' Ian looks confused before the name suddenly clicks. 'Not your pen pal Sylvie?'

'Yes, my pen pal Sylvie, or should I now refer to her as my Facebook friend Sylvie.'

'I didn't know . . . you didn't say . . . how long have you been in touch with her for?' His face looks more shocked than mine as he stumbles over his question, trying to process the news.

'We've not been in touch at all. Well, not until this second. This is the first time I've heard from her since school. I was telling Anna about her the other day and she somehow managed to find Sylvie on Facebook. I sent her a message and she's just replied.'

Ian's eyes dart up from his screen and back again, before he closes his laptop and turns to face me.

'She hasn't said anything about why she suddenly cut

all contact back then? Or why she didn't tell you she'd moved?' he says quickly.

'No, and I don't think I'm going to lead with that. I feel receiving a message from someone after forty-four years is strange enough, without them confronting you about why you stopped writing.'

'Yes, definitely,' Ian replies.

'And I don't think I'm going to mention that we're cycling to Bordeaux either or that might seem a bit too keen. What do you think?'

'I think you just agreed that we're cycling to Bordeaux!' Ian smiles.

'No, I didn't mean it like that.'

'Sure. So you and Sylvie, hey?' Ian raises his eyebrows and then winks as if the eyebrow raise was too subtle.

'No, nothing like that. She's married. She says she lives with Jacques, and she's got two grown-up children.'

'Ugh, Jacques,' Ian makes a face which makes me laugh.

'I wasn't getting in touch for that. I just thought it would be nice to find out what became of her. We spent a long time writing to each other.'

'Yeah, of course,' he says sarcastically.

'Honestly. I'm just curious, that's all. Maybe we could rekindle a friendship.'

I read the line about T. Rex again – how she still thinks of me when she hears their songs.

'Would you mind not saying anything about this to Anna when you meet her?' I look up again at Ian who has retreated behind his laptop screen.

'I thought you just said Anna helped you find her online?'

'Yes, I know. She did. But she doesn't know I got in touch, and I think I'd just like to keep it to myself for the time being. I don't want Anna meddling! I'll tell her when I'm ready.'

'Ok. Mum's the word,' Ian says, pretending to zip his lips together.

As he continues planning our trip, and I start to type my reply to Sylvie, I think these really are like old times indeed.

From: Simon, To: Sylvie

Dear Sylvie,

It's so lovely to hear back from you. I'm really relieved it was actually you – I did worry I was messaging a different Sylvie Perrin! Don't worry – I'm the same as you. My daughter signed me up for Facebook, and I don't know what I'm doing on here. I find it difficult just trying to remember my password!

Wow – a grandmother, that's amazing. Do either of your sons live nearby? Did you become a teacher like you wanted?

I'm living in Dorset, in the South West of England. I run a Bed & Breakfast. I have a daughter called Anna who is 28, and is getting married in a few weeks. I was married but my wife, Caroline, passed away ten years ago. Aside from that, just growing older by the day!

I don't know if you'd remember from my letters, but I used to talk about my best friend Raj? Very sadly, he passed away a couple of weeks ago, and thinking about him made me rather nostalgic. I actually reunited with Ian, my other friend from school, at Raj's memorial, which was a pleasant surprise. He's currently staying with me so it's been interesting getting to know him again, to say the least.

I can't believe you still think of me when you listen to T. Rex! Are you still into your music? Fortunately I've passed on some of my taste to Anna – whether she really had a choice, I'm not sure.

Sorry, my French is probably even worse than at school. We do have a few French guests staying with us every so often, but I don't think languages are my forte!

Anyway, I've asked too many questions here – looking forward to hearing back from you when you next check Facebook!

Best wishes,
Simon

22

THEN

April 1975

'Would you rather be stuck in a room with a frog the size of a horse? Or one hundred horses the size of frogs?' Ian asks.

'Can you just let me revise for two minutes?' Raj replies, grumpily.

'That's all you ever do.'

'And all you ever do is ask silly questions!'

Simon paces around the dorm room, trying to stay out of their conversation.

'What time is it?' he asks, looking out of the window, as he navigates in a circular loop in between the beds and the mess on the floor.

'It's twenty-five to eight,' Ian lies on his back horizontally across his bed, his head hanging uncomfortably off the edge. He looks across at the small clock on his bedside cabinet, trying to read the time whilst upside down.

'Ok, I still have a while to go then,' Simon replies, unable to believe how slowly time is going. It was half past the last time he checked and that felt like ages ago.

'A while to go until what?'

Simon pauses and stands still, unsure if he should say.

'I'm calling Sylvie at 8 p.m. so we can, you know, actually speak to each other for the first time.'

'You're going to phone Sylvie?' Raj perks up and puts his textbook down. 'That's a big step! How you feeling?'

'Quite nervous. It's different isn't it . . . writing a letter, well that's one thing, but you know, speaking on the phone, that's completely different.'

'Are you going to speak in English or French?'

'I didn't even think about that, I presume English, but what if she wants to speak in French . . . I don't know if I can do that,' Simon panics even more.

'You can take my copy of *Melody Maker* with you, if you'd like, and tell her what they're saying about the new John Lennon album,' Ian says kindly, his head still tilting off the bed.

'Thank you.'

'Oh no, do you know what, actually I think it says five past eight,' Ian says as he hands over the magazine, still looking across at the clock, mesmerized by watching it tick upside down.

'Can you not tell the time?'

'It's confusing when you look at a clock upside down. Have you ever tried it?'

Simon strides over to check the clock himself.

'It is five past eight! I'm late,' Simon says worriedly.

He quickly scoops up all his loose coins from his drawer and runs towards the door.

'Have you got enough change?' Raj calls out.

'I hope so. I don't know how much calls to France cost.'

'Good luck!' Both Raj and Ian shout.

'OK, what about . . . Would you rather always hop around on one foot or . . .' Ian continues, as Simon rushes down to the basement where the one communal telephone is located. It is normally vacant in the evenings, with most boys making their weekly call home to their parents on the weekends. With every step he takes, his nerves grow.

He hears the muffled sound of another voice as he reaches the last set of stairs.

'Yes, Mum, I'm doing all my homework . . . no, I know . . . don't worry . . .'

Simon peers around the corner and spots Julian – a boy in the year above – loudly gabbling away, scribbling on a piece of scrap paper as he talks, looking more interested in his sketch than the conversation.

He strides towards Julian and the phone, trying to gesture that he needs to make a call. Julian simply ignores him, and continues to shade in his doodle.

Simon tries to take the pen off him to write a message, but Julian takes the receiver away from his ear as his mother's voice still jabbers away.

'Julian, please can I use the phone?'

'No.'

'I'll give you my dessert tomorrow lunch if you let me use the phone now?' Simon barters, food being the ultimate currency for teenage boys.

Julian considers the offer as Simon hovers next to him, but instead of accepting he carries on talking.

'How's Uncle Jim doing?' He says down the phone, whilst smirking to Simon. He covers the receiver with his palm and whispers his demand. 'Desserts for the month?'

He knows he has Simon over a barrel.

With the main courses barely edible, desserts are the one pleasure Simon has. And the one thing keeping him from starving.

'A week?' Simon nervously haggles, contemplating going hungry for a week.

'Three weeks. Final offer.'

Simon sighs.

'Sure, go on then.'

'Shake on it.'

Simon puts out his hand, and Julian crushes it as he shakes it strongly.

'I was finishing now anyway.'

'Bye Mum, I've got to go,' Julian interrupts his mum, puts the phone down, and slides past Simon. 'Hope this call is worth it. I'm looking forward to my double desserts for the next three weeks!'

He laughs as he strides back up the staircase, taking two steps at a time.

Simon tries to ignore Julian's smug laughter. He stares at the phone as he waits to ensure Julian is fully out of earshot, before carefully dialling Sylvie's number, making extra sure he gets the numbers right.

'Come on Sylvie, pick up. I've given up my desserts for this,' he speaks to himself as the phone dials. The ring tone is different – he hasn't phoned abroad before.

He taps his feet nervously as it rings and rings, hoping that he's not missed her now.

Why is she not picking up?

He knows if it was the other way around, he'd have been hovering over the phone ready to pick it up as soon as it first chimed.

He finally hears a click.

'Oui, allo?'

'Hello? Sylvie? It's Simon . . . from Bristol . . . your pen pal,' he says timidly.

'Allooo?'

'Ummm, bonjour, no sorry . . . bonsoir!' He now practically shouts down the phone.

'Qui est à l'appareil? Ça coupe!'

The voice is joined by another voice, and they seem to be having their own conversation.

''Ello . . . Simon?' A different, sweeter, younger-sounding voice now speaks, pronouncing Simon as Seemon.

'Hi, Sylvie?' Simon's heart beats so loudly, he expects Sylvie can hear it down the phone.

'Sorry, that is my mum. I did not think you call. I thought you 'ad . . . euh . . . forgot. I think we say huit . . . eight?'

'Yes we did, sorry I'm a few minutes late.'

'No, it is after nine here.'

'Oh. I . . . I completely forgot about the time difference. I'm so sorry. Can you talk now?' Simon panics, worried that he's missed his chance.

'Yes I can, for a little bit.'

'Oh phew, that is good.'

He'd imagined what she sounded like when he read her letters, but as they continue to share pleasantries her voice is different from what he'd expected. He finds her pronunciation and her speech, which is punctuated by pauses and 'euhs', endearing.

'Thank you for all your letters, by the way. It's really nice to, ummm, you know, have someone to talk to, or write to, you know.' Simon is so nervous that his voice falters and he stumbles over his words, speaking worse English than Sylvie.

'Sorry, can you . . . speak a little, little bit less quick. I am more better at reading than hearing I think.'

'Of course, I'm sorry. I was just saying that I really like getting your letters.' Simon says, slowly and carefully.

'Ah I'm happy. I very like getting the letters from you too. Did you –'

'– What did –' They both go to speak over each other, Simon breathing heavily with nerves.

'Sorry, you go,' Simon says, awkwardly.

'I go to ask if you watch the Eurovision?'

'Oh no, I didn't. I'm sorry. I know I said I would, but my dad wouldn't let me watch it, so I only watched the first performance which was The Netherlands, but I liked their song. Did you watch it?'

'Yes, I did. Les Pays-Bas – or what do you say – The Netherlands? They won, so I think you watched the best. I did like the song from the UK also. I go to record store today to try and find it.'

'Ah yes, did you buy anything else?'

'No, I look to see if they have new T. Rex album you say about.'

'Ah really? I'm still trying to save up for it.'

'I tell you if I find it, OK? I love to go to concert someday for T. Rex.'

'To see them? Yes, so would I!'

'We both go?'

'Us? Together? Yes, definitely. That would be very nice.'

Simon can't believe what he's hearing. Can this be real? He's waiting for another moment like in the cafe when he realizes he's got the wrong end of the stick.

'And I take you to the record store here also? Would you like that?'

It is real. She really is saying these things.

Sacrificing his desserts was definitely worth it.

'Yes, I'd love that!' He beams, just thinking about exploring record stores together. 'Actually, I wanted to tell you that I've applied for my place on the exchange so maybe, if you'd like to, you could apply too? Then we could have two weeks in Bordeaux together and then two weeks here?'

'Oui, I do that. I look forward to it a lot.'

They continue talking for another ten minutes,

joyfully planning their time together. Simon can't help but smile to himself as they speak. He puts Ian's magazine away, not needing any prompts.

'Sorry, but I think I have to go now. My dad need to use the telephone.'

'That's OK. I'm nearly out of change anyway and we have lights out soon. It was really nice to talk to you though.' He smiles as if she can see him.

'Yes, and you too. I hope we talk soon.'

'Yes, and I look forward to getting your next letter.'

'I write it tomorrow.'

'Bye Sylvie.'

'Bye bye Simon.'

23

I put the telephone down as Mrs Cook barges into the kitchen.

'One of the guests has come down to breakfast and he's only wearing a towel!' she exclaims, her face flushed.

'And you didn't say anything?' I ask, as I help myself to a piece of toast. I really must stop snacking on the leftovers.

'What was I meant to say? I don't know what your dress code is!'

'We don't have a dress code.'

'There you go then.'

'That doesn't mean . . . oh, never mind. I'll have to go and speak to him.'

'Maybe he's sleepwalking?' Daisy pops out from behind Mrs Cook.

I didn't see her there. And I don't know why she's here so early. She's not rostered on for another two hours. I do wonder why I bother writing her a timetable.

'It's dangerous to wake someone when they're sleepwalking. I read about it online,' she continues.

'Did the gentleman look like he was sleepwalking, Mrs Cook?'

'No, he spoke to me. He ordered a Full English and was quite specific that he wanted extra of everything.'

Oh great.

I walk through to the guests' breakfast room, and as I enter, it is as I feared.

Ian is sitting there reading the paper, wrapped in nothing but his – thankfully large – white bath towel. His rock'n'roll lifestyle is certainly not in line with my quaint cottage.

'Good morning!' He looks up, nonchalantly.

'What on earth are you doing?'

'I was going to ask you the same thing. What have you been doing? I've been trying to find you! I went to use the bathroom, and I managed to lock myself out of my room.'

'How did you manage . . .?' I don't even try and fathom. 'So you thought you'd just come down for breakfast?'

'Well, I looked for you but the sign said you'd be back shortly so I thought I'd sit and wait.'

'And you couldn't have asked Mrs Cook for a spare key?'

'She came in and asked what I wanted for breakfast so I ordered. You know, I'm quite peckish. Maybe you should think about putting mini bars in the rooms.'

Not only is he staying for free, but he's now giving me tips on how to run the place.

'You need to put some clothes on now,' I say sternly.

'But my breakfast will be here in a minute.'

'You know there are other *paying* guests staying here.

I can't have them seeing you like this. We're not some kind of spa hotel.'

I start shepherding him back through the reception, up the stairs, but it's sod's law that the front door opens at that very moment.

It's Anna.

She looks bemused as soon as she sees us.

'Morning,' I say, trying to shield Ian.

'Morning to you too,' she raises her eyebrows, looking thoroughly confused. 'Should I ask?'

'Anna, this is Ian . . . Ian, this is Anna, my daughter.'

'Oh wow, this is your daughter,' Ian says.

'This is *the Ian*? Your school friend who you're going on the trip with?' She raises her eyebrows so high now that they nearly leave her forehead.

'He's told you about it then,' Ian replies.

'I think we can save the greetings for later,' she laughs, as Ian looks like he's going to walk over to hug her. 'Yes, he mentioned it. I said you could go if you both prove you're fit enough.'

I don't think Ian's half-naked body which spills over his towel is going to convince her.

'There's a spin class this morning in Bridport – if you survive that then I suppose you have my blessing,' Anna says as she takes her seat behind the desk.

'No problem. Let's get going,' Ian says confidently.

'I'd recommend putting some clothes on first!' She calls out.

*

'Who thought it would be a good idea to combine a bar with a gym?' I ask as we enter Spinning Around, located in Bridport, a more zestful market town just along the coast.

'A genius?' Ian says as he immediately takes a look at the food menu, and heads to the bar to order a drink.

'I think you're meant to take the class and then have a drink, not the other way around,' I call after him but Ian is already ordering a pint.

Given his morning antics, his constant complaints about his free room, and his incessant flirting with Mrs Cook, I'm pleased just to get Ian out of the cottage.

I pick up a leaflet from one of the tables, as Ian waits at the bar for his drink.

'Spinning Around is a unique place where the fitness conscious can enjoy a spin class followed by an alcoholic or non-alcoholic drink and something to eat.'

Fitness conscious, I laugh to myself.

As Ian staggers back, gulping down his pint, five young mums walk in chatting and laughing, all wearing zipped, branded hoodies and pristine trainers. Evidently regulars here, they head straight on to the bikes, waving friendlily to the barman.

I look across the room, at the far wall which is lined with a floor-to-ceiling mirror.

'So we have seats and tables one side of us for people to sit and watch? And then a full-length mirror? Is that so everyone can watch our red faces and pained expressions throughout the class? I'd prefer not to watch

147

myself sweating excessively, let alone everyone else being able to see!'

'You'll be fine, this is only an intermediate class,' Ian replies as if he takes spin classes all the time.

'Intermediate?! Shouldn't we have started with the beginners?'

'Beginners is for people who can't even ride a bike.'

'I don't think that's right. And anyway when was the last time you actually rode a bike?' I realize I should have asked him this before, given the circumstances.

He doesn't respond; instead he follows the women and climbs on to the bike next to them, leaving me to climb on to the one behind him in an otherwise empty row.

Ian's shorts are already falling down, meaning I am faced with the sight of his bum crack. I've already seen enough of him today.

I look around the room as the bikes start to fill up and I fear we're going to be the oldest here. In addition to the five women, there are a few twenty-somethings who spend more time photographing the bikes than actually sitting on them. Two of the girls position themselves at the front of the class so they can film themselves in the mirror as they pretend to cycle.

'Welcome everyone to today's class – I see we've got a couple of new joiners today. Are we all ready to get started?' The instructor, a young muscly man wearing a barely-there white vest, asks as he attaches his microphone around his ears.

The response is muted.

'Come on, guys, you're going to have to give me more than that. The sun is shining and we're about to get our sweat on. Who's ready to go?'

Can I leave already?

I look forward towards Ian, but to my surprise he is lapping it up, and responding to the instructor's call for enthusiasm, bellowing out, 'Yes, let's go!'

Maybe that's the effects of the pint working already.

'That's more like it! OK. We're going to start easy and gradually build it up. Remember, you can take it down a level at any time if it gets too much,' the instructor looks directly at the two of us.

'I think that disclaimer was for our benefit,' I whisper forward to Ian, but he can't hear me, especially as the music starts to blast out of the surround-sound speakers, the lights are dimmed, and the room suddenly transforms into a nightclub.

'OK, we're going to use the tempo of the music to guide us. Let's take it up in 5, 4, 3, 2, 1.'

I try to sync my peddling to the heavy beats of the music, copying what the instructor is doing. He makes it look effortless when it is certainly anything but. My legs already ache.

'Get ready, heart rates going up, stand up . . . good, yes.' The instructor continues to shout. 'Feel the burn.'

Stand up?

I look at my heart rate which is rocketing . . . 140, 150, 160.

149

God. Is Anna trying to kill me? We're definitely not at the intermediate stage.

'Drop to the saddle! Take a drink if you need it. How are you new guys doing?' The instructor asks in between aggressively barking orders.

'All good,' Ian shouts out before I can reply. Not that I have enough oxygen to breathe, let alone talk.

'Brilliant. OK, we're going to go again in five. That was an easy start, so we're going to crank it up now for six minutes.'

'Easy? Who said it was easy?' I blurt.

I look at Ian, who seems to be coping fine. How is he managing? He can't be more fit than I am, surely?

'Change the gears up, everyone.'

I watch Ian closely and notice he's not actually changing the gears each time.

He's such a cheat. No wonder he's still pedalling fast.

By the time the torture ends, I wobble off the bike and fall into one of the comfy chairs. Ian sits next to me, wiping the sweat dripping from his beard.

'Do you ladies fancy joining us?' He asks as the five women walk past us. They politely decline the offer of two very sweaty out-of-shape men who look like they're about to die.

'So how did you find that?' Ian asks after a few minutes, when we've finally managed to catch our breath, and after the instructor has checked on us – presumably for insurance purposes.

'I thought exercise was meant to make you feel good, I feel like keeling over.'

'It wasn't that bad,' Ian brushes it off.

'I saw you cheating.'

'I wasn't cheating!'

'You weren't moving the gears.'

'No, it's just I have to take it easy, I had a few heart complaints a couple of years ago. Nothing serious but –'

'You've got a heart problem? And you're suggesting we cycle to Bordeaux? Why didn't you mention that?'

I can't tell if this is another of Ian's fabrications or if he's being honest.

'Obviously we wouldn't be going at that pace, we would take it leisurely. I'll be fine. I mean, we're all going to die at some point, aren't we.'

I look at him, petrified.

'So what do you say then? Are we going to do it?'

I think of Raj. Of how much I'd like to do something to honour him.

I think of Sylvie, and wonder if maybe our trip could lead to us finally meeting.

And then I weigh up what's worse. Risking mine and Ian's lives going on the trip, or having Ian crash for longer at the cottage and the stress killing me.

Either way, it seems to end with my demise.

'Go on then. Let's do it,' I say, shaking my head.

*

From: Sylvie, To: Simon

Simon,

Yes, I should probably change my profile photo in case any more of my teenage acquaintances want to get back in touch! I can see why the photo of Jacques, my cat, might confuse them!

I'm so sorry to hear about Raj. Were you still close? That's lovely that you reunited with Ian again though. This is a proper trip down memory lane then for you. I'll have to find my old school items now, I think I've kept them somewhere.

Goodness, I'm very sorry to hear about your wife. That is awful. I don't imagine something like that ever gets easier. I was married too, but Antoine, my ex-husband, and I divorced a few years ago now. So as I said, it's just me and the cat now! Fortunately both Romain and Nicolas live nearby. It's nice that I see them a lot, and I babysit Leo often too.

How lovely you have a daughter (it's all boys in my family!) and that you run the B&B together. I didn't imagine you running a bed and breakfast. Maybe I'll have to come and stay one day. That is very exciting about her wedding. How do you feel about it?

That's very well remembered that I wanted to become a teacher (or was that just reading through the old letters?!) I actually went down a different path, and I work as an English to French translator – normally of fiction novels. So really I should thank you for helping me improve my English all those years ago – when you only sent me letters in English rather than French! It's never too late for you to learn French though; maybe I should finally give you some lessons.

Yes, I'm still a big music fan. Not so much modern music though. Romain did take me to see The Rolling Stones, and also Elton John when they toured France a couple of years ago, which was amazing. I still have lots of my old vinyl records. I will have to give them a listen now we're talking about music.

I had better not hold you up any more reading this – you had better get back to your guests! Sylvie x

From: Simon, To: Sylvie

Dear Sylvie,

I guess I have somewhat mixed emotions about the wedding. Obviously, I'm so happy for Anna, and her fiancé Ollie is a really lovely young man. But yes, it feels strange her getting married, and of course, there's part of me that feels like I'm letting go of my little girl. I think there's that little fear of where do I fit in, and am I still important any more? Is that silly?

No, I didn't see myself running a B&B either! It was very much Caroline's idea, but we've had many enjoyable years here. Of course, you're always more than welcome to come and stay here. You can look it up if you'd like, it's called Castle Cottage in Dorset. We have the most wonderful countryside around us if you like long walks. (We used to talk about glam rock and we're now mentioning countryside walks – we are getting old!)

I'm sorry to hear about your divorce. I must admit I got confused by your messages and I thought Jacques was your husband! It must be very nice to have your family still living close to you. I feel really lucky that Anna lives nearby and helps me run the B&B, although I do sometimes feel that I'm holding her back.

I'll try and not take all the credit for your successful career, but it does sound like I had a major role in it! That sounds a really interesting job. So presumably you can work remotely then?

I'm very jealous about the concerts. I can't remember the last time I went to a concert. Although I did go and see Ian perform the other night – he is a very good David Bowie tribute act. Slightly bizarrely the concert was at a retirement home – I felt it was a vision of my future!

Sorry for these long messages and if I'm oversharing. It is nice to be able to message someone – normally I just have the guests to talk to (or more accurately, deal with their complaints!). It feels strangely familiar writing to you, even after all these years.

Best wishes,
Simon

24

'Where do we start?' I ask Ian rhetorically as we walk into the large, out-of-town branch of Halfords in Dorchester. The shop, more akin to a warehouse, has aisles and aisles full of car parts, camping equipment, and – what we're looking for – bikes.

Before we're even two steps into the store, and before Ian can respond, an over-friendly sales assistant jumps out of nowhere to greet us. He looks like he's been waiting to pounce on some unsuspecting customer for a while.

'Hi guys, can I help you?'

The young man is wearing a black and orange polo shirt, which must be the staff uniform, and his dark, scruffy hair is up in a bandana. His badge, pinned to his polo shirt, reveals his name is Glenn and that he is happy to help.

Ian and I both look at each other, before Ian takes the lead.

'Yes, hopefully you can help us. We're going to be cycling to Bordeaux next week, and we need the best bikes for the trip. Which would you recommend?'

Glenn looks us up and down, seemingly less than convinced that we could cycle home, let alone to Bordeaux.

'Ok, I've got you, what bikes do you have at the moment?' Glenn asks.

'Nothing fancy. Mine is about twenty years old and rusty, and is shoved in the back of my shed,' I reply.

'Ah no worries, how much would you say you know about bikes?'

'I'd say I know a fair bit,' Ian bluffs.

'Sorry, I wouldn't say I know that much. Isn't a bike a bike? I always kind of thought you just got on it and peddled,' I step in.

'That's where you'd be mistaken, mate. There's a whole range of options depending on what you're looking for.' Glenn turns his back and starts walking. 'If you just want to follow me.'

'So, are you cycling to Bordeaux for charity?' he asks as he leads us through the store, past the other shop assistants who stand by the till, tapping their feet and singing along to the radio playing over the speakers, past shelves of baby car seats, spray paints, scooters, and finally to the cycling section.

'No,' I say too firmly, before realizing it sounds like I have an issue with charities. 'We're reliving our youths shall we say.'

There must be a hundred bikes lined up – all of which look a lot more modern and comfortable than the bikes we rode before.

'So I'm guessing you don't cycle much?' Glenn asks, presumptively, as I start trying to browse the prices.

'I cycle when I can, but I guess it's only from time to

time these days,' Ian exaggerates again. He's such a fibber.

'OK, well let's have a look,' Glenn pauses and looks at the bikes in front of us, seemingly trying to calculate something in his mind. 'I would say, it's obviously quite a big undertaking cycling to Bordeaux at your . . . you know, when you're not a regular cyclist . . . so maybe you would consider getting electric bikes?'

'I think that would be cheating, wouldn't it?' Ian chuckles.

'Would it really?' I reply, thinking that sounds a lot better.

'OK then, I'd probably recommend the Raleigh Detour for you. It's a hybrid which is popular for European bike trips. It's got a lightweight aluminium frame, it's got narrower tyres and bigger 700c wheels for greater efficiency, the twenty-one-speed Shimano drivetrain gives you great range . . .'

He may as well be talking a different language as he rambles on about the bike's capabilities.

'Would you like to hop on and try it? See what you think?'

Glenn gives us some space as Ian clambers on to the bike.

'Can you remember breaking into the outdoor pursuits storeroom to get all our gear last time?' Ian reminisces as he sizes up the bike and pretends to pedal.

'Yeah, we had to creep around in the middle of the night.'

'And we nearly got caught by the prefects!'

'It was almost disastrous, wasn't it? At least this trip should be easier in terms of having money and not having to steal the equipment. Can I try?'

As Ian swings his legs around to get off, he nearly kicks over the bike next to it. I have a sudden vision of him toppling over the whole row of a hundred bikes.

'Have you heard anything more from Sylvie since that first message?'

'Yes, I got a message from her this morning actually. I was wrong, she isn't married,' I reply as I take a seat. I rub my hands along the smooth handlebars, and I see what Glenn means that a bike isn't just a bike. This is a completely different level to the old, rusty one I have hidden in the shed somewhere, or the ones we took on our last trip.

'So you're definitely in now!' He winks.

'Stop it!'

'So what do you think?' Glenn asks, interrupting our conversation. 'Do you have any questions?'

I look at Ian for his opinion, but he doesn't respond.

'It seems good,' I reply, not knowing what else to say about a bike. 'There's just a lot to think about.'

'Sure, I'll just give you a few minutes.'

I wait until Glenn steps aside before whispering to Ian, 'Have you seen the price?'

'What?' Ian shouts back.

'I said they're quite expensive,' I whisper louder, not wanting Glenn to hear.

'Expensive?' Ian repeats loudly. 'But they sound quite good. Don't you think?'

'I suppose so.'

'If these are too expensive, I can show you some more budget options?' Glenn, who clearly hasn't been giving us any privacy, says politely. 'We do have a few cheaper options but this is very reasonable, especially with the sale. To be honest, I'm tempted to buy one myself.'

Ian and I look at each other, again, as if we're communicating telepathically. We're not.

'Go on then,' I relent.

'Perfect, I'll radio through to my colleague and ask him to get two from the back. Whilst we are waiting, shall we have a look at clothing next?'

'Clothing?'

'Well, if you're cycling to Bordeaux you will need suitable kit, and I'm guessing if you don't have bikes then you probably don't have Lycra?'

'Do we really need Lycra? We're not trying to shave a millisecond off our Olympic time, we're just going to be plodding through quaint French villages.'

'It's up to you, but I would recommend it. Shall I just show you what we have and then you can decide?'

'Yes, let's have a look,' Ian agrees.

Thirty minutes later, Glenn scans all the items through the till. The bikes, the helmets, the Lycra, the water bottles, the sunglasses, the pumps, the padded shorts, the gloves, the locks, the bags . . .

'How much is this all costing?' I stare at the screen, worried by the numbers I am seeing. 'You know we're going to have to wear and carry all this.'

'So that comes to £824.88 altogether. Would you like to split that?'

'We could have got a taxi to Bordeaux, there and back again, for less!'

Maybe stealing the equipment last time was the better idea.

'Come on, it's for Raj,' Ian replies.

I can already tell that Ian is going to use that line to get me to agree to everything.

Glenn smiles enthusiastically and waves goodbye as we wheel our purchases out of the store and he calculates his commission.

25

'Were the outfits really necessary?'

Ian and I stand outside the cottage, dressed from head to toe in our less-than-flattering Lycra outfits, our bikes propped up against the wall, and our helmets in our hands.

I catch our reflection in the window.

What on earth do we look like?

With the Lycra clinging to all of our curves, and our bellies hanging out over our shorts, it is certainly not a flattering look. I'm not sure if Ian stands out more or less in the Lycra than in his usual get-up.

'If we look like cyclists, we'll feel like cyclists,' Ian replies, sounding as if he's suddenly transformed into Plato.

I can say for certain that I don't look or feel like Sir Bradley Wiggins.

I look like an out-of-shape, sixty-year-old man who hasn't cycled since he was a teenager. I feel hot and sweaty, and we've not even started cycling yet.

What is worse is we seem to have gathered a small crowd to see us off, and they're now all staring at us in these stupid outfits.

Anna and Ollie, Daisy, Mrs Cook, a couple of

intrigued guests who poke their heads out their windows, Sue from the Post Office, and Shirley from the *Gazette*, who is there with her pen and pad, jotting everything down. I could be on the front cover again at this rate.

'I need to get a photo of you both first, especially in those fetching costumes.' Anna directs us to pose, as she snaps away on her iPhone.

'Smile, both of you!'

I manage to force a smile just for Anna.

'They're so lovely,' Anna says, checking her phone, almost tearing up.

'I suppose we ought to get going,' I say, conscious of how much time we need to get to Poole. After all, it took us forty-five minutes just to get into the outfits.

'Are you absolutely sure you don't just want me to drop you to the airport instead? It's not too late to change your mind,' Anna asks.

I look at Ian, wishing he'd relent and just say yes.

He doesn't.

'Thanks darling, but no, we're going to do this properly,' I fill the silence. I don't sound as convincing as I intend to.

'You promise not to push yourselves too much? Both of you!'

'I promise.'

'It's OK, Anna, I will look after him,' Ian puts his arm around my back.

'Why does that not fill me with much reassurance?'

Anna laughs apprehensively, having been regaled with all of Ian's stories during his stay.

'We're older and wiser now,' he says.

'Older and more forgetful, maybe,' I mumble, as I notice Ollie moving towards the cottage door, glancing across at Anna.

'Is everything OK with you and Ollie? I've noticed you've barely spoken to each other all day. Has something happened?'

'We're fine. It's nothing, honestly. We just had a little argument over something silly. Nothing to worry about.'

'Anna? I don't have to go . . . I don't want to put any more stress on you.'

'Dad, it's fine. Have you got everything? You've got your passports? Your travel insurance? The ashes?'

'Yes, yes. We're not that forgetful!' I nod to Anna as she runs through the list. 'We've got everything. You can feel these bags if you don't believe me!'

'Actually, just wait a second. I got you a little something else to add to that. Hopefully it won't weigh you down any more. Give me a minute,' she says, as she turns around and heads back into the cottage.

I smile awkwardly at Sue as I wait. If seeing me like this doesn't put her off, then I don't know what will.

'Here you go,' Anna comes running out into the garden, holding a pair of portable speakers. 'I thought some music might give you a boost. I've also made a playlist of all your favourite seventies songs on Spotify for you to listen to. The app is on your phone.'

'I don't know what to say. That's so kind, thank you darling. It should be me getting you something, not the other way round. You didn't have to do that,' I beam.

'I know it's not quite a mixtape, but I thought it might keep you going when the going gets tough. They just clip on to your handlebar like that.' She demonstrates, attaching them to my bike, before starting the playlist on my phone. 'All The Young Dudes' by Mott the Hoople starts blasting out.

'This is amazing. Really. Thank you so much.'

'They should be simple even for you to use, but there's the instructions too,' she shoves the paper notes in my bag.

'Come here,' I say as I give her a huge hug. 'I've already allocated all the rooms for while I'm gone, I've done the food order, I've left all the notes on the desk . . .'

'Dad, we've already been through it all three times. It will be fine.'

'OK, but if anything happens with you, or the wedding, or the cottage, or you just want us to come back early just call me. OK?'

'Just enjoy your trip . . . and please be careful! Remember to wear your helmet at all times,' Anna whispers as she helps clip it on over my head.

'I'll see you in a couple of weeks. Love you.'

'Bye Dad. I love you too.'

Everyone watches and cheers as we set off out of the garden, down the small country lane towards the main road, wobbling as we go.

'Dad! Watch out!' Anna calls as we nearly crash straight into the Jurassic Explorer double-decker bus, which takes the bend at an almighty speed.

'I saw it!' I shout back.

I look over my shoulder and see her covering her eyes with her hands.

26

THEN

April 1975

'She's sent you a mixtape! That's not fair. Why doesn't Jean-Luc send me anything?' Raj moans as he sees the tape drop out of Simon's envelope. Ian, at the mention of mixtape, clambers across from the other side of the room on to Simon's bed too.

Simon, in his excitement, doesn't know what to look at first, the tape or the letter. He picks the letter, and quickly skims through the reams of pages, too excited to really digest the words, whilst clinging on to the tape to ensure one of the other two doesn't look at it before him.

'This is a collection of her favourite songs,' he announces as he puts the letter down, and focuses on the tape. He looks at it in awe, as if it's a bar of solid gold. Sylvie has drawn her own cover art, and on the back she's listed all the tracks on both sides.

My favourite songs
  1. All The Young Dudes – Mott the Hoople
  2. You Ain't Seen Nothing Yet – Bachman-Turner Overdrive

3. Star Star – The Rolling Stones
4. I'm Not in Love – 10cc
5. Crocodile Rock – Elton John
6. Children of the Revolution – T. Rex
7. Cum on Feel the Noise – Slade
8. Rebel Rebel – David Bowie
9. Fox on the Run – Sweet
10. Parlez-moi de lui – Nicole Croisille
11. Le Sud – Nino Ferrer
12. Hier Encore – Charles Aznavour

'I wish I'd have kept her for my pen pal,' Raj sulks as he notices his favourite Elton John is one of the tracks. 'And Bowie . . . T. Rex!' Every artist he reels off, he's excited by.

'Go on. Put it on then, let's listen,' Ian prompts.

'Raj, can I use your tape player to listen to it?'

'Of course.' Raj walks over to his bed and chucks the tape player across the room.

Simon removes the tape that is already in the player, and replaces it with Sylvie's carefully curated selection of tracks. He would like to savour it on his own, but there's no chance of that with Raj and Ian as keen as him to listen.

'Hello Simon, I hope you are well. I wanted to make you a tape. Here are songs I like. I hope you like too. Until I can take you to the record store, I hope you enjoy this. And maybe in a future day we listen together,' Sylvie's voice speaks from the player.

'Man, this girl really likes you,' Ian pushes Simon.

The tape crackles before a French radio host talks for a couple of seconds, and then the music starts playing. Whether it's the lyrics, or the thought that Sylvie has compiled these tracks for him, music has never sounded so good.

They spend the next forty-five minutes listening to the tape, and only then do Raj and Ian head out, leaving Simon to lie on his bed, close his eyes, and listen to the beauty of each and every track, over and over again, imagining him and Sylvie together. Despite not understanding the lyrics, he even likes the French songs, guessing what the artists are singing about.

He rewinds Sylvie's brief introduction over and over again, listening to her voice on repeat. He reaches into his drawer, where he's kept all her letters. He pulls out the photo of her, stares at it, and realizes that, for the first time in his life, he is falling in love.

*

Simon walks back into the dorm room, after going to do his chores, humming 'All The Young Dudes'. He's not been able to think about anything other than Sylvie for the past few hours.

He stops humming when he realizes Raj is dictating his homework into his tape recorder, and mouths 'sorry'. He climbs over his bed, rather than walking around, and reaches straight into his drawer to take out

Sylvie's letter, wanting to read it again. She talks about the record store she wants to take him to, that she only included a Charles Aznavour song as he's the only French singer Simon knows, and that she will translate the lyrics for him when they meet some day. His smile grows as he reads each sentence. He pulls out the mixtape case and admires her handiwork. He's already decided he's going to return the favour, and record his own one for her, as long as Raj lets him use the tape recorder. He's just got to decide on the perfect tracks.

'So long as men can breathe or eyes can see . . . So long lives this, and this gives life to thee,' Raj recites the text into the microphone.

'What is that?' Simon asks as soon as he sees Raj raise his finger off the record button.

'It's for English. We have to learn a Shakespeare sonnet. I thought if I record myself reading it then I can listen back and hopefully learn it that way, but I kept mucking up halfway through.'

'Do you even understand it?'

'Apparently it's something to do with friendship, and death, I don't really know,' Raj shrugs.

'Where did you put Sylvie's tape?'

'Have you not got it there?' Raj nods to the cassette box Simon holds in his hand.

'No, it's just the case. I left the tape in your player as I was going to listen to it again. Where did you put it?'

Raj's face freezes. He immediately drops the tape recorder.

'I . . . but . . . why did you leave your tape in my player?'

'I wanted to finish listening when I got back from my chores.'

It suddenly dawns on Simon what's happened.

'You're joking, right?'

'I'm not joking, Si.'

'Come on. Where did you actually put it?'

'I'm really sorry. Obviously I thought you'd taken it out after you listened to it, and put my blank one back in. I wouldn't have . . .'

Simon jumps on to Raj's bed and snatches the device off him, forcing the tape player open. He pulls out the tape.

As he sees the French branding on the side of the tape, his face drops.

'How was I meant to know you'd left your tape in there?'

'How long have you been recording for?'

'I don't know. A few minutes.'

'Play it back.' Simon almost shouts.

Raj nervously rewinds the tape and hits the play button. They stand there listening to him reciting the same sonnet over and over again until he gets it right, before it finally cuts away from his voice into 'Crocodile Rock'.

Simon picks up the empty cassette box.

'That is the fifth song. You've recorded over four songs – and worst of all, Sylvie's voice!'

'Look Si, I'm really sorry –'

'– Just because your pen pal can't even be bothered to write to you, why did you have to ruin my tape?' Simon looks at the cassette box, devastated.

'No, I didn't know . . . I don't know what to say. What can I do?' Raj holds his hands up, as if surrendering, and nervously bites his lip.

'Nothing. Don't do anything. Ever again. I don't want to talk to you any more.' Simon snatches the tape off Raj and storms out of the room, not that he can play the tape anywhere else, or that he has anywhere to go.

He slumps to the floor on the landing outside their room, looking down at the tape, and can't stop the tear which starts to fall down his face.

27

Water drips off my brow as we pull over in a lay-by, just beyond Dorchester, and I look at my watch. How have we only been cycling for just over an hour? I feel like we should be almost in Bordeaux already.

I don't know how I'm going to get to Poole, let alone across France.

To make matters worse, the sky which was blue and beautiful now looks grey and miserable; rain is spitting down on us.

I try not to take this as a bad omen.

'Are you sure you don't want anything?' Ian asks, climbing off his bike, less than elegantly. He nearly trips himself over in the process.

'No, I'm OK thanks. We only had lunch just before we set off,' I say as I pant loudly.

I watch the queue of traffic, which we were holding up along the narrow countryside roads, flood past us – the drivers all staring out of their windows, looking disgruntled.

'Suit yourself.' Ian heads over to the extremely dodgy-looking burger van parked up between a large freight lorry and a smelly Portaloo. He scrambles around to find some loose change in his bag, as I study the menu from a distance.

A cultural trip, he said.

I look on as he seems to have a good chat with the woman flipping the burgers. I wonder if he factored in stoppages to his schedule. The Google Maps prediction seemed overly ambitious, even without burger stops.

'You're missing out,' he says as he returns, his full mouth making it difficult to understand what he's saying. 'You see life on the road is full of kebabs and burgers.'

As he speaks, he drops a couple of his chips, overflowing from the paper tray, on the ground. Without hesitation he bends down and puts them in his mouth.

'Got to refuel regularly to keep up our energy.'

'I'm not sure it looks the best quality,' I say, as the smell of the portaloo mingles with stench of the grease.

'I must have eaten from hundreds of places like this over the years on the way to and from gigs. Never had an issue, but suit yourself. What's the time?'

'It's just gone three,' I check my watch again.

'OK. I reckon we should be there by five. Comfortably.'

It is in fact four hours later when we finally arrive at our hotel in Poole, after being delayed by Ian's faulty internal compass – and dodgy stomach. The full-body Lycra outfits prove the worst possible outfit choice when needing to make regular toilet stops. A muffled 'Summer Breeze' by The Isley Brothers played ironically from Anna's speakers as we battled with cross-winds, slippery tarmac, and a constant stream of lorries speeding past inches away from us.

I'm now lumbered with the bags, waiting beside the reception desk, water dripping off me, whilst Ian laughs and jokes with the young female receptionist. I look around, worrying he's blown our entire budget on this first night's stay. It's certainly an upgrade from our last journey. He eventually strolls back from the check-in desk, and hands over a white, plastic card key.

'Here you go. The room is number . . .' He's forgotten already. 'Sorry, what did you say the number was?' He shouts back across the entrance hall.

'One-zero-one. I've written it on the card for you,' the blonde-haired woman calls back, miming writing.

'Room 101,' Ian relays the message, as if I couldn't hear.

'Well, now that is ominous. What am I most scared of . . .'

'And breakfast is served from 6 to 10 a.m. tomorrow,' Ian doesn't get the reference and continues talking.

'Thanks. What time do we have to leave for the ferry?'

'Good question. Let me just check.' Ian pats himself down, trying to remember where he put his notes. He eventually pulls out a torn scrap of paper from his bag, with notes which don't seem to correlate to English.

He studies these for a while, trying to comprehend his own writing.

Why did I let him organize everything?

'The harbour is only about ten minutes away,' I say, trying to help him.

'Yes, OK, so we just need to leave here at 7.30 a.m. then, that will give us plenty of time.'

'So I'll meet you in breakfast at seven? Goodnight then,' I say wearily, picking up my bag and heading towards to the lift.

'What do you mean? Where do you think you're going?'

'To my room.'

'Your room? We're both going to the same room. I just got us two keys.'

What?

I look back confused, too tired after the day's exercise to think.

'We're sharing a room. I got us a twin,' Ian clarifies my worst nightmare.

He's got to be kidding.

'Why?'

'Well, firstly, you told me you were on a budget because of paying for the wedding, and secondly, I thought it would be nicer to share, for old times' sake.'

It would be nicer to share?!

'Did you now?' I try to keep my cool, wanting nothing more than some peace and quiet, and distance from Ian. 'Does that mean we have to camp at some point too?'

Ian bursts out laughing, which doesn't reassure me.

We both enter the silver, mirrored lift and stay silent as the automated female voice updates us when we reach the second floor. I stare at my reflection.

We really do look ridiculous.

We lug our bags down the corridor until we find Room 101, having to complete almost an entire loop of the floor before we find it back by the lift.

It takes Ian three attempts to get the card key to work, putting it in the wrong way up, pulling it out too quickly. Every time the red light flashes, I want to jump in and do it myself.

'Can I?'

'No, I've got it now . . . oh no, I haven't.'

'Do you want to let me?'

'What was wrong with old fashioned key keys, not plastic cards.'

'It's the wrong way around. Come on, move out the way, I'll do it.'

When we eventually manage to break into our own room, it is overbearingly white, and minimalist. We drop our bags by the door and inspect our accommodation for the night. It is the first time we've shared a room since we were sixteen, and there are no posters of Bowie or Bolan on the wall here.

I realize it is the first time I've shared a room with anyone since Caroline.

'Well, this is an interesting design,' Ian calls out as I take off my shoes by the door, having watched Ian walk mud straight through the room.

'What's that?'

'Come and take a look.'

I walk, now barefoot, into the room, and stand next to Ian who admires the bathroom. A bathroom which has no door, whatsoever, and a shower which is separated from the beds only by a thin sheet of translucent glass.

'Is this what people pay money for these days?' I look horrified at the pretentious design.

'Keep your eyes to yourself, mate. No peeking.'

'Trust me, I've seen enough of you already over the last couple of weeks.'

'I apologize in advance for my bad stomach. You know, I'm not sure that burger agreed with me,' he says, as he heads straight into the bathroom.

'I know, Ian, I know.'

I crash on to my single bed, thinking maybe camping would have been preferable.

From: Sylvie, To: Simon

Hi Simon,

No, please, share away. It's very nice to talk to you too. At least you have the guests to talk to, I only have Jacques! I'm not sure who causes the most nuisance. At least I hope your guests don't scratch you for no reason, but then again?!

I know exactly what you mean about the feelings ahead of the wedding. I felt the very same way. It felt like a goodbye of sorts, even though I knew both the boys would be staying in Bordeaux. I think especially as Antoine, my ex-husband, and I had split by then, so it was just me on my own. I don't know how you've found it, or if you have had any relationships since your wife, but I've found it can be really tricky to meet new people. Especially as my job is solitary.

Trust me, though, you're always her dad, and she will always want you. I worried about my boys, but they're still coming home. The youngest still wants me to do his washing even though he's almost thirty! The one good thing with an empty house is I had more chance to be spontaneous, and I'm fortunate with my work that I can pick and choose the jobs I take on, and work remotely. I can drop Jacques off at Nicolas' and just head off on an adventure. It's been lovely as it's meant I have been able to travel a lot over the years. Last year, I visited Cambodia and Sri Lanka. Have you travelled much over the years?

I looked up your B&B on the internet and it does look lovely indeed. We are showing our age, but yes I like countryside walks. I'll certainly have to come and stay one day. That must be a full-time job running it though? I don't imagine you get much time off?

Sylvie x

From: Simon, To: Sylvie

Hi Sylvie,

You joke but you'd be surprised/horrified by what some of the guests do. Caroline and I used to write a notebook with the worst things. I thought it'd be amusing to publish but I think people would say it's too unbelievable. Although if it ever got published, you could translate the French edition!

No, I've not dated anyone since. I've certainly missed the company – someone to talk to, someone to laugh with. I'm very lucky that I have Anna, although I don't want to burden her with all my thoughts and problems. However, the time has just never felt right, and with the B&B, I've never really had much free time. Anna has started to push me to meet people over the last few months. She even tried setting me up on online dating but it wasn't for me. I went into town a couple of months ago and I recognized a woman – for the life of me I couldn't remember where I knew her from – and then I realized I'd seen her profile and all I knew was she was 'over-competitive at Monopoly'! I know what you mean about finding it hard to meet people. I feel the same, even with friends. There are not that many opportunities as you get older. That's why it's been nice to reunite with Ian – even if he has started to drive me somewhat crazy! So have you dated at all since Antoine?

That's amazing you've been able to travel the world so much. Cambodia and Sri Lanka sound very exotic. I was reading an article about tourism in Cambodia in the paper a couple of weeks ago. It sounds fascinating. Maybe one day I'll make it there. Do you have any other trips planned? Did you ever make it to England?

Caroline and I used to travel a fair bit before we bought the cottage, and then we had family holidays with Anna to the usual places – DisneyLand, etc., but since Caroline passed I haven't got away that much. Unfortunately, you're right. I normally don't get much time off – it's really a 24/7 job. We have some guests who like to wake me up in the middle of the night with their problems!

Funny that you mention it, as Ian proposed that we go on a rather impromptu trip so we've just set off on an adventure of sorts. I apologize if my responses are even more delayed than usual, as I'm not sure how much signal we'll have.

I'm pleased you liked the look of our cottage – I may be biased, but we are really in a beautiful corner of the world here. Yes, maybe your next adventure could be in Dorset. I mean it's slightly different than Cambodia but we do have nice cream teas!

Best wishes,
Simon x

28

'Good morning everyone, welcome on board this crossing from Poole to Saint-Malo, via Guernsey and Jersey. My name is Jonny Steel and I'm your captain for today's journey.'

'There's no way that's his real name,' Ian laughs, clearly talking from experience, as we climb onboard the ship, having left our bikes below deck. Thanks to us forgetting to set our alarm, we only just make it as the gates are shutting. As the last two passengers to board, we're hurried along by the stewards. I pant loudly as we climb the steps, still out of breath from our rush here.

The boat is packed full of holiday-makers, all scrambling around trying to find their seats and already raiding the duty-free gift shop. There are a few older groups, who are queuing for their cooked breakfasts, and a large gathering of young Scouts, who seem to be very loud and lively for this time of the day, off on their own adventure. We have to walk back and forth several times, trying to work out where our seats are located, needing to check the map for help. The long rows of identical bright-blue patterned seats match the carpeted floor.

'Sorry, would you mind if I just squeeze through,

thank you,' I ask a small child, who has commandeered the floorspace right by my seat, seemingly travelling all on his own.

The little boy continues staring straight ahead. I look around to see what he's looking at and realize that our allocated seats are right next to the kids' cinema zone.

Despite its fancy name, it's essentially a large TV screen, with a couple of soft furnishings inside a gate, but still, even before the ship has set sail, it's proving popular. In fact, there are already too many kids to fit in the demarcated zone so they have started cramming and climbing over the passenger seats to watch *Finding Nemo*.

I wait for Ian to comment on our unfortunate seat location, but no complaint is forthcoming. On the contrary, Ian, like one of the children is glued to the screen.

'What have I missed?'

I look up, thinking Ian is talking to me, before realizing he's asking one of the toddlers about the movie.

'You can't talk to the kids!' I whisper, as I notice Ian has tomato ketchup, from our hurried breakfast, dripping from his beard. 'How long is this journey meant to take?'

'I think it's meant to be about six and a half hours altogether,' he says, looking annoyed at being distracted from his movie.

'Six and a half hours?' I repeat, thinking that ferries would have gained a bit more speed in nearly half a century. My retort is lost as laughter erupts at something happening in the film.

As Ian continues chuckling at the movie, I check my phone but there are no new messages from either Anna or Sylvie. Instead I close my eyes, and try to relax. My muscles ache from our first few hours on the bikes yesterday, and what with sharing a room for the first time in so long, I barely slept. I forgot just how loud Ian used to snore at school, and it seems that with greater age comes even louder snoring.

'Are you OK? Simon?' Ian prods me in the arm and I realize this time he's actually talking to me.

'Sorry . . .' I open my eyes.

'You're not feeling seasick like last time, are you?'

The memories of our horrendous overnight ferry last time flash in my head.

'No, sorry, I'm just thinking about Anna.'

'What about her?'

'I don't know exactly, I'm just worried there's something the matter between her and Ollie. He didn't come over to watch Eurovision with us, and then every time I've seen them together recently, they don't seem to be themselves. Didn't you notice yesterday that they barely spoke to each other?'

Ian shakes his head, looking oblivious.

'In the whole time they've been together, sure they've had squabbles, but I've not seen them like that before.'

'It's probably just pre-wedding jitters. Loads of couples argue over small things before their weddings, don't they?'

'Well, exactly, that's why I'm worried. What if I'm putting too much stress on them leaving her to look after the B&B on top of the wedding?'

'She said she's fine, didn't she?'

'Yes, she did.'

'There you go then. She'll tell you if there are any problems. Come on. Just concentrate on enjoying our trip. When was the last time you even went on holiday?'

'Oh gosh. Not for ages. I haven't had a proper holiday since Caroline passed. It must have been ten or eleven years now. We went to the States with Anna the Christmas before she took her A Levels.'

'You've not been anywhere for that long? Not even in the UK?' Ian looks stunned.

'Well, Anna and I went away for a few days just to Devon when we were having work done on the cottage.'

'That doesn't count! Wouldn't she go away with you again?'

'I'm sure she would if I was paying! No, of course she would, but she's got Ollie, and they go away together. They've invited me before, but I wouldn't want to gatecrash. And it's not that easy with the B&B, certainly to do anything spontaneous. Caroline and I used to close for a month at Christmas, but I've kept it open since . . . In the first few years I wanted it as a distraction.'

'Surely you could be doing something more enjoyable with your time? Have you thought about retiring? Selling up even?'

'I've thought about it. More so when we get a spate of annoying guests!' I don't name any names. 'Obviously I could sell it and downsize, which would work financially. It's just tricky as I have to think about Anna. She runs it with me, it's her job too. I can't just make that decision as I'd be putting her out of a job!'

'Have you spoken to her about it?'

I shake my head again.

'Well, maybe you should?'

'But it's not just Anna, there's also Caroline.'

Ian looks confused.

'It was Caroline's dream to open it, and I'd feel guilty cutting it short. I feel I owe it to her to keep it thriving, to keep it living on in her memory. And it's also the place that we all lived, it's where Anna grew up. I'm not sure Anna would forgive me if I sold it.'

'You won't know if you don't talk to her. And obviously, I didn't know Caroline but I can't imagine she'd have wanted you to feel tied to it.'

'No, I suppose she wouldn't,' I mutter back.

'You talk about Caroline and Anna, but what about you? What do you want?'

I smile at Ian, not knowing how to answer.

'Anyway, at least try and enjoy this trip! Come on, we're going to have a great time!' he says, slapping my thigh before he returns to *Finding Nemo*.

I return to my thoughts, looking out to the endless sea on the horizon, and I realize – despite my already sore limbs and my initial fears – how nice it is to be out on an adventure.

As we eventually – six hours and a few naps later – make our way into the beautiful port of Saint-Malo, we stand outside on deck, watching land come into view. I look out across the panorama of the coastline and the shimmering, light-blue sea, full of wind-surfers and para-gliders. Tiny figures clamber along the coastal path all wearing sunglasses and caps. Bathers escape the heat in the crystal cool sparkling water. A jet boat races across, leaving a vanishing white streak in its wake. I watch one of the white yachts bob up and down. The young men on board, all with tanned, chiselled faces and sun-bleached, salty hair, the women young, attractive, all looking carefree.

Maybe I could get used to this, I think as the sun shines.

29

I try not to laugh as Ian tucks into a Full English breakfast on our first morning in France.

'How did you sleep?' I ask him, as I eat my – in comparison, rather paltry – fruit salad.

'So-so,' he mumbles between mouthfuls. He is already on his second plate, piled high with scrambled egg, sausages and bacon. 'Why don't you just let guests help themselves like this?'

'Because people like you would eat us out of business!'

We quickly left behind Saint-Malo's glimmering sea, the strong smell of suntan lotion, and the countless shops selling Nutella crêpes, making the most of the late afternoon sunshine to continue our journey south to the picture-perfect Dinan, a beautiful medieval town which from every angle looks like it should be on a postcard.

In contrast to the town, the hotel buffet breakfast room is rather soulless. Aside from us, there are only three other tables, and the bright yellow walls do little to brighten the mood. Traffic-light system posters are blue-tacked around the building to inform guests of the best times to get a table, but we're currently on amber and there's no queue. I turn to look at the table behind who take mouthfuls of their cereal in between large yawns. At least I slept better – I must be adjusting to Ian's snoring.

'Is that all you're going to have?' Ian looks at my bowl disparagingly.

'I'm trying to be healthy, haven't you noticed?'

'Why you doing that?' he asks, as if it's an utterly outrageous concept.

'Because we are about to try and cycle across France for a start! Secondly, I guess Raj's death has made me think about my health more. I think I probably eat too much gluten and dairy, or that's what Anna tells me anyway.'

'Nonsense! Everyone's a bloody vegan, or vegetarian, or intolerant to something these days! We always used to just eat what we wanted!'

'And then we got older, and they discovered high cholesterol.' As I speak, Ian shakes his head. 'I just want to be as healthy as I can be. At our age we have to start thinking about these kinds of things more.'

'What are you extending your life for? To spend the rest of your days working?' He's still going on about me needing to take more breaks from the B&B. 'Surely Raj dying makes you think you have to live for the day? If I'm going to drop dead tomorrow I don't want to waste my last few hours not enjoying them. Any meal could be my last, and certainly I'm not going to waste it. I promise you'll regret it if your last meal is that miserable bowl of melon and grapes!'

I laugh at our two opposing takes on the situation as I take my pill box out of my pocket. Each compartment is labelled with the day of the week so I know if I've had my statin. In contrast, Ian pulls out a loose tablet from his pocket and swallows it, without water. I don't know whether he's taking paracetamol, viagra, or ecstasy, and I'm not sure he knows either.

'We may as well take something for lunch,' Ian indicates the buffet spread as he polishes off his second plateful.

'We can't do that.'

'Of course we can. It's fine, I always take something when I'm on the road. Everyone does.'

'That's probably why they have a sign which says quite clearly "don't remove food from the breakfast hall". I nod my head to the big sign by the entrance, which is translated into multiple languages so that everyone can clearly understand it. I can't believe they have that many guests visiting from Croatia but it's still translated into Croatian.

'No one pays any attention to that. It only goes to waste. I expect they throw it all out if it's not eaten. We're actually helping the environment. That Greta what's-her-name would definitely encourage it.'

'Do you know what? I've not actually seen her discussing the benefits of stealing from hotel breakfast buffets at one of her rallies yet.'

'Come on, these hotels started all this by using the tiniest glasses and plates. I mean, who drinks out of glasses this small? You can barely get one sip of juice from it.' Ian holds the glass, which is more akin to a thimble, into the air. 'If they're going to limit us to a sip of orange juice, then it's fair game to take some extra food.'

I look around the room, wondering if we can get away with it. The maître d' circles around checking on the spread, and the small and quiet nature of the room makes stealing an even greater challenge.

'OK, what do we want?' Ian asks as if he's making a shopping list for the week.

He looks across at the usual array of continental offerings. Croissants, pains au chocolat, pains au raisin, yoghurts, cereals, cheeses, hams, bread, fruit, and some nice muffins which I think we should start stocking at the B&B.

I'm not going to be able to convince him otherwise, and so I anxiously watch as he wanders over and, less than subtly, piles a handful of bread rolls and a mountain of sliced ham and cheese on to his plate. I immediately realize that trying to cut out gluten and dairy in a country which is famous for bread and cheese isn't the best idea.

'It's your turn,' he says as he starts making up the rolls at the table.

I hesitantly walk up and grab a selection of fruit and a couple of pastries, trying to think what we might want to keep us going later on the road. As I take my seat again, I look around, seeing if I can get away with putting the food straight into my bag.

'Hurry up, she's coming back!' Ian whispers loudly, as I stuff the croissant into a napkin, drop it into my backpack, and kick it under the table, just before the maître d' returns from the kitchen. She stares at both of us suspiciously as we pretend to talk and continue eating our breakfasts.

'She definitely saw us,' I whisper, paranoid, as soon she looks away.

'Just act calmly,' Ian whispers, trying to soothe my nerves. His tactics are not working. I fiddle with my glasses as my eyes dart round the room, waiting for us to be kicked out of the hotel.

'I am acting calmly,' I shout, sweat dripping from my head.

We are conducting our theft as if we are operating a sophisticated jewellery robbery in Hatton Garden. Only we're more like those old men who got caught and spent their last years in prison than anyone who has ever successfully got away with the diamonds.

Ian leans under the table and drops his stash into my bag, then gets up again and less-than-discreetly pockets another banana. The way he's going, I'm quite surprised he doesn't put the cornflakes in his pocket, and then pour some milk in.

'Are you ready to go?' Ian says, not even bothering to sit down again.

I wait and watch the maître d' stroll into the kitchen. 'Yes, let's go now. Quick.'

I walk towards the door, with an apple in my left pocket, a satsuma in my right, the crumbled croissants, squashed ham and cheese rolls, and crushed muffins in my bag.

My walk quickly turns into more of a jog. I look like one of those funny Olympic race-walkers.

Why did we sit at the table furthest from the exit? The room suddenly seems bigger than before. The exit looks miles away.

How did I let Ian rope me into this?

As I sidestep one of the other guests who abruptly brushes past with his miniature glass of pineapple juice, I feel something drop from my bag. Please let it be my pill box. My phone even. I don't care if the screen has smashed. Just not one of Ian's bloody bread rolls.

As I look down, my fear is confirmed.

It is the bloody roll and it's doing exactly what it says it does. It rolls down the incline of the room. I debate whether I should quickly pick it up or pretend not to notice. I'm caught in two minds and I hover, staring at it.

As I look up, out of nowhere the maître d' has returned. She glares down at the bread roll, and then back at me, and then at the sign on the wall, as if the glances are enough to let us know that we are in trouble.

I shake my head, tut, and nod accusingly towards the poor man who has just sat down with his miniature glass of pineapple juice.

As soon as we're out into safety, I look across at Ian, laughing, feeling like we're teenagers again.

30

THEN

May 1975

Ian takes the largest plateful of lunch as he joins Simon and Raj in the vast school dining hall. The meat and veg don't look of the highest culinary standards but he doesn't seem to mind as he digs straight in.

'You're not still arguing, are you?' he mumbles as he chews. 'I can't put up with another day of silence!'

Raj looks across at Simon's distraught face, and then over to Ian, as if checking for permission to talk.

'It's not about that. Mr Sullivan just announced the names of the boys going on the French exchange, and Si isn't on the list. He found out that Si had forged his dad's signature.'

The mixtape mix-up is now yesterday's news.

'Oh, damn,' Ian nearly chokes on his food, as Simon still sits stony-faced, barely touching his plateful. 'How did he find out?'

'He rang his dad.'

'Crap. What's the punishment?'

'He said he was going to let Si off as he was pleased

he was so keen to improve his French,' Raj continues, speaking as if he's Simon's spokesperson.

'Well, that's good, ain't it?'

'The punishment is not going! I wanted to go to Bordeaux. I wanted to see Sylvie,' Simon sulks, breaking his silence.

'I'm sure there will be another chance.'

'I don't know how. Or when. This was my one golden opportunity. And I told Sylvie I was coming to see her. What is she going to think now? I really wanted to see maybe if there is something there – you know, more than just friends.'

'Like your first girlfriend?' Ian says proudly. 'Surely you knew you would get caught though? How did you think you were going to get away with it? Where was Sylvie going to stay when she came?'

'I'd have thought of something,' Simon mutters, realizing that his plan was doomed from the start. 'And what's worse is my dad knows I forged his signature. He's going to kill me!'

'Your dad has said you can go on the camp to Wales though . . . . that could be fun,' Raj says, knowing full well that camping in wet Wales will be anything but fun.

'Come on, we'll think of something. And at least you can finally have your pudding today,' Ian points to the jam sponge on Simon's tray. 'That's got to cheer you up!'

With everything else going on, Simon had forgotten

that the three weeks of having to hand over his precious desserts to Julian have come to an end.

And even better, jam sponge is his absolute favourite.

For a moment, at least, he forgets the disappointment, he forgets wanting to beg Mr Sullivan to change his mind. Simon reaches out and grabs the silver jug to smother his portion in custard.

Except it's not the custard jug. And he doesn't realize this until he has smothered his entire pudding in gravy.

His face sinks as he stares down at the brown liquid which now drowns his sponge, and mingles with the red jam.

'You've got to be kidding me,' Simon puts his head into his hands and despairs as the whole table erupts in laughter and ironic cheering. 'Well, that's just bloody great.'

He looks at the dessert and moves his spoon through the gravy, considering just eating it anyway.

'Come on, you can have mine,' Raj slides his untainted pudding across the table.

'Really? Thanks Raj, you're the best,' Simon smiles as he carefully checks the other jug, before demolishing his dessert.

The resentment over the mixtape debacle is already forgotten.

31

Whether it's the blue sky or Ian's pep talk on the ferry, I smile as we get back on our bikes.

The only downside, as we leave Dinan, is the cobbled stones which bump us up and down, and force us to get off and walk our bikes through the warren of narrow streets. We follow a man carrying his painting gear and easel, past the town's famous half-timbered houses, down the steep cobbled hill, browsing the arts and crafts shops, until we reach the impressive port, and begin our ride along the Ille-et-Rance Canal.

I don't mind that we're rapidly overtaken by a peloton of young cyclists – who Ian hopelessly tries to keep up with. I don't even mind when we're overtaken by a couple walking faster up a hill than we can cycle.

As we follow the beautiful, if slightly hazardous, gravel path, I switch on my new speakers, and we work our way through the set list of songs Anna has curated, all our old favourites. We sing and laugh, and replay Sweet's 'Fox on the Run' multiple times as we belt out the lyrics at the tops of our voices, seemingly having the majority of the French countryside to ourselves. I smile, thinking what a kind gesture it was from Anna, and how these same songs have made me happy for so many years.

We cycle past countless locks, boats, and fields and fields of unwrapped hay bales. We're stopped by a parade of black and white cows crossing the road, thinking that zebra crossings are for them. We pass the occasional house, and the even rarer little village. We see a couple of dogs fighting in front of a church, who pull their helpless owners into the conflict. We smile at a man who sits out on his front lawn drinking a glass of wine. We wave to a woman watering her plants. And every so often a cool breeze blows over us like someone is blowing out a candle, keeping us from over-heating.

By the time we make it to Rennes, having given 'slow travel' a new meaning, we collapse on a bench in the luscious gardens of Thabor Park, surrounded by thousands of roses. As we rest our weary legs, watching the world pass us by, I reach into my bag and pull out the postcard I bought in Dinan.

'What are you doing?' Ian immediately asks.

'I thought I'd write to Anna.'

'Do people still send postcards? We'll probably get back before it arrives!'

'You're probably right, but I thought it would be a nice surprise for her.'

As I scrawl the message, my handwriting gets smaller and smaller as I run out of space, and I end up having to continue writing around the address along the perimeter of the card.

'Talking of writing letters, what's the latest with

Sylvie? You've been very coy about it all,' Ian nudges me, knocking my pen.

'There's nothing much to report,' I say, as I watch a couple of dancers take to the bandstand. They start waltzing to a Bruno Mars song playing from their mobile, who I only know as Anna used to be obsessed with him.

'Don't give me that! You're like a teenager, constantly checking your phone.'

'What can I say? It's been nice to write to her again, and hearing how she is. It's kind of felt like it used to.'

I realize that despite the intervening years, I'm in a similar position as I was back then. The two times in my life I've needed someone to talk to.

'So has she said anything yet about why she stopped writing before?' Ian asks.

'No, she hasn't. We still haven't talked about that. As I said, I didn't want it to be the first thing I asked her about, but I am tempted to bring it up now. I would like to know what happened, just out of curiosity if nothing else. It's still niggling away at me.'

'Do you think that's a good idea?' Ian replies quickly, turning to face me, as a couple walk past us hand in hand, reciting aloud the different names of the roses from the green metallic signs in front of each one.

'Why not?'

'Well . . . what difference will it make? She's talking to you now. Why go over old ground? She must have had her reasons.'

'Would you not want to know why someone stopped

writing to you? Why they didn't tell you they'd moved house?'

'OK, but maybe it's not something that you should talk about in a message. I don't know. It's complicated. It could get messy. As you just said, it's been nice talking again. You don't want to ruin that.'

'I suppose not,' I say half-heartedly, confused by Ian's strong stance.

'Or, at least why don't you wait until you meet her and then ask her in person? That would make more sense?'

'Yeah, I don't know if I am going to meet her though. I've not told her that we're visiting Bordeaux yet.'

'What do you mean? We're literally going to be there in a few days and you can finally meet her after all these years!'

'I don't know, I was thinking it might be better if we don't meet?'

Ian looks at me, his eyebrow raised, as the couple who were reading out the names of the roses now take a myriad of photos of the flowers, their camera constantly clicking away.

'What happens if neither of us lives up to the expectations we have of each other? Maybe we're just better as pen pals?' I shrug my shoulders as I finish writing the card, and put the cap back on my biro.

'Better as pen pals? Honestly. You've got some hot French woman who likes you and you just want to write her letters?'

'You know, sometimes I don't think you've changed at all since we were at school!' I laugh. 'Did you ever grow up?'

'And you've changed completely! What happened to the Simon who followed his heart? I don't believe you just want a pen pal? I think there's something you're not saying.'

Ian may be right, but I'm not willing to admit that to him, or even to myself just yet.

'Let's just get there first, shall we, and then we'll see? In fact, let's get to our hotel, for starters.'

32

I'm not sure you can call it an actual hotel.

As soon as we step inside the dingy and dark front room of the B&B, I realize that bathroom doors are going to be the least of our problems.

I've never seen so much stuff everywhere. The room is chock-a-block full of knick-knacks, ornaments, vases, jugs, dolls, books, frames. It looks the kind of house you see in the newspaper where some hoarder has been found dead amidst all their possessions. In fact, there could be any number of bodies under all these items and nobody would know.

What was Ian thinking when he booked this place? What did the photos look like?

'Bonsoir!' the owner says as she greets us with a kiss on both cheeks.

I know it's French tradition, but I think my guests would be horrified if I welcomed them in this manner.

'Come on in,' the woman, who must be in her eighties, speaks slowly in a thick French accent, the lines sounding rehearsed, as if this is a stock phrase she has learnt.

She continues to lead us through the maze of mess.

Maybe Daisy could get a job here.

As I nearly trip over, I notice – on a rare part of the wall which isn't hidden – a series of framed certificates for her ecological awareness.

Clearly she is not disposing of any rubbish because she keeps it all in her house instead.

'Oui, yes, I am big supporter environment,' she says, noticing me spot the certificates. 'In my house, we no have lights.'

'No lights?'

She nods happily.

How on earth am I meant to see where I'm going between all this mess with no lights?

'I have only one room for guests,' she explains.

Presumably the other rooms are all for her possessions.

She leads us into the one bedroom, and I wonder if we'll be able to see the beds under the clutter. Remarkably it is fairly clean and tidy. Although even a teenager's bedroom would be considered clean and tidy compared to the rest of the house.

'This is nice room,' I say, limiting my English to her level, for some reason, and putting my thumbs up. I look around, realizing there are no lights, or even plug sockets.

'How long . . . the two of you?' she says, pointing at both of us, and then makes a kissing gesture.

'Oh no, we're not . . .' I try to explain, but Ian interrupts.

'We're just friends. His wife died.'

'Thanks, Ian.'

'I was just explaining to her.'

She looks at us smiling, not understanding what we are saying.

'Don't worry. I'm very . . . I have open mind, oui?'

I don't try and explain. I just want to sit down for a few minutes in some peace and quiet. But she continues to loiter in the room, and I wonder if she's ever going to leave. It looks like she is working out how to say something.

'Le soir, euh . . .'

'In the evening?' I help her out. Ian gives me a look as if he's impressed I managed to translate one word.

'Yes. I have glass of wine. You join.'

I'm not sure if it's her English, but it sounds more like an order than an invitation.

'Thank you, that's very nice of you. But I think we're going to look around the city,' I say, accompanying my words with a variety of hand gestures, and pointing to the map.

She nods her head, but I'm not sure she understands what I am saying.

'Do you need, euh, directions?'

'No, I think we're OK, thank you.'

She takes the map anyway and unfolds it.

'We. Here.' She starts pointing to places. 'Here. Bon. Here. Bon.' She curls up her mouth. 'Here. Non. N'y allez pas.'

'We don't go there, OK. Thank you.'

I now wonder what is wrong with where she's pointing.

'Here is key. For principal door. And for chambre,' she hands over two keys.

'Thank you.'

She stands there smiling for a few more moments until she eventually walks out.

'À plus tard!' she says, as she closes the door, leaving us alone for the first time in our dark room.

I wait for a couple of seconds to check that she's actually gone, and then I immediately turn to face Ian.

'Can I ask what your criteria were for booking these places?' I whisper, raising my eyebrows.

'It had good reviews! It said she was very friendly.'

'That's one way of describing her!'

*

'We can't ring the doorbell, she'll be asleep. I expect she goes to bed about 6 p.m.,' I say, as we fumble around with the door key trying to re-enter the house, having ventured out to have dinner, see the famous half-timbered houses, and watch the impressive *son et lumiere* show projected on to the Parliament building.

We are relying on the glare from the nearby street light so we can see what we're doing, but neither key seems to fit in the lock.

'This is the right house, yes?'

'It's the only one without any lights on, so yes!'

A man walks past along the pavement, and stares at us suspiciously. To be fair, it does look like we're trying to break in.

'We're in!' Ian says, more excited than I am to re-enter the chaos.

We tiptoe back into the front room which is now fully submerged in darkness. It is impossible to see where to go, and I don't want to send the piles of mess crashing to the floor.

'OK, there's being eco-friendly, and then there's just being ridiculous. She could have at least given us torches, or a candle,' Ian complains.

'I really don't think a flame would be a good idea here,' I whisper back.

'Can you turn the torch on your phone on?'

Neither of us knows how to turn on our phone torches, so we resort to using the glare of the screen.

I hold it up in front of me, and I jump into the air in shock as it casts a light ahead of us.

The old lady is sitting in the darkness, with a glass of wine, presumably waiting for us to join her.

'Oh God. I didn't see you there,' I say as my heart thumps from the surprise.

It would be ironic if I died of a heart attack now, rather than on the bike.

After making awkward small talk for fifteen minutes, we eventually make it back into our room with the remainder of the wine bottle, and close the door behind us.

'Did you unpack our bags?' Ian asks as he opens his, reliant on the glare from the street lights outside to illuminate the room.

'No, when would I have done that?'

'I don't know, but where are all of our clothes?' He looks up confused. I immediately worry that we've misplaced the urn again.

I open up my bag and notice that my clothes have vanished too.

'They're hanging up!' Ian says as he opens the wardrobe.

'That's a bit weird, isn't it?'

'I'm not sure if that's really good service, or just weird.'

'She's unpacked all our toiletries too, and laid out our toothbrushes,' I say as I walk into the near-pitch-black bathroom.

I return to the room and make a face at Ian.

He is still looking for something. He lifts the pillows up on his bed.

'She's put our pyjamas under the pillows!'

'OK, I'm now swaying towards thinking she might murder us in the middle of the night,' I say, as for the first time on the trip, I am glad to be sharing a room.

'Have you checked the door is locked?' he asks.

'She's obviously got a key so what difference does it make!'

We stare at the door, waiting for the handle to turn.

Whilst it is scary that some octogenarian French

woman may break into our room in the middle of the night, I am more scared by the thought that this may be me in a few years' time.

Still working, still alone.

I fall asleep feeling sorry for her, and worrying about what I may become.

I appreciate that she is simply looking for company.

From: Sylvie, To: Simon

Morning Simon,

Oh, don't get me started on online dating. It's horrendous. In France, dating comes very much from your social circles, but we do have these new sites now, like which you speak of, which are becoming more popular. I should probably put myself out there more. I've dated a few men since my divorce but nothing has lasted very long. I've not found someone I share things with. I've certainly not yet met 'Mr Right', or l'homme idéal, as we'd say. I've decided I should sneak a few French expressions into our communications so you can start learning!

It sounds like you've found yourself some company in Ian at least! Where have you gone on your spontaneous trip? This sounds very exciting. I hope you're having a good time. Don't worry about the slow responses, this is still much quicker than waiting for those letters to be delivered. I still vividly remember rushing to meet the postman to see if he had a letter for me.

I'm jealous of your trip as I'm currently very busy with work. The publishers are trying to rush out a new book so they want the translation quickly.

Cambodia was amazing. When I was there, I tried grasshoppers and tarantulas so I think a cream tea sounds delicious!

Yes, I've been to England a few times. To London, York and Oxford. I've also been to Edinburgh. I'm sorry to say I've never made it to Bristol though, despite all your recommendations. I wonder if it still looks like the postcards you sent me?

I don't have any immediate travel plans. I'm hoping to get away later in the year, all being well, but we'll see. If you could go anywhere, where would you go?

P.S. A book about your life running a B&B – and all the curious guests – sounds like a great idea. You should absolutely write it!

From: Simon, To: Sylvie

Hi Sylvie,

We're actually in France, in Rennes! The weather is glorious. Keep adding a few French expressions and I'll do my best to finally learn. That's a promise! Maybe I'll even try them out whilst I'm here.

I remember doing the very same, running down from our dorm room, to check the pigeonholes where our post was left. I used to run down every day to check if there were any letters, and I'd always be excited to see your flowery handwriting, and the French stamps.

That's a tough question about my preferred destination. I read the travel section in the papers every week, and there are so many places I always think it would be nice to visit one day. It's a bit clichéd but I've always wanted to see the pyramids, maybe take a cruise down the Nile. I haven't been back to Bristol much myself in recent years. We drove through the other day for Raj's memorial, and it looked very different than I remember from my schooldays. Anna and Ollie have been regularly and enjoy it, so maybe I will have to spend more time there when I have a chance. Likewise there are loads of places I've not seen in the UK. Is it bad that I've never been to York myself? Edinburgh and Oxford are lovely though.

I hope your translating is going well. I've always been curious how that works, it must be difficult trying to translate accurately between languages – do you have to change some parts?

Maybe when I eventually have some time, I'll pen some notes!

I'm intrigued to know what grasshoppers and tarantulas taste like . . . I'm not sure we'll add them to our menu!

Best wishes,
Simon

'It's not my fault that my mobile has died!' Ian shouts through the thunderous downpour.

'It was your fault that you booked a B&B which didn't have any electricity to charge our phones though!'

'If you hadn't been on your phone writing to Sylvie all morning we could have used yours!'

Our mutual annoyance about getting lost in the middle of nowhere, somewhere between Rennes and Redon is not helped by the weather. The clouds have suddenly burst, as if they've been saving up the water for the past month, and a deluge floods down from the skies.

'I don't know what was wrong with paper maps,' Ian shrugs his shoulders, scrunching his face up in disgust at the torrid weather. 'And I don't know why they call these stupid things smartphones when they run out of battery so quickly. Pretty dumb phones if you ask me.'

Ian was meant to be guiding us today, yet his mobile has died halfway through our ride, and mine died this morning, meaning we don't have a working phone between us, and we seem to have somehow got lost following a river.

This morning, the sunny riverbank was packed with crowds of other cyclists and walkers. Now, the path alongside it is dark, muddy and rocky, the people all long gone. We've raced the weather, desperate to get to our destination before nightfall, yet the storm has fast-tracked the night, and amidst the settling fog, we've found no town, no directions, no people. Just a disappearing, slippery path. The mud splashes up over our legs, and the torrential rain loudly beats down on our helmets, soaking both our bodies and our bags.

'So we have no idea where we are? Or where we're going? And we can't even call a taxi?' I have to shout to be heard, as the low growling rumble of thunder competes with me.

We climb off our bikes, venture off the river path, and hug into the side of the country road, seeking shelter under a tree, which doesn't have many branches, and is putting us more at danger from any passing cars.

'Since when did we become so reliant on phones? We managed OK last time without one,' he says, clearly having forgotten everything that happened on our last trip.

As we stand still, both frustrated by the situation, and neither of us having any idea of what we should do about it, a rare car speeds past, but before we can flag it down, it splashes an ever-growing puddle over us and leaves us in its wake.

'Oh great. Thanks very much for that,' Ian calls out after the car, not that we could get any wetter.

My feet are now squelching around in the puddles inside my shoes.

'What was it you said to Anna about us being older and wiser?'

'What do you think we should do?' Ian asks, ignoring my retort, and unwilling to take responsibility for any choices.

'I don't think it's safe to carry on like this, it's so slippery. And I don't think we're that close to Redon, so I guess we will just have to stop at the first place we can and stay there for the night.'

'The next town could still be miles away though.'

'Well, what else do you suggest? We sleep under this tree?' I shout louder, as much due to my frustration with the situation as the sound of the thunder this time.

'You live in the countryside . . .'

'In a house, not a tent. Living in the countryside doesn't automatically make you Bear Grylls!'

'It looks like there is a church in the distance.' He points to the silhouette of a spire which appears through the fog, towering above the trees in the distance. Everything looks dark, dingy and sinister in these conditions.

After twenty minutes of battling the elements we reach the spire, but the few houses nearby are all barricaded up for the night. There is certainly no hotel, or B&B for us to check into.

'The church might be open? We could shelter in there?' Ian suggests.

'Is that allowed?'

'I don't know. Isn't the church meant to look after

people?' Ian says, as if that's the only message he took from us attending Sunday services every week at school.

'I don't remember the parable about helping the two idiots who got lost on their bikes and forgot to charge their phones!'

'Oh, come on, we may as well try.' The rainwater now drips out of Ian's mouth as he speaks. He continues anyway through the entrance to the churchyard and we tip-toe around the masses of tombstones. I'm not sure how such a rural place can have so many dead bodies.

'It's bound to be locked.' I twist the large metallic handle one way and then the other, trying to unlatch and push the main door open, but it's too stiff and my hands are frozen.

Ian, of course, knows best, and he pushes me out the way to yank at the handle. Eventually the door creaks open.

'There we go,' he says, too smugly.

We slowly creep inside the pitch-black church, the large stained-glass windows not letting in much light from the darkness outside, and the faces of the engraved figures in the windows staring down at us as we tread over the stone slabs.

'Come on, it's a church, what's going to happen?' Ian says, sensing my trepidation.

As if on cue, thunder and lightning crash outside.

We both look at each other.

'We'll just light some candles, and it'll be fine,' he

smiles, as the water continues to drip from both our faces.

I'm just pleased to have a moment of shelter from the downfall, and we immediately rest our bikes behind the door and pull off our soaking outer layers.

'Everything in our bags is soaked too . . . how much did we pay for these bags? I thought they were meant to be waterproof!'

'I'm not sure we should have trusted anything Glenn had to say.'

As Ian goes to light the candles, I can just make out the noise of the gate opening and closing, over the sound of the continuing rainfall.

'Shhh. I think someone's coming,' I whisper.

Given the fact we probably shouldn't be here and that we definitely don't want to be kicked out, we decide to quickly hide, shoving our bags away, and ducking down underneath the pews. Luckily the bikes are hidden by the darkness, behind the doors. The footsteps from outside pitter patter quickly, the sound growing louder, the wooden latch rises, and then the church door bursts open.

'Who is it?' Ian mouths to me, as I hide in the opposite side of the aisle, with a view of the door.

In the dim light I can just make out a pair of shoes entering the church. The feet stop, and pause for a second, before carrying on along the side of the church. I quickly bob my head up.

'It's the vicar!' I mouth back.

We continue lying there in silence, as the footsteps wander around the church, the violent rain outside masking the sound of our heavy breathing.

I can hear the footsteps getting louder again. I try to stay still, but the dust from the stone floor and the old kneeling cushions fills my nose. I can feel myself about to sneeze.

I try and stop myself, but I can't.

Aachoo.

Fortunately, just as I sneeze the thunder rumbles.

That's divine intervention for you.

The vicar's shoes pause again, before the door creaks open again, closes, and then we hear the sound of a key turning.

'I guess we're definitely staying here for the night then!'

34

THEN

May 1975

'In the beginning was the Word, and the Word was with God, and the Word was God.' The ancient chaplain – who looks old enough to have been at The Last Supper himself – reads the same passage of the Bible that he repeats every single Sunday morning.

For such a big book, Simon can never understand why he can't switch the passages up occasionally. The service in the church near school marks the end of the week – the boys who board part-time are greeted by their families and allowed home for the night, whereas Simon, Ian and Raj are given a few hours of freedom before they have to be back in school.

Simon knows the service verbatim, so instead of listening, he usually risks the wrath of Mr Montgomery by playing noughts and crosses against Raj on a blank page in the hymn books.

Today though, he's too focused on his new letter from Sylvie which he holds in his hands. He reads the line over and over again about her applying for the exchange, and of her excitement at the two of them getting to spend the summer together.

She doesn't know yet about the bad news, and now he's got to reply saying that none of it will be happening. He's got to tell her to pull out of the exchange. He's got to let her down.

As he sits there, listening to the chaplain ramble on, he decides that he can't do that. He decides that he's got to see her.

He's so preoccupied by his thoughts that he doesn't try to put Ian off as he sings in the choir, or even look up as he comes bounding over to his pew after the service.

He continues staring at Sylvie's words, lost in his thoughts.

'Did you see Julian's sister today?' Ian asks, raising his eyebrows to Simon and Raj, who are left sitting alone after the other boys have been reunited with their families.

'He's still only interested in Mademoiselle Sylvie,' Raj replies.

'I thought we decided that since you couldn't go on the exchange, we'd try and find you someone else?'

'We never decided that!' Simon shakes his head. 'Anyway I've actually been thinking this last week . . . well, I've got an idea.'

'Go on.'

Simon waits for the chaplain to walk past, and leave the three of them in complete privacy.

'I think I should forget all about the stupid exchange, and go myself.'

'To Bordeaux? On your own? You're going to make your own way there?' Raj looks at him curiously.

'Yes, why not?'

'How do you think you're going to do that?' Ian now joins in the questioning.

'You haven't got the money to get there.'

'And you've never been anywhere by yourself before!' The two friends look as dismissive of Simon's idea as each other.

'I'm going to cycle there.'

Ian and Raj both burst into laughter.

'Don't be silly.'

'I'm being serious,' Simon snaps defensively.

'Can you even ride a bike?'

'Everyone can ride a bike.'

'But to France?'

'It's still riding a bike. It's just, you know, quite a long bike ride.'

'OK, but . . .' Ian tries to think of another flaw, before Raj steps in with his own concern.

'How are you going to go without your dad knowing?'

'So this is what I've been thinking about. Dad thinks I'm going to be in Wales for three weeks, right? But I still haven't handed in the form so if I don't, school will expect me to head home straight after exams when term finishes, then I have three weeks where neither school nor my parents know where I am.'

'Your dad will think you're in Wales, and school will think you're at home. Giving you three weeks to do whatever you want,' Raj smiles as he thinks through Simon's grand plan.

'Exactly. Three weeks in which I could cycle to Bordeaux, see Sylvie, and come back,' Simon smiles.

'It's risky. But it could work. I suppose. As long as you intercept any correspondence then neither will be any the wiser, and if you get back before the trip does, then you could probably get away with it. And you could even fund your trip with the money your dad gives you to go on the camp. But if you get caught . . .'

'I know, but I can't think about that now.' Simon pauses.

Raj and Ian look at him, impressed.

'What about all the equipment you'd need?'

'I can take it from the Outdoor Pursuits cupboard. After Duke of Edinburgh is over, no one will check whether it's there or not.'

Raj and Ian continue nodding, remarkably surprised by his plan.

'And then I was thinking . . . maybe you could come too?'

'I don't know, Si, my parents would never let me go,' Raj shakes his head.

'OK, then you do the same. If you ask them if you can go on the camp, we can just get copies of the letters being sent home and pass them on to our parents. If we tell them to pick us up on the same day, but we get back before the camp, then how would they know?'

'I suppose so, but we've got our exams too. We've only got a few weeks now. We haven't got time to plan a whole trip if we're meant to be revising. We need to do well in these exams!'

'Come on, you're going to ace your exams anyway. And I promise it will be fun.'

Raj looks unconvinced.

'I'll come,' Ian suddenly declares, without question.

'I thought you just said it was a silly idea.'

'I've changed my mind. You're right, maybe it will be fun, and what's the worst that could happen? It's better than going home.'

Simon smiles at Ian, before turning his attention back to Raj, as the church bells chime the hour.

'OK, we're both in. Raj, you have to come now.'

'Ohhh. Fine then,' he says anxiously.

'Have we just decided we're all going to cycle to Bordeaux?' Simon smiles.

As they step out of the chapel, the three boys all look at each other, their faces a mixture of excitement and absolute trepidation.

35

With the candles flickering, and the crashing rain softening to gentle pattering against the windows, the atmosphere inside the church is almost tranquil and relaxing.

I empty our wet bags, propping the urn up alongside us, making sure that no water has seeped inside, and then I take out the remainder of the two-day-old food we took from the hotel buffet.

'Good thing we stole them, right?' Ian says as he returns from lighting the candles. I've already scoped the whole place for electricity but none of the sockets seem to work.

'I'm not sure we should be endorsing stealing in a church,' I smile. 'There you go, we have one very squashed ham roll each.'

I hand the less squashed one over to Ian.

'Oh, we also have that bottle of wine from last night!' Ian says as he digs into his own bag. 'Bread and wine. This seems very fitting . . . In the beginning was the Word, and the Word was with God, and the Word was God,' Ian mimics our old school chaplain.

I laugh as I watch his performance. Just like when we were kids, it's hard to stay annoyed at Ian for too long before he makes you smile again. I've missed that.

'Do you know what? If you'd asked me at school, what I'd be doing at this age, I don't think I'd have said this,' I say as I dig into my roll and look around at our surroundings.

'What did you think you'd be doing?'

'I don't know. I suppose just not sitting in Lycra in a rural French church, eating a stolen ham roll, hiding from a priest, with my old school friend and an urn of ashes.'

'Strange, because that's just how I imagined our lives going.'

Despite my earlier annoyance, I can't help but laugh about the whole situation. The vision of fancy hotels and appreciating local culture has already succumbed to crashing in a church, yet, as we eat together under the candlelight, it seems more fitting than being in any five-star establishment.

'I've been meaning to say . . . I'm sorry that I ran off, you know, when we got back to school last time,' Ian announces out of the blue.

'I know we're in a church but you don't have to start making confessions.'

Whether it's because after a few days on the road we've exhausted every trivial subject, or due to the setting prompting reflection, Ian takes me by surprise.

'It's just after what we were saying yesterday. I realized, well, maybe there's some things I need to apologize for.'

'That was years ago.'

'I suppose it was, but I'm sorry anyway for that, and –'

'Honestly, it's fine, thank you.' I look at him, his face remorseful, almost relieved to be getting an apology out.

'Unfortunately we can't change the past,' I say. 'However much sometimes we'd like to.'

'That's true, we can't change it. It's actually something I've been thinking a bit about over the last few weeks. I was wondering, do you think we'd be different if we hadn't been sent to boarding school?' Ian asks as I take my last mouthful of our food rations.

'That's quite a hypothetical question.'

'I know, but what do you think?'

'I was actually having a similar conversation with Anna the other day, about what it was like. I think it probably had both a positive and negative impact on me. I guess I never understood at the time why my parents sent me. For a long time I felt they just wanted to get rid of me.'

'Do you still feel that way?'

'No, I think I see things differently now. I think having Anna has changed my perspective.'

'In what way?'

'Would I have chosen to send Anna away? No. But equally I'd want the best for her, and I think that's what my parents wanted for me. Dad had worked himself up from nothing, and he thought he was giving me the best start he could, sending me to a good school. I think he just showed his love in his own way, probably a different way to how I'd have liked, or how I'd have done it myself, but equally it was a different time, wasn't it. Even when we got back, and he was so furious with me, I think he was just worried and then disappointed about the repercussions for my future.'

'That's interesting. Obviously, I've not had the insight of being a parent myself, but I remember at the time definitely feeling unwanted. You know I never had a close relationship with my folks. Even after school, we were never very close. They carried on moving every few years which was probably where I got my nomadic spirit from, but I'd only see them once every so often. And then they both died relatively young.'

'I'm very sorry to hear that.'

'No, it's OK. But I think it had a big impact on what I was like, why I was always playing up, trying to be the centre of attention. I always thought you and Raj didn't seem to mind too much. You just kept your heads down and got on with it. For me, I just felt I didn't fit in at all. I wanted to be liked. And apart from you two, no one else liked me. I wanted to be popular. I wanted to be someone else.'

'Like Bowie?'

'Yes, exactly, and look, I've done that my whole life. It would be funny if it wasn't so sad. I don't need to pay a psychiatrist thousands of pounds to tell me what my problem is.'

I look at Ian, having never heard him be so candid.

'You say it's a problem, but equally I think it's amazing that you've followed your dream, and you've been able to see the world. I'm very envious of that.'

'I suppose so.'

'And I'm not just saying this, but you've actually got a really good voice. Like really good.'

'I know, I do,' Ian jokes, and the candour is masked by humour again.

'Did you ever consider performing as yourself?'

'I thought about it years ago, but now who wants to see an old, fat, balding ginger man on stage?'

'I do!' I smile.

'Thank you, I'm pleased I've got one fan!' He swigs the wine. 'We got on so well at school, but we never really spoke about this kind of stuff, did we?'

'Not really, no. I used to write to Sylvie about stuff like that.'

'I thought you just wrote about music.'

'We did write about music, but also deeper stuff. She was having problems with her parents at the time, she was worried they were going to get a divorce. And I wrote to her about my issues.'

'Why didn't you talk to us about them?'

'Probably the same reason you never spoke about any of the stuff you're saying now.'

Ian looks flummoxed.

'Why don't we talk about feelings more?'

'We haven't talked at all for over forty years!'

'But in general? Men?'

'I don't know. I've found it hard to talk about things since Caroline . . .'

'You know you can talk to me about it if you want?'

We spend the rest of the evening talking before we fall asleep, lying on the pews, using the embroidered kneelers for pillows.

My cushion, rather ominously, has RIP stitched into it.

*

I awake to the coloured light filtering in through the stained-glass windows, and the morning calls of the birds.

No alarm. No customers complaining. No having to worry about Mrs Cook insulting, or worse, killing one of our guests.

This is the life.

I was expecting my neck to be sore, but no, even the embroidered kneeler was surprisingly comfortable.

It is completely idyllic for a few seconds, until I open my eyes fully and look around.

Standing over me is the priest from last night. His face furious.

Crap.

And behind him is what must be the entire village, waiting for the first communion service of the day.

Double crap.

I quickly jump up, before I remember that I slept in

just my underwear. No wonder the congregation all look shocked – albeit apart from one lady who seems to be checking me out, getting far more than she bargained for from today's service.

'Sorry, pardon . . . we're . . . aller . . . we're going,' I try to explain, unable to think of the right French words, my face now a shade of purple.

I panic as I can't find where I put my glasses, and as I bend down to look for them, I give those gathered even more of a sight. Ian's influence is clearly rubbing off.

The priest picks them up from the pew and hands them over, shaking his head violently, looking like he's going to do himself an injury.

'Je suis désolé,' I cup my hands in an apology, but it looks more like I'm praying.

Half-dressed, we gather up our stuff, hop our way to the door and retrieve our bikes. The congregation remain in silence.

As soon as the large wooden church door slams shut and we make it out of the graveyard, Ian and I can't help but burst into laughter. That's given this sleepy village something to talk about for a while.

He puts his hand round my shoulder.

'Do you know what? I think that must be the first time since school that I've been in church at this time of the morning!'

36

As soon as I switch my phone back on, it pings exuber-antly with a mass of missed calls and concerned messages from Anna.

I stand up and step away from the wooden table to return her calls, leaving Ian to continue sipping his tea at the small cafe along the river where we've stopped for breakfast. We're the only customers, but with calmer cyc-ling conditions this morning, we've already passed a few people tentatively re-emerging after last night's storm.

The owner has kindly let us charge our phones and given us directions. It turns out that we were closer to our hotel in Redon last night than we realized, but for-tunately that means we don't have to cycle too far extra today to make it to our scheduled stop in Nantes by this evening.

Anna picks up immediately.

'Hi Dad, are you OK?' she says hurriedly, sounding concerned.

'Yes, sorry Anna, I'm fine. I'm sorry to worry you . . .'

'Oh, gosh. I'm so relieved to hear from you. I was worried something had happened. I didn't hear from you all day yesterday. I tried to call you last night but I couldn't get through.'

'I'm really sorry, darling, my phone died. I promise I won't worry you like that again.'

I hold the phone close to my ear as the wind whistles, and I look up to see a couple of cyclists pass by, while another stops to use the makeshift toilet shack. I imagine this place, with its waterfront, scenic location and wooden jetty will be busy later, even if the battered marquee is currently looking worse for wear.

'How's everything going?'

'It's all been a bit of a whirlwind. I've already lost track of what day it is. It is strange without the usual routine. But everywhere's been very scenic so far. We've been enjoying listening to your music.'

'I'm glad. What about your accommodation?'

'Yes, good thanks. Last night was . . . divine.'

I decide to lie about our stay in the church so as not to worry her any more.

'And Ian? How are you two getting on?'

'Put it this way, we haven't killed each other yet.'

'That's a positive,' Anna laughs.

'I think I'm just about getting used to his snoring, and his midnight trips to the bathroom! No, it's actually going really well. I think we had a bit of a breakthrough last night, it felt like we really bonded for the first time again.'

'I'm so glad, Dad, do you think you'd hang out more after this?'

'Let's get through this trip first and then see!' I chuckle, looking across at Ian attempting to make conversation with the owner who is more interested in clearing away the residue of the storm, and erecting the red Coca-Cola-sponsored umbrellas above each table.

'What about the cycling? It's not too much?'

'It's been tough, and I think every single part of my body is aching now. We've got a rest day tomorrow, though, which I'm looking forward to. But, dare I say it, this was a good idea. It's been nice to have a break, to get away, to have time to think.'

'Yeah? I'm so pleased to hear that . . .'

Anna's voice quietens, and the line suddenly goes muffled.

'Hello, are you still there?' I say as I hear bickering in hushed tones. I try to make out what is being said, but I only catch a few words about it being 'better to tell him'.

'No, it's really good you're getting on so well,' Anna's voice resumes a few seconds later, as if nothing happened.

'Was that Ollie? What was he saying?' I continue pacing around the gravel car park, which is empty apart from a grey Nissan Scenic which I presume is the owner's.

'Sorry, he was just asking me something.'

'It sounded more like you were arguing about something. Is everything all right?'

'No, it's just . . . it's nothing. Don't worry about us.'

'What is it, Anna?'

'Honestly, it's nothing, he's just being silly.'

'Are you sure?'

'Yes, yes, what were we saying?'

'We were talking far too much about me, I want to hear how everything is with you.'

'All OK. But it's been busy. Not helped by the fact Daisy has got chicken pox so I've had to sort everything here today.'

'That's strange as Daisy has already had chicken pox three times this year!'

'You're kidding me? That girl! I'll give her a call now, and tell her to hurry up and get to work!'

'What about the wedding?'

'It's . . . Sorry, I've got to go. A guest is just coming. But I'm pleased you're OK. Remember to charge your phone!'

'OK, you're sure there's nothing else? Anna?' Before I can finish my sentence, I realize she's hung up.

I look down at my mobile, worrying there's definitely something the matter, and wondering what I should do.

It's times like these that I really wish Caroline was still here to help me.

37

'Caroline would have absolutely hated this,' I say, as we admire Nantes from the 360-degree viewing platform at the top of the soaring Tour Bretagne, which Ian's guidebook tells me is France's third-tallest building.

With a whole day set aside, we've already covered the majority of the city on foot, following the green line painted on the streets leading us through the city's best cultural stops, contemporary installations, and must-visit sites. Even we can manage that without getting lost.

Everything in the city seems to be amusing and light-hearted, from ironic statues to hilariously sized benches. This skyscraper is no different, with a model of a ginormous white bird wrapping around the circumference of the floor and doubling as a bar, while massive eggshells form the seats and tables.

'She didn't like heights?' Ian asks as he peeks through the mesh wiring at the panorama below.

'She was awful with heights! I remember when we went to the top of the Rockefeller Center in New York. Anna loved it, but Caroline was absolutely terrified. She couldn't go anywhere near the edge,' I muse. 'Sorry, I'm talking to myself really.'

'No, not at all. Tell me more about Caroline.' He smiles.

I think about what Ian said in the church about us sharing more, about how nice it felt to talk to him properly.

'What can I say? Apart from her fear of heights, she was unstoppable. She was amazing . . . all the guests used to love her. They really came for her. She'd spend ages chatting to everyone. So much so, I'd have to drag her back into the kitchen to help me with the cooking.' I laugh to myself as I remember this. 'We used to have people from the village round every weekend. She loved being part of the community.'

'I really wish I could have met her. She sounds amazing.'

'She was. And of course, she was just a wonderful mum, a wonderful wife.'

'Can I ask what happened to her? I mean you don't have to talk about it if you don't want to.'

I pause. It's been a while since I've spoken about it. Since I've told anyone.

'No, it's fine . . . it's not a secret.'

I wait for a couple of other tourists to wander past. They must be following the same green line as us, as I noticed them at one of the stops earlier, when we were squirted with water by a moving mechanical elephant inspired by Jules Verne.

I look around, checking that we're alone again, and take a breath.

'We'd run out of clotted cream at the cottage, and so one of us had to pop to the supermarket. Caroline offered to go. I let her. An hour or so later I got a call, telling me some boy racer was driving too quickly along one of the bendy country lanes. He forced Caroline off the road. That was it. It was that simple. She didn't even make it to the hospital. I didn't even get to say goodbye to her.'

'I'm so sorry,' Ian whispers.

'Just like that, everything changed. For ages, I kept thinking why didn't I go? Or even why didn't I delay her going? Why did it have to be that very second? The small fractions of time which change everything. Why did she have to be driving around that corner at that very split second?' As I talk my voice wobbles.

Ian pulls out a used hankie from his pocket and offers it to me.

'Sorry, this is embarrassing,' I snivel. 'I don't know, I feel I've been keeping this in for ten years. Trying to keep busy, trying to keep positive for Anna. This is the first time in ages that I've had time to think about everything. To almost process it.'

'Honestly, don't worry. Let it out,' Ian says sympathetically, putting his arm around me as my eyes fill up.

Goodness knows what passers-by think as Ian consoles me in front of the massive bird beak.

'And the thing is, I honestly don't know what I'd have done without Anna at the time. It was such an awful time for her, she had started her architecture degree at university literally the week before. It was meant to be the best time of her life, and then during her freshers' week, I had to tell her that her mum had died. I can't even imagine what she must have been going through.'

'God, that's awful.'

'I tried to convince her to stay on studying, but she decided to drop out. She came back to the cottage to help me with everything, and then she never went back to university. She stayed on running the place with me. But that's why, the other day, I was saying it's difficult with the cottage. I can't just say to her, thanks a lot, but now I want to get rid of the B&B. It's because of me that she gave up on her dreams.'

Ian continues to pat me on the back.

'I bet you wish you never asked now,' I muster a smile.

'No, not at all. I'm sorry. I can't begin to imagine what it must have been like. And how you've coped afterwards. I don't even know what to say.'

We stand there in silence for a few minutes. For once, Ian seems to know when not to talk. I stare at the miniature city below me, replaying that day in my head, but also the good times Caroline and I shared. I think about how happy we were. And then I think about how sad I've been since. I think about Anna, and what Ian was saying. About how I've felt on this trip. About the B&B owner. About Sylvie. About the future. About how happy I've been today exploring this fun city.

'How much more have we got to do on the trail?' I say eventually, blowing my nose, and smiling to Ian. 'We must have walked nearly the whole city, haven't we? It was meant to be our rest day!'

'Yes, I think we've done nearly all of it. There's one last thing I want to do though,' Ian flicks to the relevant listing in the guidebook, hiding the page from me.

After we catch the lift back down to ground level, we walk from the modern skyscraper to the old castle, The Château des ducs de Bretagne, next to the Tourist Information Centre where we started, completing the loop. It's only on second glance that I notice even the castle has been enhanced. A long, steel slide wraps around the contours of the outer wall of the castle, running from the battlements to the moat. We stop for a couple of minutes to watch a stream of people – mostly kids – whizzing down it.

'This is the last thing!' Ian nods towards the slide.

'The slide? Isn't that for kids? We can't do that! We'll probably get stuck!'

'No, it's art. It's for everyone. Come on, let's have a go!'

He's already marching off across the drawbridge before I can object, almost pushing his way past the children in his rush to have a go.

By the time we reach the top, we're much higher than I expected. We must be about forty feet up in the air.

I read the sign, hoping that there may be a disclaimer which means we're forbidden.

!!! Paysage Glissé is forbidden to anyone under 130 centimetres (4 foot, 2 inches) tall.

!!! Only one person is permitted to use the slide at a time.

!!! Bare feet, heels and flip-flops are forbidden.

I guess we're doing this then.

I watch as Ian launches himself down the slide first, holding his hands in the air as if he's on a rollercoaster. He bumps up and down along the silver metal, which glistens in the light.

The young man on duty nods that I am allowed to follow. I hesitantly walk up to the start of the slide, looking around to check who's watching.

I awkwardly sit down, placing my legs in front of me, and see Ian waving from the bottom, encouraging me to follow.

I throw myself down.

Despite my achy body hurting as I whizz down the metal slide, I can't help but chuckle to myself and smile.

I realize it's time to get the old me back.

I realize it is time to start living again.

From: Sylvie, To: Simon

You're in France! What made you decide to visit Rennes? How long are you there for? If you get a chance you should pop down to Bordeaux! It would be lovely to see you.

OK your phrase of the day is: Je n'en crois pas mes yeux, which means I can't believe my eyes. You can use it when you see something dazzling during your trip. Report back?

Do you know what? I've never been to Egypt. It's also somewhere I'd like to visit one day. And Jordan too. I know what you mean, I've seen more of the rest of the world than I have seen of France. There are lots of places closer to home I need to visit. I have never been to Rennes, would you believe. I'd love you to tell me what it's like.

That's interesting to hear how much Bristol has changed. It's similar here. Bordeaux is very different to how it was when I was growing up. It's almost unrecognizable. It's become so much more popular with tourists in recent years, and also many Parisians having second homes, or they visit for the weekend. There is a new high-speed train line connecting Paris to Bordeaux so some people even commute now. It was about twenty years ago when everything started changing. Lots of the less desirable areas were transformed into 'bourgeois' areas. And the areas either side of the river were transformed with restaurants. It's really lovely now . . . I'm not just saying this so you visit!

Translation is going well thank you. Yes, sometimes I have to use some creative licence. There is a lot of nuance in translation so often you have to look beyond translating directly, especially in novels.

And tarantulas taste a bit like crab!

From: Simon, To: Sylvie

Bonjour Sylvie! So we're actually travelling through France. And funnily enough we're actually planning on being in Bordeaux in a few days' time, so it would be lovely to see you too. There's also something that I would love to speak to you about.

Sorry I didn't say anything before about visiting but I thought it might be a bit strange if I got back in contact with you and said straight away I was coming to Bordeaux.

I'll let you know our plans ASAP, and then we can arrange when you're free.

We're having an interesting time so far – put it that way! We ended up having to spend a night sleeping in a church – don't ask! Rennes was very pretty – you should visit if you get the chance – and I really enjoyed Nantes. It's a wonderful city with lots of interesting modern art, which I'm not normally into. I did try and use your phrase, although it was greeted mostly with confused faces so I might need a lesson on pronunciation too! x

38

THEN

June 1975

Simon stares hopelessly up at the oversized clock which hangs at the front of the cavernous school room, where all the O-Level exams take place.

It ticks loudly. Every second sounding like a drum beat. The movement of the hands almost hypnotic.

Dr Johnson, the stern, elderly physics professor, patrols up and down the aisles in between the tables, on adjudication duty, looking over the pupils' shoulders as he goes. His footsteps are irritatingly out of sync with the ticking of the clock.

Neil, who sits two tables to the right of Simon, taps his pen against the wooden table.

William, sitting behind, grinds his teeth.

It is almost impossible to concentrate.

Simon panics, knowing he should have revised more. He should have listened to Raj, who frantically scribbles away. Having spent the last seven months writing letters, creating mixtapes and planning a highly secretive cross-country trip, he neglected to actually prepare for his exams.

He's already struggled through the other subjects, but this, the final exam, is the worst. History. He is dreading receiving the results before the exam is even over.

He can already hear his dad's voice, the anger and the disappointment.

He looks helplessly around the large room, at all the other boys who have their heads down and are furiously writing away. Ian is the only other boy looking up, which is never a reassuring sign.

And all this time, the clock is still ticking down, and he still hasn't answered the question.

'You have five minutes left,' Dr Johnson calls out.

Simon looks up again at the clock in panic. Where did the other two hours and twenty-five minutes go, he wonders.

If there was an exam on how to get from Bristol to Bordeaux, he'd certainly pass. Thanks to his regular trips to the library, he's planned out their entire route. 'Mission Sylvie' has consumed every waking hour for the past month. No wonder he can't remember anything about the Treaty of Versailles.

'OK, that's it. Time's up. Pens down.' Dr Johnson barks the very second the hand ticks the hour. 'I said pens down. Brown. Put your pen down right now. If I have to tell any of you again, you will be disqualified.'

Simon puts his pen down, despairingly.

Dr Johnson collects all the papers before the boys filter out of the room, remaining silent until they reach the doors, and then erupting into conversation. As

Simon overhears the others discussing their answers he quickly realizes he has done even worse than he feared.

'How do you think it went?' Raj asks as the three boys veer off from the pack.

'I guess we'll find out in August,' Simon grimaces.

'Oi, you two! I don't want to hear any more mention of exams. What can we learn from history anyway? It's time to celebrate! We're done with exams! We're done for the term! We're done for the year! We're off to France!'

'Shhhh, keep it down!' Simon hushes Ian as they rush to their dorm room to finish packing for their clandestine adventure.

'What do you two look like?' Simon can't help but laugh as he looks up from packing his bag and sees Ian and Raj dressed in true glam-rock attire – flared trousers, silk shirts and platform boots. 'We're cycling to France dressed like that?'

After five years of boarding school, they're adept at packing their bags, even if this time they're not going home immediately. Most of the other boys in their year are staying on site, with the Welsh camp and the French exchange departing school tomorrow.

'So we all know the plan, right? All we have to do is make it look like we're leaving school to go home. We'll leave our bags to take to France under our beds,' Simon reminds Ian and Raj in a hushed tone, making sure no one outside can hear.

Raj nods as he slides his bag underneath his single

bed and ensures the duvet is hiding any glimpses of it. Their dorm room looks bare with their possessions packed away, and their music posters removed from the walls.

'We're going to carry our suitcases to take home with us through the school, sign out, and just say that our parents are collecting us by the road. Then we'll double back around the side of school, climb through the dorm window and hide our suitcases under the beds, and switch them for our bags to take to France. Got it?'

'Do you not think anyone will check under the beds after we've gone?' Raj asks, looking far more nervous now than he was before their exam, as Ian props open the window.

'No. Do you not remember what we found under the beds at the start of the year?'

'Yes! That old bra catalogue!' Ian remembers fondly.

'Just don't panic,' Simon whispers to Raj, sensing his stress as they walk through the school to the small reception located in the entrance hall.

'Where are you boys off to?' The voice of Mr Montgomery booms from behind the desk.

This wasn't part of the plan.

It was meant to be the school secretary. The nice old lady who doesn't know anything. Not the intimidating marshall guarding the front door.

'We're going . . .'

'Home. We're going home,' Simon prompts Raj, who forgets his words. He's absolutely fine answering questions against the clock about Lenin's rise to power in 1917, but lying to Mr Montgomery is another matter entirely.

'You're not coming on the Welsh trip? Some physical exercise would be good for you boys.'

They try not to smirk.

'No, sir, our parents are picking us up now.'

Montgomery looks dubiously at them, and Simon can feel a bead of sweat drip from his face. He doesn't dare look across at Raj, who he can imagine is shaking like a leaf.

'Have you left your dorm tidy?'

'Yes, sir. We've taken everything,' Simon indicates their suitcases, before grabbing a pen and swiftly signing out.

'I'll come and see you all off.'

'It's OK, sir, we're . . .'

'No, I have to make sure you are all picked up safely.'

Simon's face drops.

He can hear Raj saying I told you so.

Everything is over before it's even started.

As Simon frantically tries to work out a new plan, suddenly a tennis ball drops from the top of the stairs, bouncing high off the stone floor.

'Who threw that?' Montgomery yells, looking up at some younger kids running along the landing. He chases the culprits, taking two steps at a time. 'Come back here.'

'Quick, let's go!' Simon senses their opportunity.

The trio hurry through the front gates, down the drive – avoiding the incoming postman on his bike – and, after checking that no one is following them, they track back on themselves and head round the corner of the school building until they reach the outside of their dorm room.

'In you go then!' Ian prompts Raj to climb through the open window.

'Why me?'

'You're the smallest!'

Raj looks back, nonplussed.

'Come on, the quicker we do it, the quicker we get away. We're going to get caught if we don't hurry!' Simon says.

'If we get caught . . .'

Simon and Ian hoist Raj through the window before he can finish complaining.

'I don't know why I'm friends with you sometimes,' Raj moans as he takes the suitcase off Simon.

'Have you got it? It's heavy.'

As Raj hides the bags under their beds and exchanges them for their pre-packed bags containing all the equipment they stole from the outdoor pursuits cupboard, Ian, who is meant to be keeping watch, pulls the window down and pretends to leave Raj behind.

'You're so funny, aren't you,' Raj rolls his eyes.

'Come on, we haven't time to mess around! Let's get out of here before anyone sees us,' Simon says, taking control, and a deep breath.

They continue round the back of the school, behind the science labs, where the old school bikes are kept. No one will notice they're missing.

Simon looks across to his left at Ian, and then to his right at Raj. The three of them lined up ready to go.

'Ready?'

'As Alice Cooper says, "school's out for summer"!' Ian shouts loudly, as they cycle down the hill, before realizing thirty seconds later they've already gone the wrong way, and they have to head back past the school.

39

Jay waves as soon he spots us, putting his redundant mobile into his pocket as we approach.

As much as Ian and I have started to bond again, it's nice to see a different, familiar face. And in spite of only meeting at the memorial, he does seem so familiar.

'Funny seeing you here,' I joke, as he shakes my hand.

'Welcome to Noirmoutier! You're both still in one piece, then?' He smiles, welcoming us to the island where they have their holiday home. I'm excited to see it, to see the family, to see where Raj found his happiness.

'Just about, although I have to say this bridge is quite precarious,' I reply, indicating the cobbled causeway, Le Passage du Gois, which we've just traversed. 'You don't usually see many road signs warning you about a risk of drowning.'

'Yes, it's the longest submersible bridge in the world, I believe. You can only cross it twice a day at low tide, so you timed it well.'

'It's pretty cut off this place then,' Ian remarks as he looks around at the sparse sun-scorched fields which greet us. 'I remember us cycling past along the coast last time, wondering what this island was.'

'Yes, I think Dad liked the idea of this island being a

kind of secret haven, hidden from everyone else. He actually used to make up stories when we were kids, telling us we were in some magical kingdom. And it's the perfect place to cycle. Everything is nearby, and the whole island is flat.'

'Lazy sod, no wonder Raj picked here! He moaned constantly every time we cycled up a hill!' Ian jests.

'I see you're taking after your old man,' I point to the bike he holds next to him.

'Yes, although I'm a bit out of practice!'

'You think *you're* out of practice?' I laugh.

We follow Jay as we cross the island, immediately feeling a world away from the modern industrial city of Nantes. Unlike other islands, there are no luxury golf courses or massive hotel resorts. It feels like it's from a bygone era. It feels like the France we encountered the first time.

There don't even seem to be many cars, with everyone getting around on bikes, or the little white tourist train which runs past all the beach huts along the island's sandy coast. As such, we ride three abreast, filling in Jay on our travels so far, as he points out places of note and tells us about the island.

'This is us,' Jay announces after about half an hour as we arrive at a sumptuous house which – with its whitewashed walls, terracotta tiles and pastel-blue shutters – looks like it's been transposed from a Mediterranean island. It stands beside the yellow beach, looking out to an endless panorama of turquoise sea.

'Come on in,' Priti – wearing sunglasses, large, colourful dangly earrings, and a red and navy patterned dress – greets us warmly. It's lovely to see her smiling.

Raj's daughters, who I didn't really get a chance to speak to at his memorial, stand behind their mum. Zara, the eldest, has long dark hair, hoop earrings, and a silver necklace which dangles over her mustard-coloured t-shirt. Mishti's hair is cropped shorter, she appears shy but smiley. The girls both look more like their mother, but each is recognizable as Raj's child, whether it's their eyes or their smile. I watch them closely as they speak, trying to see which mannerisms they inherited from Raj.

'You must be starving, we've got lunch all ready for you. Make yourselves at home.'

Ian's eyes light up as he follows the kids to the outside dining table on the terrace which overlooks the beautiful sea view. I go inside to offer my help to Priti, but she is insistent that she's got everything under control.

'How are you doing?' I say, realizing what a daft question it is in the circumstances, but one which I was pleased to be asked after Caroline died, remembering how people would tip-toe around me.

'I don't think any of us were sure about still coming this year after everything, but it's been really nice to have the children together, for me to have their company, for us to get away from home for a bit. Escape from it all. It's been good for us. It's been a few years since we were all here. I wish we'd done this more as the kids grew up, but you have to let them fly the nest and do their own things, don't you.'

I feel lucky, and then a little guilty, that I've had Anna for as long as I have. As I consider Priti's words, I wonder if I've held Anna back.

My attention is suddenly caught by a small framed photo on the wall. It is of the three of us on our trip, similar to the one that I found in the attic.

'Have you just put that up?' I ask Priti, as she carries another plate of food to the outside dining table, still refusing my help.

'No, no, it's always been there,' she smiles. 'It was one of the first items Raj put up when we bought the place and renovated it. It was a reminder for him of why he loved this area of France so much.'

I stare at the photo, which still conjures mixed emotions. Happiness for the memories, sadness for the regret of not reconnecting.

'He'd be very pleased you two are here. He always wanted to reunite and invite you here. It was on his to-do list, forever. He didn't realize he wouldn't have time . . .' Priti says, smiling at me. Before I can reply, she continues outside and joins the others who greet the food with great excitement, primed with their cutlery in their hands.

We dive into the array of beautifully prepared, locally sourced food. I help myself to the freshly caught pollock, and seaweed-enriched new potatoes, which taste even more delicious after the monotonous hotel buffet spreads and stolen sandwiches. The fruit and vegetables look bright and colourful, against the wondrous backdrop of the sails dotted in the sea.

'It must have been lovely spending all your summers here,' I say, admiring the view.

'Yes, it was great growing up, spending our holidays here. Mum and Dad let us walk and cycle around by ourselves,' Jay replies.

'As long as we didn't pass the bunker!' Zara laughs. It is her laugh that comes from Raj.

'There's an old World War Two pillbox up the beach. That was their cut-off point when they were younger. They could do what they wanted but couldn't go beyond there,' Priti explains to Ian and me.

'Although we always used to sneak off to the other side of the island . . .' Mishti says quietly, seemingly still worried about getting in trouble now.

'Did you? I didn't know about that!'

'Dad did!'

Priti shakes her head, exaggerating the movement for effect.

'He always used to say that he wanted to raise our children with the freedom and spirit that you three had on your trip. But when you have children you worry about them, don't you? You have these ideals, but then you panic when they go off. Fortunately it's always been very safe here.'

'I have to ask, what was Dad like at school? He

made out that he was a bit of a rebel because he got expelled.'

'I'm sorry, Jay, your dad was many things, but he certainly wasn't a rebel.' As I respond, both Ian and I can't help but laugh. 'No, I reckon our trip was the first rebellious thing he'd ever done.'

As we sit and talk around the table, lunch soon merges into dinner, day into night, and the present into the past. Remembering, reminiscing, smiling, laughing, sampling oysters, and savouring flan maraîchin. Ian and I take it in turns to share stories of teenage Raj, before listening to his family's tales, putting all the pieces together.

*

It comes as something of a shock when we have to get back on our bikes the next morning, after our idyllic, and far too short, time on the beautiful island. The sociable night reminded me of the dinners Caroline and I used to enjoy with our friends, the dinners I have missed – as much due to my own fault – for the last few years.

'Are you sure you're happy for us to join you for this leg?' Priti asks as she climbs on to her yellow bike. 'Raj used to take the children cycling down the coast every summer.'

I look across, smiling as Ian and I are joined by Priti, Jay, Zara and Mishti, all on their bikes.

'Of course we are. It's a lovely idea. I still think you should come all the way with us. Or you could catch the train down and just join us in Arcachon if you don't want to cycle?'

'No, I think Raj would have liked it to be just the two of you, but Jay thought last night that it would be nice to join you for a little way. I'm not sure how far I'll be able to go.'

'To be honest, I think Ian will be pleased for some different company!' I say as I watch him chatting away to Jay, Zara and Mishti, who he seems to have struck up a real bond with.

As we cycle together, taking the alternative bridge off Noirmoutier due to the tide, and head past pine trees, along a sandy path beside the coast, it makes me wish even more that Raj was here with us.

We reach Saint-Gilles-Croix-de-Vie for lunch, enjoying the sardines recommended by Priti, before she decides that it's time for the four of them to turn back.

'Thank you very much for honouring Raj like this,' she says, as we exchange rather sweaty hugs goodbye.

'Not at all, thank you for letting us. I'm just sorry that I haven't got to know you before.'

'Hopefully we can rectify that now. Please don't be a stranger.'

'I won't,' I say, knowing how grateful we both are for company.

'You're welcome to come and stay here anytime if you fancy a break. Both of you . . .'

'Be careful what you say or you will have a permanent lodger in Ian!' I whisper to Priti, as Ian says bye to the kids, and we swap positions.

'I'd love you three to meet my Anna next time,' I say to Jay as we shake hands.

'That would be great, hopefully see you soon!'

'Enjoy the rest of your trip,' Zara says, as I put my helmet back on. 'You're on the home straight now! You should easily get to Arcachon for the fireworks on the fourteenth!'

'Yes! Nothing's going to stop us now . . .'

40

As we are directed to the hotel conference room where the wine tasting is being held, I can immediately tell it is a bad idea.

'Come on! Jay said we should go wine tasting while we are in France,' Ian says as I pause in my stride, wanting nothing more than to spend our evening in Les Sables-d'Olonne resting my legs and getting a good night's sleep.

The cumulative effect of each day's cycling is really starting to take its toll. Saddle sores, swollen feet, aching joints, windburn, cracked lips. All problems we took in our stride at sixteen. But it is the emotional toil which I didn't expect. After the last couple of days spent with Raj's family, I want time to digest everything, to decompress.

'I think he meant going to a scenic vineyard, not a hotel,' I say in vain.

'Tomaytoes, tomatoes. It's the same thing,' Ian ploughs on, once again showcasing his differing stance. Our time with Priti and the children only confirmed to him that we should be making the most of every second.

It is clear that the wine tasting, which Ian saw advertised on one of the in-room flyers, is targeted at foreign tourists. There are only a few others in the room. A couple from Germany, and their ten-year-old son who will have to make do with juice – his face exudes disappointment at being dragged along. And a pair of Australian women, who are probably in their fifties, who Ian makes an immediate beeline for.

They introduce themselves as Melissa and Annette as if they're a TV double act.

'I'm Ian, and this is Simon.'

'Are you on holiday?' They say in unison, before giggling about speaking at the same time.

'We're actually cycling to Bordeaux,' Ian answers.

'No way, how funny, we're on a cycling trip too.'

'Really? We're going on to La Rochelle tomorrow.'

'So are we!'

'We should cycle together?' Ian proposes to these two random women we've known for thirty seconds, without any consultation. I stare at him incredulously, but he's more interested in his new company.

'Let's do it. I hope you can keep up with us,' Melissa winks to him.

Fortunately, the instructor interrupts Ian's flirting as he enters the room with his bottles of wine and his welcome spiel. Unfortunately, he's not the most engaging of speakers which only prompts Ian to mess around more.

'Are we meant to swallow it or spit it out?' I ask, before I take a sip of the first glass he pours for all of us.

Rather than answer, Mel and Annette simply start giggling.

I think they've already been on the wine before they got here.

'Naughty!' Ian joins in their laughter. I feel like I may as well go and sit with the young German boy who is now playing on his phone.

The instructor passes the spittoon down the long table, not that anyone opts to make use of it. Ian gulps his glass down in one mouthful.

'I'll let you have a few moments. I'm just going to go and get a few different bottles,' the instructor says, having lost the attention of the group already.

'We're going out after this if you want to join us?' Annette turns to ask us both.

I go to argue that we should get an early night given tomorrow is our longest journey, but Ian jumps in before I can have a say.

'Yes, definitely, where were you thinking?'

'I read that there is a karaoke bar nearby,' Melissa says excitedly. 'It could be fun.'

'Or –' I try to get a word in.

'Sounds great. Actually I'm a tribute singer,' Ian replies.

'Oh really? Who do you do? Oh no, wait. Let us guess,' Melissa says before Ian can get a word in.

I fear this is not going to go well.

'Who do you think?' She turns to her friend as they both study him.

'I reckon the guy in Simply Red?'

'Mick Hucknall?!' Ian spits out his wine for the first time this evening.

'I was going to say Meatloaf.'

Ian looks to me, as I do my best not to laugh.

'I'm trying my best not to be grossly offended right now,' he says, as they laugh.

Ian covers his eye with his hand.

'Now who do you think?'

'Oh OK . . . what was their name? That one who sang "Dreams"?'

'Gabrielle? Was it?'

'Do I look like Gabrielle? I'm David Bowie!'

'Oh, OK. Yes, I kind of see it now,' she says unconvincingly.

An hour later, I'm watching Ian and Melissa duet to 'Under Pressure'.

'Here you go,' I say as I return to the dark wooden table, feeling self-conscious as I carry two cocktails in flamingo-shaped mugs, complete with little pink umbrellas. I've been left with Annette, the less bubbly of the pair. She has shoulder-length, dark-blonde hair, and wears oversized earrings.

We don't exactly fit in. The rest of the bar is full of local students who jump up and down as they chant some French song, the large TV screens show the football, and Ian and Melissa continue to flirt in between their drunken renditions. I quickly remove the pink umbrella from my drink.

'So, who would be your dream dinner guest, Simon?' She shouts to be heard, which makes her questioning seem quite aggressive.

We've already run out of conversation, and our chat now seems like a job interview as we scrape the bottom of the barrel with questions. I already feel like I've had at least one drink too many, and I struggle to focus.

'Are we talking dead or alive?' I ask.

'Well, they're not going to be great company if they're dead, now are they?' she laughs.

'I was going to say my teenage self wouldn't have forgiven me if I didn't invite Marc Bolan but unfortunately he's dead.'

'Who?'

'You don't know T. Rex?'

'The dinosaur? You're inviting a dinosaur to dinner? What's a T. Rex going to eat?'

I shake my head.

'No, T. Rex were a band in the seventies.'

'Oh I don't know much about music. I don't really like music.'

'Who doesn't like music?'

'I leave that to Mel. She's the musical one. I'm more of a sports fan.'

'Have you heard of Sweet?'

Whether it's due to the number of drinks I've had, I decide not to give up.

'No.'

'10cc?'

'What are you on about?' She looks at me as confused as I am by her lack of musical knowledge.

'Surely you've heard of Slade at least?'

She looks into the sky.

'They sing that annoying Christmas song, right? No, the only people I really like are Maroon 5 and Take That.'

I continue to shake my head in disbelief.

'I'm just going to the loo. Be back in a minute,' she shouts before I can bore her any more with my impromptu music quiz.

As she wanders off, trying to squeeze through all the students, I check my phone.

I smile when I see there's a new message from Sylvie.

From: Sylvie, To: Simon

I can't believe you're actually visiting Bordeaux. How exciting! You definitely should have told me before though. I'll paste my number below if you want to give me a call before to arrange meeting up. Talking about phone calls takes me right back! It will be so nice to finally see you.

I had some spare time yesterday and I managed to find our old letters in my attic. It was so lovely reading through them. They did make me laugh. I'm not sure how much I told you in my letters, but I remember that year at school was so difficult for me. I didn't have many friends at college, and I was being bullied by a couple of girls. And at home my parents were constantly arguing (they divorced the year later). It was your letters which kept me going. I never got to thank you, so I wanted to say thank you now.

Anyway hopefully speak (or see you!) soon before these messages start turning into essays like our letters used to.

Tiens-moi au courant! (Keep me up to date!) x

As I read Sylvie's message, for the first time I start to allow the feelings I had for her as a teenager to creep back in. I realize I wish I could be sitting opposite her right now.

In spite of the amount of alcohol I've had, I rather foolishly decide to reply.

From: Simon, To: Sylvie

Think you Sylvie. I'm in bar and is Ian singing karaoke. I loved ours letters too that year. I wish you didn't stop writing to me.

41

THEN

July 1975

With great razzmatazz, Ian pulls out two bottles of white wine from behind his back as he saunters towards the tent that Simon and Raj have spent the last half hour struggling to put up. Their efforts not helped by being unable to find one of the tent poles.

'It looks quite lop-sided,' Ian looks at their creation very dubiously. His eyes glance across to the family camping nearest to them who have the identical tent, but are using it solely to store their bags in.

'You were the one who said you've been camping loads and know how to put up a tent. And then you disappear every time we put it up! We thought you were just going to the loo!'

'I took a detour to the shops, and hello, you're forgetting what I've got,' Ian waves the bottles in the air again. The horses in the neighbouring field look more interested, as they neigh and poke their heads over the hedge.

'How did you even manage to buy wine?' Simon asks.

'There's no way that you look eighteen,' Raj adds before Ian can respond.

'There were a couple of guys outside the shop and I gave them the money to get the bottles for us. Very entrepreneurial I thought.'

'Let's have a look at the bottles,' Raj reaches out to get them from Ian. 'They look all right as well.'

'Yes, I've heard Blue Nun is meant to be good,' Ian bluffs.

'Since when did you know anything about wine?' Simon retorts.

'I drink all the time at home actually. My parents always let me drink wine with dinner,' Ian says defensively.

'Of course they do,' Raj and Simon look at each other, raising their eyebrows. 'Are these the same parents who take you camping all the time?'

'Or the ones who complained to the school when you had an extra sip of wine at communion?' Raj laughs.

'Shut up. I've drunk more than both of you put together, OK?' Ian finally joins the other two in sitting on the ground, and snatches the bottles back off Raj. 'Anyway I also got us some meat!'

'What kind of meat?'

'I'm not sure, I couldn't understand the sign. It looks like beef, I think,' Ian replies as he takes out the non-descript meat from the blue bag.

'Maybe it wasn't the best idea to let the non-French speaker go,' Raj remarks.

'How many times do I have to say, it's not my fault I

don't study French! If we were in Germany, I'd be talking fluently to everyone.'

Simon and Raj share wry smiles.

'It's probably horse. Apparently that's what French people eat according to my dad,' Simon says, as he starts to unpack the gas stove from one of the other bags.

'Ugh, I'm not eating horse meat,' Raj creases up his face in disgust.

'What does horse meat look like?' Ian holds up his purchase, and then looks at the horse in the next field and feels bad for waving the meat around. 'I don't think it is. And come on, at least it's not more jam sandwiches.'

'You do know that the money has to last us our entire trip?' Simon says.

'OK, OK, I'm not stupid,' Ian starts to rip off the foil around the top of the bottle.

'Aren't you? You know we don't have a corkscrew, how are we even meant to open the bottles?' Simon shakes his head despairingly.

Ian turns his back and wanders off again trying to find someone with a corkscrew. The campsite amidst the French countryside is full of families staying in brightly coloured frame tents or caravans. A couple of kids play football on the far side, annoying their dad as they use the family car as a goal. His annoyance quickly evolves into anger as he shouts at the boys to take their penny floater elsewhere, before carefully inspecting the car for any dents or scratches.

The boys have positioned themselves in the corner of the site, away from everyone else, not considering the reason that no one else wanted to pitch their tents here. The ground is uneven and boggy, and each time they want to use the toilet they have to trek half a mile there and back. Despite trying to look and act older than their years, for any onlookers in the campsite, it would appear that the boys' parents have simply abandoned them.

'I'm not really sure we should be drinking,' Raj says quietly as Ian eventually returns.

'What do you mean?' Ian takes a sip as he walks, and does his best not to give away how disgusting the wine tastes.

'I just don't think it's a good idea.'

'Nonsense, we're in France so we have to live like French people. Drinking wine and eating horse.'

'I thought you said it wasn't horse!'

'My point is we're on holiday, we've got some wine, let's enjoy ourselves.'

'As long as we leave on time tomorrow,' Simon looks up from examining the stove.

'We'll be fine. We're not going to get drunk on two bottles.'

As the sun starts to set, they all sit around the stove, each taking it in turns to swig from the bottles of wine, listening to their portable tape player. Despite none of the boys enjoying the taste of the wine, they each persist with taking their sips, not wanting to be the one who says they don't like it.

'I swear we've been cooking the meat for ages?' Simon mumbles quietly, feeling light-headed.

'Oh, I forgot all about it!' Ian shouts.

'Do you know what? I really don't want to eat anything . . . I think I'm going to be sick,' Simon says, holding his head.

'Can't handle a little bit of wine?' Ian now laughs.

'Actually . . . now you say it . . . I don't think . . . I am feeling that well either,' Raj belches.

'Oh God, you're such lightweights,' Ian says as he wobbles to his feet, trying to check on the meat which is now overdone.

As he gets up, he stumbles, and accidentally kicks over the stove.

It takes him a moment to realize what is happening, by which point it's too late.

Simon notices Ian's mouth drop, and turns around to see what he's staring at.

'Fire! Fire!' Simon points helplessly as the flame from the stove catches the tent material. 'Quick!'

Ian still stands motionless, as faces peek out of tents and camper-vans around the field, wondering what the noise is about.

'Where are the . . . water bottles?' Raj asks, still dazed.

'We drank all the water! What do we do? What do we do? The toilets are all the way over there.'

'The wine?' Simon meekly suggests.

'But it's . . . it's . . . flame . . . flammable?' Raj picks up the bottle.

'Just do it. Throw it!' Simon's heart races, as his head spins.

Raj hesitantly throws the remainder of the disgusting white wine over the flame.

As the fire smokes and fades, the three boys all stare at the tent, which now has a gaping hole extending across one side.

'Do we have any jam sandwiches left?' Ian asks, looking miserably at the burnt, wet, dirty horse meat lying under the wreckage.

Simon holds his hands to his head.

'Oh God, I'm never drinking again.'

42

My eyes hurt so much I can barely open them. I hold my hand to my right temple, hoping it will stop throbbing.

Last night was most definitely a mistake. I can't recall the last time I had a hangover, and now I remember why.

I head out of the hotel's revolving doors in desperate need of some fresh air, unsure how I'm going to manage to cycle today.

I slowly do a loop of the building, trying to remember where we left our bikes when we checked in. I eventually find one, and as I go to unlock it Ian calls out from behind me, making me jump.

'Good morning!' he bellows, seemingly not as affected as me. His alcohol intake threshold has changed over the years.

'Morning. Have you got your bike already?' I turn to face him, looking confused at why there is only one bike tied to the railings.

'No, that is my one.' He points to the saddle which is higher than mine.

'Where's mine then? Has someone taken it?' I panic, thinking back to yesterday when we arrived. It takes me a while, given I can barely remember most of last night.

'I remember I was desperate for the loo when we got here, and I asked you to lock it up because I had to rush on into the hotel.'

'You never asked me,' Ian says defensively.

'I did.'

'Oh, yeah, actually maybe you did. No, you're right. Yes, I definitely locked it up. I swear I did. It was next to mine.'

'So someone cut the lock?' I look at him suspiciously.

'I guess they must have done,' Ian replies, not meeting my eye.

I'm not sure who is the more likely culprit – Ian or Glenn's dodgy locks that we paid a fortune for.

'So what do we do now, then? As if this morning couldn't get any worse.'

'Well, before you blame me, shall we check with reception? Maybe they moved it, or know where it is?'

We walk back into the hotel, waiting for an age for the electric glass doors to recognize our presence.

'Hi again,' I say, despairingly, to the receptionist who we only just bade goodbye to, before I fill him in on the situation.

This is the last thing I need to be doing now. Amongst the A3 paper maps, guides and questionnaire forms cluttering his desk, I notice a leaflet for the Museum of Shells, which sounds like it would have been a much more sensible activity for us, rather than wine tasting.

'No, sorry. I don't know anything about your bike. I can check the handover notes to see if my colleague has reported anything. Maybe she moved it, or knows about it. Just give me a second.'

I look around as he flicks through the pages of paper on his clipboard.

'Sorry, there's nothing here. Let me just go and check the store room. Maybe someone has put it there. I will be back in a minute.' He disappears into a door behind the reception desk.

'What do we do if it's gone?' I look back at Ian, who firmly grips on to his own bike.

'I guess we'll have to claim on insurance?'

I exhale loudly and close my eyes, wanting to be horizontal in a darkened room. As I reopen my eyes, the receptionist returns.

'Is this it?' He asks, pleased with himself for finding it.

Thank God, he's got it.

The bike is concealed by the desk, and it's not until he wheels it to the front of the reception that I can see what he is holding.

It is a bike.

But it is certainly not my bike.

It is a small, bright pink pushbike, with white tyres and a light-brown wicker basket in front of the handlebars. It even has purple sparkly streamers gushing out of the handlebars.

My face fades.

'Sorry, no, that's not my bike. Mine is the same as his,' I point to Ian's bike. 'It's identical.'

'Oh, sorry, this is the only one we have back there.'

It's a teenage girl's bike! Did he really think that it was mine?!

'Let me call my manager and see what she says.'

I take a seat next to Ian on the sofa.

'Can this morning get any worse? I've got the worst hangover, and now my bike is gone.'

'That's two bad things. What's the third going to be?'

'Oh thanks! Don't say that! I don't know why you made us drink last night.'

'So it's my fault for both the bike being stolen and your hangover, is it?'

'Yes,' I mumble inaudibly.

The receptionist speaks in rapid French, with lots of head nodding, and 'oui'-ing. After a few minutes he puts the phone down, and I stand up.

'So my manager said unfortunately there is nothing we can do about your lost bike as you left it outside our premises. However, this bike has been left here unclaimed for weeks now so if you'd like it we're happy for you to take it.'

'What else can we do?' I turn to Ian. The question is more rhetorical.

'Report it to the police? Find a bike shop and buy another one?'

'Sorry but it's a Sunday. I don't think you will find a bike shop open in the city today,' the receptionist interrupts.

'So, I suppose there's only one answer then?'

I shake my head, despairingly.

'Thank you,' I say to the receptionist as I take the small pink bike and wheel it outside. The irony of having a sticker plastered on it which says *cycliste professionnelle* isn't lost on me.

'Are you going to be OK on that?' Ian tries to conceal his laughter as I swing my leg over. 'Mel and Annette are going to love this.'

'It's not funny!'

'It is a little funny, come on.'

'You're not the one who has to cycle for five hours on this today!'

43

Having gone from twenty-one gears to just three, and from shock absorption to some sparkly purple streamers, by the time we eventually arrive in La Rochelle my whole body is broken.

As hard as I pedalled on the small bike, I seemed to go backwards, while Ian effortlessly moved further and further ahead, trying to impress Annette and Mel. It didn't help that the coastal cycle path was also rammed, meaning my excruciating embarrassment had an audience. I was even overtaken by a young girl who was excited that we had the same bike.

I collapse on to my bed as soon as we enter our new room, and I contemplate just sleeping in my Lycra. It doesn't matter that for the first time on the trip, Ian has chosen a well-located, central hotel right next to the port, the museums and the centre of town. I'm not interested in any of that.

'Are you getting ready then?' Ian asks, changing out of his cycling gear.

'Ready for what?'

'We're all going out again.'

'No way. I'm not going anywhere.'

'Oh, come on, don't be boring. Annette really likes you.'

This simply means he wants me to keep Annette company whilst he cosies up to Mel.

'Go if you have to, but I'm not. I'm too tired. We have to leave early again tomorrow. Can we not just both have a quiet night tonight?'

'You're such an old man now.' Ian decides not to take my advice.

As he gets ready, I take shelter in the bathroom. I need a few moments alone. Fortunately this bathroom actually has a door. With a lock. How old fashioned.

I perch down on the lid of the toilet seat, pull out my mobile to see if Sylvie has replied, and try to log in to the guest Wi-Fi, reading the message which pops up on my phone.

'Please verify you're not a bot.'

Why would I be a robot?

I read the instructions as nine small, hazy, square images suddenly appear.

'Select all images with fire hydrants. Click verify once there are none left.'

I thought robots were meant to be taking over the world but they can't identify a fire hydrant. They can't be that clever.

I survey the boxes and tick all those which show a fire hydrant – the system trying to catch me out by having some in white as well as red. As I select each one, the box then reloads with a new image. All I want to do is check if Sylvie has messaged, and now I'm playing Whac-A-Mole with fire hydrants.

After ticking seven boxes, there are finally no fire hydrants remaining. I click done and wait to be able to proceed to Facebook. But no, it prompts another screen of nine images.

For goodness' sake.

'*Select all images with bicycles.*'

'What was wrong? I ticked all the fire hydrants!' I whisper to my phone, starting to get frustrated.

'Why are you taking so long in there?' Ian calls from outside the door. 'I'm heading out now.'

'I will be out in a minute,' I call back, turning on the tap so it sounds like I'm doing something in here other than checking my phone.

'Are you going to say bye?' Ian shouts out.

'Just wait, I'm coming!' I say passive-aggressively.

I start clicking all the squares, randomly, fed up of these questions. Surely it shouldn't be this hard.

Bloody hell, I know what a bike looks like, I've seen enough of one.

No wonder robots can't do this. How is anyone meant to do it?

'*Select all images with motorbikes.*'

'Oh for Pete's sake . . . I'm not a bloody robot!' I shout at the top of my voice and, even above the sound of the running tap, the noise travels out of the door.

'I don't know what you're doing in there, but I'll see you later!' Ian calls back.

As Facebook eventually loads, I gasp as I reread the message I sent last night at the karaoke bar. And then I gasp even louder when I digest Sylvie's reply.

'Ian . . . wait!'

From: Sylvie, To: Simon

Hello Simon,

I'm guessing from your message you had a good evening!!

I want to hear more about this karaoke now. Did you sing yourself? It's been a long time since I did karaoke! Maybe I should try that for my birthday in September?!

It was good to get your message, as I was beginning to worry that something had happened to you on this spontaneous trip of yours.

I'm not sure if it was just the alcohol talking, but to answer your question, I didn't stop writing. You were the one who stopped writing to me!

I know we've been skirting around the subject, but maybe we should address it.

I wrote to you multiple times, and I remember even writing to Ian and Raj via your school to ask them what had happened, and when they didn't respond either I presumed you just wanted to stop writing. It was so sudden that I was worried that something had happened to you.

Anyway, that was years ago, and we were only teenagers. The past is the past, and it's nice to be in touch with you again.

Sylvie x

44

What does she mean I stopped writing?

It was Sylvie who stopped writing to me.

And why didn't Ian ever mention any letters? He was the only one not expelled. He would have still been at school to receive them.

I am still trying to understand and process Sylvie's message the following morning. I want to ask Ian about everything, but it's 8 a.m. and he still hasn't returned from his night out. We were meant to have been on the road an hour ago.

I pace up and down our room, already fully dressed in my Lycra. The electronic beep of the key card registering against the door suddenly wakes me from my whirring thoughts.

I quickly look across the room and see a sheepish Ian plod in.

'Where the hell have you been? We were meant to have left by now,' I snap.

'Good morning to you too,' he groans. My head may be feeling better, but I can tell his certainly won't be. Even from a few feet away, he reeks of alcohol. His eyes, which he can barely open, are puffy and bloodshot.

'I've been trying to call you all morning. I didn't have a clue where you'd got to.'

'OK, OK, calm down, please don't shout, my head is a bit sore.'

'I've just been sitting here all morning waiting for you,' I decide to raise my voice more.

'What's the rush? I thought we were meant to be taking it leisurely this time, you know, enjoying the sights.'

'The sights of what? Of Mel?'

He doesn't respond as he sits down on his bed, holding his head in his hands, yawning.

'I need to ask you something about Sylvie.'

'Do you have to ask right this second? Can it not wait?'

'Did she write to you?'

'What do you mean? When?'

He looks away from me.

'After our original trip, did you get any letters from Sylvie?'

'Why would she have written to me?' Ian shrugs his shoulders before picking up his Lycra from his bag. 'As you say, we're late, so I'd better hurry up and get ready.'

'After we got back from our trip, did you ever find any letters for me at school? I never got a chance to go and check.'

'I don't think so.'

'Sylvie said that she wrote to both of us? It doesn't make sense that you didn't see any of these letters.'

Ian holds his hands to his head.

'I don't know. There may have been a letter from her, and, perhaps as you say she may have written to me afterwards but it was so long ago, I can't remember. It's history now. Can we just move on? You're the one making us late now.'

'So you did receive a letter from Sylvie?' I push him. His confirmation that Sylvie did continue writing hits home as I realize I had it wrong for all of these years. That all the hurt and pain were unnecessary.

'I don't know why you're getting so worked up. You're back in touch now, so it's all good.'

'What do you mean it's all good? It was your fault we never met all those years ago, thanks to your complete inability to read a map, and then you didn't even let me know she wrote to me afterwards. How is that all good?'

'You're really still blaming me for her not being there all those years ago?'

Both of us continue to raise our voices.

'I just don't understand – why didn't you try to get the letter to me? Or write back to her explaining what had happened at least? You could have told her that we came to visit? You could have said that I'd left school. You could have put us back in contact!'

'I don't know. I was sixteen. I think maybe I sent the first letter back return to sender? Look, I'm sorry. What do you want me to say?'

'But you're not sixteen any more. Haven't you grown up at all? Why didn't you tell me now? On this trip?'

'I tried to apologize in the church, but you said I

didn't need to apologize for things that happened all those years ago.'

'I didn't mean this! We've been spending every minute together. We've talked about her. Why did you carry on letting me believe something you knew was wrong? Didn't you think that I'd find out eventually from her?'

'I thought you wouldn't mind if you two finally met. And I guess . . . I didn't want this. I didn't want it to come between us.'

'So you thought you'd just lie? Pretend it never happened? Like you live your whole life pretending you're someone else? Someone better?' I realize as soon as I've said this, that I've gone too far.

Ian stands up off the bed, his face turning red.

'OK, do you want to know the reason why I never did anything? I didn't do anything as it was because of her that I lost my two best friends. That stupid trip was all your idea. We went along with it. We came back, and then what? You and Raj fucked off, didn't you. What about me? I had to stay on living at school for another two years, with no one. So yes, I didn't feel like writing to her, or passing on her details – because she ruined our friendship.'

We both fall silent for a moment, as I pause, struggling to digest everything.

'Sorry, but we didn't decide to fuck off, as you put it. We were expelled. You were the one who fucked off and left us to take all the blame –'

'Oh, it's always woe is me with you, isn't it? And yes,

as you say, maybe I pretend to be someone else, but I've done things I wanted to do. What about you? You're barely living! You say I'm stuck in the past but you're the one who hasn't moved on in ten years . . . you're never going to move on with your life!'

I can feel my blood boil. I can feel the tension that I've suppressed for so many years finally exploding. All the annoying hotel guests, all the grief of Caroline's death, all the worries that I've kept locked away.

'Do you know what, I can't do this any more. This whole thing was a stupid idea from the start. Why don't you just piss off, Ian? It must be time you ran off again!'

I storm out of the room, slamming the door behind me, leaving Ian looking dazed and confused.

I prod the elevator button over and over again, hoping it will make the lift appear faster. But it doesn't.

I can't wait. I rush down the four flights of steps to the reception. I've wasted enough time today waiting for him. I'm not going to waste any more. I stride across to the storage room where we left our bikes.

I take Ian's.

He can try cycling on the little pink bike and see how he copes.

I wheel it out of the building, before climbing on. With no one for company, I switch the speakers on and turn the music up loud. I pull out of the hotel car park, on to the main road, and head off – the accusations, regret and remorse whirring around inside my head. I don't pay any attention to the sweeping landscape, or pause to compare it with how it looked all those years ago.

I don't even know where I am going. I just want to get away from Ian.

Somewhere, anywhere.

I think about what would have happened had Ian passed on Sylvie's letters to me.

I think about what he said.

As I try to breathe, and calm down, I realize that, as annoyed I am with Ian, I am more annoyed with myself. I am annoyed that he is right.

I pedal faster and faster.

As I reach a T-junction, I don't see the car speeding along.

I don't even hear it.

Not until it's too late.

45

July 1975

'I think we're going to die!' Simon whispers, his heart beating out of his chest.

'Stop pretending! It wasn't funny when Ian pretended to see a bear,' Raj replies dismissively.

'Shhh, I'm not pretending. I really did see something.' Simon's face has turned pale as he anxiously looks around the French forest, his eyes darting back and forth.

His palms start sweating as he walks his bike along the path which has vanished into thick grass. Ferns swallow the boys' bodies, reaching up to their waists, and snapped branches block their route. The vast pine trees which tower above them are now more closely packed together, and the narrow strip of blue sky which had been guiding them is now barely visible.

The supposed shortcut through the forest wasn't the best idea.

'It was probably just a bird,' Ian says coolly.

'It wasn't a bird. It was something big. I swear.'

As Simon defends himself, a tree shuffles loudly. All three boys jump. Ian, the highest.

'See, I told you it was just a bird,' Ian says, quickly continuing over the uneven and unkempt ground, hoping the other two missed his frightened reaction.

'I saw it again. I think . . . I think . . . it's a . . . tiger,' Simon says, now stuck to the spot. He points with his right arm.

'A tiger? Don't be daft, what's a tiger doing in a French forest?' There is now a slight wobble in Ian's voice, replacing the bravado from before. 'There are no tigers in France are there, Raj?'

'No. Tigers can be found in the wild in India, China, South East Asia and Russia.'

'See, Simon, Raj knows everything and he says there are no tigers in France.'

They all stare into the distance where Simon is still pointing, looking closely to see if they can spot any movement.

'What happens if it's escaped? Or maybe it's something which looks just like a tiger then. I don't know. I just really think we should turn back.'

'You're such a scaredy-pants,' Ian laughs, as his hands start to shake.

'Shut up! Why did you make us take this shortcut? It was a stupid idea to go through a forest,' Simon argues back. The tensions of the trip, and lack of sleep, are starting to come to the fore.

'Do you not think it's weird we haven't seen anyone else?' Raj asks, as they continue looking around. All they see is an endless panorama of trees. Every angle looks the same.

Suddenly, a panting, gnarly roar echoes through the trees.

The boys immediately freeze.

'How did you do that, Si?' Raj asks nervously.

'I didn't do anything,' Simon whispers.

'Oh shit. Oh shit. Oh shit,' Ian says, hyperventilating, catching sight of a flash of orange in the distance, and then seeing it clearly as it stops about a hundred metres away. 'It's . . . it's . . . over there,' Ian points, his hand shaking.

The boys look at each other, panicking.

'Come on, Raj, you're the clever one. What do we do? Do we run or stay still?' Simon asks hurriedly, his voice trembling as much as his body.

'Umm, I don't know.'

'How fast can they run?'

'Very fast. Probably about thirty-five miles per hour.'

'How fast can we cycle?'

'In this grass? Not that fast.'

'What about if we climb a tree?'

'Tigers can climb trees. They also have very good vision and hearing, and they're regarded as the strongest and most dangerous of all cats.'

'OK, genius. We've got it. What you're saying is we're screwed.' Ian now looks as pale as a ghost. 'And . . . and how do we know there's not more than one? They might be everywhere. We're going to be eaten. We're going to die.'

'I don't want to die. This was all your idea!' Raj argues back.

'Shhh, shut up, both of you,' Simon whispers. 'Let's just stay still. It might go away.'

The three stand rooted to the ground, their legs shaking.

'If we're about to die right now, I just want to say that I love you both, and you've been the best friends, and I'm sorry that I made us come through the forest,' Ian cries.

'If I don't survive, I leave my tape recorder to you, Si. And Ian, you can have my magazine collection.'

'As nice as this moment is, I don't think maybe this is the time to be talking . . .'

As Raj steps back slowly, he snaps a twig on the ground, and a flash of orange immediately appears to their right.

'RUN!'

As the tiger roars again, Ian jumps on his bike and pedals as quickly as he can through the woods.

Simon and Raj are left with no choice but to follow him. All three cycle frantically neck and neck, three in a row. Another roar blows the leaves off the trees. The ground begins to shudder.

'Is it chasing us?' Ian shouts out panting, as Raj pulls away, pedalling furiously. He's never cycled so fast in his life.

'I don't know, just keep cycling,' Simon replies, praying that he doesn't hear the sound of the tiger again.

Ian does the opposite, and turns around.

'Oh God, it is. Shit. Shit. Shit. We're going to die.'

As he looks back at the imposing beast, he doesn't see the branch sticking out in front of him. His front wheel catches it and the impact sends him spinning to the ground. He scrapes his arm, perforating the skin.

His screech of pain stops Simon in his tracks.

Simon takes a deep breath before he turns his head around, expecting to see that the tiger has pounced on Ian and is devouring his body.

But he can only see Ian rolling around on the ground.

'Get up! Ian, get up!' He slams on his brakes, and yells back.

'I can't,' Ian is immobilized, more due to fear than injury.

'Bloody hell, Ian.' Simon jumps off his bike and sprints back to where Ian is still lying on the ground. 'You have to get up.'

Simon desperately tries to pull him up, but he is too heavy to lift.

'Go on without me.'

'Don't be stupid, just get up. Now!'

Simon desperately pulls Ian to his feet, before they both jump back on their bikes, and pedal for their lives until the light at the end of the forest beckons. They don't look round once, not until they reach the edge of the forest and collapse on to the tarmac which greets them.

'Oh my God. Has it gone? Are we safe?' Ian shouts out, barely able to breathe, as they hear the sound of slamming car doors and screaming babies.

They look up to see Raj standing there, unable to hide the smile from his face.

'What's so funny? We nearly died!' Simon says, his heart still racing.

'You didn't nearly die.'

'We did too. The tiger nearly caught us! Si saved my life!'

Raj shakes his head.

'It was a zoo!'

'Huh? What do you mean?'

'The tiger wasn't in the woods. We were cycling along the back of the zoo. It must have been the tiger enclosure. There must have been a fence separating him from us, that's why he never came any closer.'

Simon and Ian look at each other, unsure whether to laugh or cry, and then look at their surroundings.

The signs dotted throughout the car park all point towards the entrance to La Palmyre Zoo.

46

As my eyes flicker open, I see Ian looming over me.

Is that what Hell looks like?

I slowly glance around, without moving my head, and realize I must be in a hospital. The room is sparse. The walls are painted in bright pink, and a single window looks directly on to a brick wall. There's one blue flimsy fold-down seat positioned next to the radiator, which I presume Ian has been sitting on, and the rest of the room is filled with random apparatus – weighing scales, a moveable table, and stacks of plug sockets. The clock reads eleven o'clock, but I'm not sure if that is in the morning or evening.

'You nearly gave me a heart attack!' Ian shouts in my face, as if the accident has rendered me deaf. He holds a disposable plastic cup of water in his hand, which he nearly spills over me in his excitement.

'Don't have a heart attack. There's no point in us both being in hospital,' I reply, quietly, still flickering my eyelids, adjusting to the light. The pain throughout my body is not fully quelled by whatever painkiller they've given me.

'I told you there would be a third bad thing.'

'Thanks for your wisdom. Why did all three bad things

have to happen to me? That doesn't seem very fair,' I smile ruefully.

'How are you feeling?'

'Like I've been hit by a car.'

'Very funny.'

'What have they said?' I ask.

'They've done a few scans and the doctor is meant to be coming any minute to give an update, but it looks like you've just lost the one leg.'

I reach down in horror.

Both my legs are still there.

'You idiot.'

Ian looks very happy with himself.

'What about the driver?' I try to recall what happened but it's all a blur.

'Don't worry, he is fine. He just didn't see you.'

Ian perches down on the bed, proving that my leg is definitely still there as I can now feel him sitting on it. He quickly moves when he sees me flinch.

'I should have been paying more attention to the road.'

'Yes, you got lucky. The bike, however, was not so lucky. You seem adamant that you don't want us to end this trip with a bike! I cycled after you as soon as you stormed off, although I could barely keep up on that small bike.'

I blink my eyes, as I try to recall anything. I can hear the screech of a car. I can feel my body skid across the road.

'You were the one who found me?'

293

'Yes. It was really frightening to see you there, like that, on the ground. The crash must have happened a couple of minutes before I got to you. Fortunately, for once my phone had battery and I was able to call an ambulance.'

'In your perfect French?'

'Don't mock me, I saved your life!'

'I suppose that means we're finally equal now!'

We both smile. We both get it. We both know how far we'd go for one another.

'I also called Anna to tell her everything that happened. I explained you were in the hospital but you were OK, and I would update her when you were awake. Obviously she's very worried.'

'Oh, she must be. Thank you for calling her. I'm sorry, Ian, for taking the bike, and for storming off.'

'No, you don't have to apologize. I'm the one who should be sorry. I'm sorry about the letters. There's no excuse. I don't know why I . . . I guess I was annoyed at Sylvie. I lost my two best friends because of that trip. Maybe there was part of me that was jealous, too. I was envious that you had a girl who wrote you these wonderful letters. But I should have told you when we reunited. It's just . . . to be perfectly honest, I don't have that many friends and I was excited about this trip with you, and I just didn't want to lose you again. When you mentioned you were back in touch with Sylvie, I was actually hoping I could help rectify my mistake, help you finally meet her.'

I smile at Ian for his honesty.

'It's OK. I understand. And without you I wouldn't have left the B&B, or had this adventure, which, as you say, might lead me to Sylvie, so I'm very thankful to you for that. Really.'

'I'm sorry as well for saying what I said about you not living your life. I know the last few years must have been difficult for you.'

'No, you were right with what you said. It is time I started living again. Although getting hit by a car is not the best way to begin that!'

We stop talking as soon as we hear the door opening. I look up, but my neck twinges as I do so. A doctor – young, dark haired and ridiculously good-looking – walks in.

'We are used to English patients here. But normally those with sunstroke, not people who have been hit by cars,' he smiles. 'How are you doing?'

'I think that's what you need to tell me,' I manage to utter back, feeling tired again already. Ian returns to his fold-down chair, getting out of the doctor's way as he looks at his clipboard.

'I've just had a look at your scans and you seem to be unscathed. You've got a nasty cut on your head, and some severe bruising to your body, but there are no broken bones. You were very lucky.'

'That's good, isn't it,' Ian chips in.

'You may experience nausea, blurred vision and headaches over the next few hours. The best thing to do is just try and rest.'

'How long do I have to stay in for?'

'We need to keep you here overnight, and then you need to rest at home for a few days.'

'But we are cycling to Arcachon,' I interrupt him.

He looks at me like the concussion is worse than feared, and I've completely lost the plot.

'I'm afraid there's no way you're cycling anywhere,' the doctor replies.

'But we need to be in Arcachon in two days to spread our friend's ashes –'

'– And we need to see Sylvie,' Ian calls out, smiling.

'I really wouldn't advise cycling for a few weeks,' the doctor says sternly now.

'We don't have a few weeks, we need to be in Arcachon for the fourteenth. And then I need to be back in England for my daughter's wedding.'

He looks at his clipboard again.

'If I was you, I'd let us monitor you here, and then you can fly home when you're ready, and take it easy for the next couple of weeks, try to avoid any stress, and enjoy your daughter's wedding.'

I look across at Ian, devastated, feeling like I've let Raj down.

With his damning verdict, the doctor renders our trip a failure once again.

47

I say goodbye to Anna, put the phone down, and gently nod to Ian, who peers through the door to check that it's OK for him to re-enter my hospital room. His face smudged up against the glass reminds me of him looking through our classroom door at school. I almost expect him to stick out his tongue.

'Thanks for giving me some privacy,' I say, as he walks back in with two glasses of water, passing me one.

'How was Anna?'

'Understandably worried, but reassured that I couldn't be too badly hurt given I still made a couple of awful dad jokes.'

'It could have been a lot worse.'

'The jokes?'

'The crash!' He rolls his eyes.

'Obviously, I know it could have been much, much worse, and I do feel fortunate that it wasn't. But I'm still absolutely gutted that both times we've attempted this trip, it's ended in complete and utter disaster. I'm so upset that we're not able to get to Arcachon for Raj. If I hadn't gone off . . .'

'There's no point in going over what we could or should have done on either occasion.' Ian still loiters beside my bed. 'I guess we'll just have to finish the ride later in the year?'

'But we wanted to be there for the fireworks again! That was the whole point.'

'Next July then?'

'Who knows what will be happening next year? We can't leave it that long.' I look across at Ian, exasperated.

'And we can't leave it that long for you to meet Sylvie either. You've waited quite long enough, no thanks to me.'

'I don't know. Don't you think someone is trying to tell us something?'

'What are they trying to tell us? That exercise is dangerous? That it's much easier to fly to France?'

'I just wonder, for whatever reason, maybe I'm not meant to meet Sylvie,' I sigh, as a couple of nurses peek through the door window as they pass.

'Don't be silly.'

'It's been lovely getting back in touch with her, and it's felt really natural. The other night when we were at the karaoke, for the first time I felt something else, something more.'

'Yeah?'

'Which is daft, I know, because we've still never met, and even if we did meet, there's nothing to say she'd feel the same. But, I feel like that for the first time about someone again, and bang, look what happened. Maybe this is a sign from Caroline?'

'A sign from Caroline? Are you being serious?'

'Why not?'

'Please don't tell me you actually believe that. I'm going to go and get the doctor back here right now if you talk any more nonsense like that. I don't think your head can be all right.'

'I just think someone or something is trying to stop me meeting Sylvie,' I reason.

'If Caroline was going to send you some kind of mystical, magical sign, trust me it's not this. She wouldn't put you in hospital! You didn't get hit by a car because you fancy someone.'

I simply nod, and then glance at the machine next to my bed which makes a strange beeping noise momentarily.

'I know it must be strange, but you are allowed to feel that way. It's been ten years now. You said Anna has been trying to set you up on dates, right? She thinks it's OK for you to meet someone new. I'm sure Caroline would, too.'

'Would she? I don't know that. There was no lengthy process where she deteriorated over months, and we could have heart-to-heart conversations about what she wanted me to do, or for her to give me her blessing to move on. I hear what you're saying, but I'm not sure if it's as easy as you make out. That's why I was saying the other day that I wasn't sure about meeting Sylvie. I don't know if it's the right thing to do. I don't know if I want to risk falling for someone.'

'I can understand how difficult everything must be,

but don't let the past hold you back. You've got to look forward – even if forward is with someone from the past – oh, you get my drift!'

'Anyway, this is all a pointless conversation. You heard the doctor, it's all over.'

'Maybe it doesn't have to be over quite yet? I've got an idea . . .'

48

'Are you sure you're comfortable there?' Ian asks, as I gingerly shuffle across into the window seat.

'Yes, I'm good thanks,' I reply, trying to mask the pain.

Ian lifts our bags into the overhead compartment, taking his new role as my carer very seriously. He tries to make the lifting look effortless, but he nearly topples over under the weight.

'Have you got enough leg room?'

'I'm fine, honestly. Thank you very much, though,' I reply, encouraging Ian to sit down next to me, in case someone takes the empty seat, and before he injures himself too. The trip was meant to make us fitter; we can't both return to the UK as invalids.

'Arcachon here we come, hey!' Ian smiles as he finally sits down at the table seat.

The doctor may have said we couldn't continue our journey by bike, but he didn't ban us from using the train.

And so, that's how we find ourselves on the 14.47 to Arcachon. With an approximate four-hour journey time, we'll have caught up with our lost days, make it in time for the fireworks, and be back on track to catch our flight home from Bordeaux in a couple of days' time.

Despite boarding early to make sure we got seats, the train is already busy; the aisle jammed by people likewise struggling to lift their baggage into the storage above their seats. There is also the inevitable confusion regarding seat reservations, and someone seems to be sitting in the wrong seat, or the right seat but the wrong carriage, which slows everyone else down. One man is sticking two fingers up, and I'm not sure if he's looking for Carriage Two or he's simply swearing at someone.

I look out the window, watching the floods of commuters rushing along the platform – families arriving in La Rochelle, day trippers going to catch the bus onwards to Ile de Ré. I can't help but chuckle as a love-struck boyfriend waves from the platform to his girlfriend, not realizing that she has moved to a different carriage and that he's actually waving at a very flattered old woman who simply smiles back through the tinted glass windows, wondering who her new admirer is. He continues waving until he's shouted at by an over-officious guard telling him to stand back from the platform edge, and the train slowly stutters out of the station.

'Have you messaged Sylvie yet to tell her we are going to be in Bordeaux tomorrow?'

Since admitting the truth about Sylvie's old letters, he seems to now be as outwardly invested in our potential reunion as I am.

'Not yet.'

'What are you waiting for? I thought we decided that you were going to see her. We're going to have two days in Bordeaux, so that's plenty of time for you two to meet up.'

'Yes, I know. I suppose I am just a bit nervous about it all.'

'Pre-date nerves are normal.'

'I told you, it's not a date! It's just two old friends finally meeting. Let's just take things slowly. I'm just nervous about what happens if we don't click in real life. I mean, this meeting has had a long build up! Talk about raising expectations.'

'Well, you're not going to find out unless you meet each other. Hurry up and invite her on this non-date date. Tell her you'll meet her tomorrow by . . .' Ian flicks his guide book open that he has on the table ready to read. 'Meet in front of the Opera House.'

'Should I say anything else?'

'Well, you need to give her a time!'

For some reason, we both look at our watches.

Hi Sylvie. Sorry for the delay – had a rather crazy couple of days. I'm actually going to be in Bordeaux tomorrow. Are you free to meet in front of the Bordeaux Opera House at 12pm? It would be great to see you if you're free.

I finish typing and read the message aloud.

'Do you think that's OK?'

'Perfect.'

'Remind me again why I'm taking advice from you,' I smile at Ian.

We don't have to worry about the girl opposite eavesdropping on our conversation. The teenager is listening to music through her headphones, but she has the volume so loud that the whole carriage can hear every lyric of the song that is playing. She holds her phone up and takes selfie after selfie, checking each one before discarding them and attempting a different pose – with the window in view, without the window in view, looking at the camera, looking away.

Her camera flashes manically as we speed past fields and fields of sunflowers which merge into a blur of yellow.

'Nice scenery, isn't it.'

'Yes, it's beautiful,' Ian looks out of the window too. 'It's nice we can appreciate it now rather than have sweat dripping down our faces.'

We speed past the land that we covered last time by bike, and we try our best to look out and spot any familiar locations, but the train moves too quickly.

'Why didn't we just take the train the whole way?' I laugh.

'It does feel a bit like cheating, though, doesn't it?'

'I actually remember reading somewhere that in one of the early Tours de France there was a cyclist who was disqualified after he was caught using trains rather than cycling.'

'I'm surprised Lance Armstrong didn't try and get

away with that one! We gave the cycling a good crack, for two old timers,' Ian says, patting his hand against my leg before realizing he's hurting me.

'But we have managed to end our trip without either of our bikes, so I'm not sure we can count it as a complete success,' I joke.

'But, we are still both alive.'

'And Raj is still with us.'

'Winning, really.'

My mobile vibrates on the table.

'What did she say?' Ian asks immediately, before I've even picked it up.

You're going to be in Bordeaux?! Tomorrow?! That's more than a bit of a surprise! But yes, I can certainly be free at midday.

I hold the screen in front of Ian's face, who simply winks back at me.

Perfect. I look forward to finally meeting you then. See you at 12!

I quickly message back before I close my eyes and drift off for the rest of the journey to Arcachon, dreaming about our meeting.

49

THEN

July 1975

Simon stares incredulously at the sign welcoming the boys to the seaside resort of Arcachon.

'What?! We were basically in Bordeaux! You've taken us in the wrong direction!'

'It looked like we just needed to cycle straight so that's what we've been doing,' Ian shouts back defensively.

'Yes, but clearly we've been cycling straight along the wrong road for the last two hours. You were meant to be looking at the map,' Simon moans as a blue Renault 12 beeps and drives past the three of them as they loiter in the road.

To avoid being run over, they decide to pull over. Raj quickly snatches the paper map off Ian, which he should have done three hours ago.

'Look! When we came in from the coastal path, we were meant to turn left there, not right! I honestly don't even know how you've managed this.' Raj doesn't know whether to laugh or cry. He moves his finger across from Bordeaux to Arcachon, to show Simon where they are exactly as he huddles behind him.

'I knew we weren't going in the right direction!'

'I don't know why you're blaming me, you could have looked at the map yourself. Anyway, I wanted to come here,' Ian looks across at the sign. 'I've heard Archa . . . Arcachon is really nice.'

'Yeah, who told you that?'

'Just someone. You don't know them.'

'So you mean to say, you've not mistakenly led us miles out of our way when we could have been in Bordeaux by now? But in fact, you deliberately decided that we should visit and you just thought you'd leave it as a surprise?'

'Yeah, exactly.'

They both look at Ian, sceptical of every word which comes out of his mouth.

'So I guess we're going to have to find somewhere to camp here, and then head to Bordeaux tomorrow?' Raj talks to Simon as he checks his watch.

Simon nods back, disappointed that his union with Sylvie has been delayed.

'Look how nice it is here. I just thought we could enjoy the beach first before we go to Bordeaux.' Ian, oblivious to their conversation, continues to defend himself.

As the boys look out across the beautiful sandy coastline, Ian's eyes bulge as he taps Raj's arm excitedly.

'Now I see why you took us on a detour . . .' Raj gawps as two topless women walk out of the blue water.

'I told you, lads . . . trust me, I know what I am doing!'

*

'See! All these people must know it's the place to come.' Ian keeps up his pretence as the trio walk across the packed beach, in between hundreds, probably thousands of others. Some wave French flags in the air, others have colour coded their outfits in red, white and blue. There is a joyful, celebratory mood in the air.

'It's the fourteenth of July, it's Bastille Day! France's national day. That's why it's so busy,' Raj says smugly.

'How do you know so much? It's weird,' Ian laughs, as they find a patch of sand to sit on. 'I've never heard of it.'

As he finishes talking, a beach ball lands next to them, and they see a blonde-haired woman chasing after it.

'Pardon, sorry,' she says.

'That's OK,' Raj blushes as he passes the inflated ball back to her.

'You are English?'

'Yes.'

'Ah, that is nice. We are from Munich in Germany.'

'Germany? Ian here is fluent in German, aren't you?' Simon turns to Ian.

'Es ist schön dich zu treffen,' the girl smiles at him.

Ian freezes on the spot, much to Simon and Raj's amusement.

'Uhhhh, yes, sorry, ja.'

The girl bursts into laughter.

'Möchtest du uns beitreten? That means, do you want join us?' She winks at Ian who is still dumbstruck.

'Yes, yes, we'd like to, thank you,' Simon answers on his behalf.

The trio, not believing their luck, follow the girl to the mixed group of six Germans sat in front of them, all smoking and drinking cans of beer. They are probably only in their late teens, but compared to the immature, wide-eyed boys they look about ten years older. The blonde-haired girl introduces them to her friends as they join them, forming a circle.

'What are you doing in France?' one of the other girls slurs, in between drags.

She passes the cigarette round to Raj, who looks at it unknowingly.

'We are cycling to Bordeaux. Simon's going to see his French pen pal he's in love with tomorrow . . .' Raj explains, before he attempts to puff the cigarette and bursts into a coughing fit. The girl takes it back off him, giggling, finding his reaction cute.

'But we're single, both of us,' Ian quickly adds, making sure the girls all hear.

'That is very cool. We are on road trip. We drive through Europe currently, just seeing where we get to.'

'How old are you?'

'Eighteen . . . yeah, we're eighteen,' Ian quickly answers, winking at Raj.

'So what do you do?'

'We're still at . . .'

'I'm a singer,' Ian announces, interrupting Simon.

'Really? What do you sing?'

'Anything!'

'Come on then.'

Ian looks shocked at having a willing audience.

'Really?'

'Yes, come on.' The German teenagers start clapping. 'Jurgen, play your guitar.'

One of the strapping German teenagers grabs his acoustic guitar and starts strumming.

'You know this one?'

He starts playing the first chords of 'Starman'.

Without needing any more encouragement, Ian joins in and starts singing, at first hesitantly, and then as the group all start cheering, he gets into it more. By the chorus, he's on his feet, putting on a show, encouraging the rest to join in. He's never had an audience like this before, he's never had a crowd singing along with him.

All of a sudden, Ian's performance is interrupted by a loud bang, with everyone cheering as the black sky is illuminated with fireworks.

Simon looks up to the sky, before smiling at Ian, who is loving his moment. He smiles even more when he notices one of the girls kissing Raj, as the fireworks continue to explode. Simon knows that his moment will be tomorrow, but for tonight he's delighted that his friends are having fun.

They've finally found a place where they fit in.

They spend the rest of the night singing, dancing, talking, kissing, drinking, and coming of age.

*

As the crowds eventually dissipate and the boys say goodbye to their new friends – Raj looking longingly at his German crush as she heads off – they're left alone on the large dune which towers high over the water.

Given the condition of their tent – which barely still counts as a tent now that the hole has grown exponentially – they decide against erecting it, and instead opt to simply wrap it around their bodies.

'Do you know what? I think this is the most amazing place I've ever been,' Raj lies on the sand, staring up at the night sky, awed by the brightness of the stars dotted across the dark background.

'So you're happy I brought you here now, then?'

'Yes, of course, Ian,' Raj rolls his eyes.

'It's slightly better than being stuck in our dorm room, ain't it?'

'Just slightly!' Simon combs his fingers through the fine, white sand, looking down at the rolling waves below.

'Who'd have thought a few weeks ago that we'd be sleeping on a beach in France?'

'Who'd have thought that us three would have cycled all the way here?' Ian adds.

'And who'd have thought that you'd be meeting Sylvie tomorrow?' Raj smiles.

'Can you imagine what the others would say if they knew we were here?' Ian says.

'They'd never believe us,' Raj replies, looking around, taking in their beautiful surroundings.

50

The sun is setting across the Dune of Pilat by the time we arrive. A yellow glow playfully scampers across the sand and bathes in the sea. The shadows of the pine trees start to slowly shrink and fade until they disappear completely. Footprints in the sand trail behind the other revellers who have come to celebrate and watch the fireworks.

I hobble up the steep sand incline, with Ian on hand to support me should I need it. The warmth of the glistening sand engulfs our feet.

'We've actually done it!' I exclaim as we reach the peak. 'We've made it.'

A real sense of achievement flows through my body as I smile from cheek to cheek. It may not be the top of Everest, but for us two to reach Arcachon at least in part by bike again, this moment feels more than special.

'It was never in doubt.' Even Ian struggles to keep a straight face as he says this.

I chuckle, thinking about all the obstacles on our journey. Even more bumps in the road than during our first trip.

'I was worried it would have changed, but my gosh,

it's still so beautiful,' Ian gasps as we look out across the same sumptuous bay where we camped out and slept under the stars. We enjoy the same sunset we witnessed all those years ago.

'Do you still insist that you intended to bring us here last time?' I ask, smiling.

'Of course, a hundred per cent it was deliberate!' He chuckles.

We pause for a couple of minutes as much to catch our breath as to take in the magnificent panorama. Eventually, we carry on along the dune, kicking the sand in our path, until we reach an area by the sea, away from anyone else. Ian, holding the urn in his hands, looks at me, and I look back at him.

'Shall we?' Ian asks hesitantly, not knowing the protocol for spreading ashes.

'Should we say something first?' I suggest.

'Yes, good idea,' Ian turns to face the urn as if he is talking directly to Raj inside. 'Raj. You were the brightest person I've ever known, even as a teenager. Thank you for the times we shared . . . the bond we had. Times weren't always easy back then, but you always had my back. I don't really know what else to say, but I'm really pleased we could do this for you.'

I put my arm round Ian as he speaks, before reaching into my bag and pulling out an old portable tape player.

'What are you doing?' Ian looks across confused. 'No wonder your bag was so heavy.'

'I found the old tape in my attic, I couldn't bring myself to listen back to it yet, but now seems a good time to do so.' I turn to the urn of ashes. 'I remember never wanting to talk to you again after you recorded over this tape, but now all I wish is I could have one more conversation with you.'

I press play as Ian still tries to work out what I'm referring to. Before he can figure it out, Raj's teenage voice starts speaking.

> 'Shall I compare thee to a summer's day?
> Thou art more lovely and more temperate:
> Rough winds do shake the darling buds of May,
> And summer's lease hath all too short a date . . .'

Both of us can't help but smile, as we hear Raj stumble over Shakespeare's sonnet. We stand in silence, simply listening.

> 'Sometime too hot the eye of heaven shines,
> And often is his gold complexion dimm'd;
> And every fair from fair sometime declines,
> By chance, or nature's changing course untrim'd;
> But thy eternal summer shall not fade,
> Nor lose possession of that fair thou ow'st;
> Nor shall death brag thou wander'st in his shade,
> When in eternal lines to time thou grow'st:
> So long as men can breathe or eyes can see,
> So long lives this, and this gives life to thee.'

As soon as Raj finishes the final word, the tape machine clicks and goes straight into playing the second verse of Elton John's 'Crocodile Rock'.

'This is what I was talking about. This is what he would have wanted,' Ian smiles as Elton sings.

I can't help but laugh as a tear rolls down my cheek.

'Goodbye, my friend.'

I let the music continue to play as we each take a handful of ashes out of the urn, and together let them fly into the air, and out to sea.

I realize, in this moment, that I'm saying goodbye to both Raj and, finally, to Caroline.

*

'It kind of makes you think about everything, doesn't it,' Ian says, out of the blue, as we sit on the sand looking out at the sea. The urn is now empty beside us, and the tape has finished playing.

In normal circumstances, the woolliness of Ian's statement would make me laugh, but he's spot on here.

'It does.'

'You know you're very lucky,' he turns and says.

'I haven't thought of myself as lucky in many years.'

'I know, but from what you've told me, you were fortunate to have had a wonderful wife, you have a lovely daughter, and who knows, tomorrow maybe you find out you have a real connection with someone else.'

I look across at him and smile, realizing I have to stop mourning and appreciate what I have.

'Likewise, Raj had a successful career, a beautiful family. It was so lovely seeing them all. And also all those people who came to his memorial. What do I have to show for my life?'

'You've lived your dream, you've travelled the world, been to places I could only dream of. I'm extraordinarily envious of everything you've done whilst I've been killing time.'

'But who is going to do this for me? Who'd turn up at my memorial? Who can I share anything with?'

'What about all your legions of female fans in every port?'

Ian looks across at me, debating what to say.

'I might have slightly exaggerated about that. I don't think I've been with anyone for – what? – probably twenty years now. And even then they only wanted to sleep with Bowie . . . when someone actually called me David in bed that was kind of the final straw.'

I try not to laugh.

'What about Mel the other night? She didn't even think you looked like Bowie – I don't think she was trying to sleep with Gabrielle!'

'No, she was nice, but nothing happened . . . I don't know . . . I guess I'd like to find someone who I can share my life with. God, did I just say that? I'm sixty and I'm only just realizing this.'

I smile at him.

'And it's not like I have many friends either to talk to,' he continues.

'You're not the only one. Caroline was always the social butterfly, the one inviting people round constantly, she was the one who made friends for both of us. It's not easy as you get older to meet people.'

'And I'm stuck on the road with a man who is the worst Rod Stewart impersonator you'll ever see, who only communicates using Rod's lyrics.'

'I don't want to talk about it?'

It takes Ian longer than it should to get the joke, and then he chuckles.

'Yes, exactly. I don't want to sound all schmaltzy about it, but this has been nice . . . you know, this trip.'

'You're right, it's been . . .'

I pause to think of the right word, and Ian jumps in.

'Crazy?'

'Yes, it's certainly been crazy. I'll be honest that I wasn't expecting us to recreate the first trip quite so literally with so many things going wrong again!'

'Come on, it'd be boring if everything went right!'

'I suppose so! No, seriously, it's been good. As you get older, you get more fearful, don't you? And those things that you do as kids without thinking, you stop doing them. Just riding a bike becomes more scary, let alone riding one to France. I think that first trip, with our first hangovers, our first time abroad, Raj's first kiss, your first public performance . . . I think we believed that was our coming-of-age trip, but now I wonder if this one is.'

'Do you think Raj is up there somewhere looking down at us, pleased that he's reunited us?' Ian asks.

'I think Raj believed in reincarnation,' I smile. 'But I take your point. I reckon he'd be happy wherever he is. And, you know, you're stuck with me again now.'

'Shall we set the details now for where we're meeting in forty-four years?' Ian asks.

'I think we can meet up slightly sooner than that.'

'Forty years?'

I laugh.

'I'm not sure we'll be able to cycle at all then. Maybe next time we'll forget the cycling. I think we've realized once and for all that cycling isn't really for us. Maybe something else? And perhaps with separate rooms? Or at least rooms with toilet doors!'

'Yes, definitely. Fishing? Are we at that age now? Playing golf? Watching cricket? What else are we meant to do in our sixties?' Ian shrugs.

'I think we can do whatever we want.'

'What was it Bowie said? "I don't know where I'm going from here, but I promise it won't be boring."'

'And what does Ian Pratt say?'

Ian looks out to the sea, thinking of something fitting to say.

'Ian Pratt says, it's funny that our favourite place on the trip was here, a place where we weren't meant to be, somewhere we hadn't planned. Maybe we should both take a few more risks going forward?'

'Very philosophical,' I smile.

We continue sitting in the sand until darkness falls, talking at first and then in silence, just content to sit and watch the world, and be in our own thoughts. We look over at the groups of teenagers enjoying their night, and then smile as the fireworks crash above our heads, illuminating the sky as if Raj and Caroline are decorating it with glitter and gold.

51

'I can't meet Sylvie looking like this,' I say despairingly to Ian, as I stare at myself in the mirror of our hotel room in Arcachon's Winter Town the next morning.

Each house in the neighbourhood is more eccentric, extravagant and exotic than the one before. Bright colours, ornate balconies, turrets, colonnades, unusual roofs, unique staircases – a complete mismatch of styles as if the architects let their imaginations run completely wild. The room is similar with a hotchpotch of furniture and fittings – a fold-down wooden desk, a vintage rocking chair and a series of framed cartoon prints on the pastel blue walls.

'What? Old?' Ian eventually replies.

'Very funny. I'm bright red, I look like a bloody lobster!'

Whilst yesterday's late night on the beach was a fitting tribute to Raj and good for the rekindling of our friendship, the deceptively strong setting sun wasn't so good for my complexion.

'You're not that bad . . . oh no, actually you are,' he says as he looks across from watching some obscure French quiz show on the TV.

'Brilliant. So now, not only am I bruised all over and

have a bandage around my head, but also the rest of me is bright red!'

'Don't women like battle scars? I thought you were going for the rugged look.'

'Who was I in a battle with? The sun? This is the first time Sylvie's ever going to see me, and I look like this?'

I stare forlornly at my reflection. It's not exactly how I envisaged turning up for our first meeting.

'It'll be fine, I'm sure there is some quick fix. Let's look up how you can cure really, really bad sunburn,' Ian says, smiling gormlessly, as the French TV presenter continues asking questions neither of us can understand.

He picks up his phone and types two-handed, as I continue looking at my sorry state in the mirror.

'What if I still look like this for the wedding photos!'

Ian can't multitask and he is too busy reading to listen. He talks to himself as he scrolls through an article.

'So, apparently you need to eat mango?'

'Mango? How does that help? And how much mango do I need to eat? Are we talking a slice, or a whole tree load?'

'Look, I'm not a mango expert but that's what it says.'

'Is there another suggestion?'

'You're not happy with that one? OK then . . .' He goes back to mumbling. 'We could do this one.'

'Do what?'

'I'm just reading!'

I shake my head, laughing, playing to my own reflection.

'We need to cover you in shaving foam.'

'How's that meant to help? We're going to shave off the sunburn?'

'It says if you leave it on for half an hour it will help cool it,' he announces, putting the mobile down.

'Really?'

'Do you want to try it or not?'

'I suppose so.'

I've applied shaving foam thousands of times in my life, but for some reason Ian is insistent that he helps. I sit on my twin bed whilst he smothers it over my face as if he's giving me an overly vigorous massage.

'Ouch, that's enough. OK, thanks,' I lean away as he starts patting my face where it's sore.

'This better work.' I swallow a bit of the foam as I speak. 'I now look like a rosy Santa Claus.'

'Just stay still, and it will do its thing.' Ian says as he washes his hands, seeming overly confident in something he's read online. As he does so, his phone rings. He stares at the screen, trying to read who is calling.

'It's Anna.'

He hands me the phone, and I smudge the shaving foam all over it as I hold it to my ear.

'Hello, darling. You OK?'

'Ummm, not really, Dad, everything's just gone wrong.'

52

I freeze as Anna speaks, my body immediately paralysed with worry.

'What's wrong? Are you OK?' I say hurriedly, instinctively fearing the worst.

She doesn't respond. I can just hear her breathing heavily.

'Anna? Has something happened to you? Is there a problem with the cottage? The guests?'

'No, no. That's all fine,' she replies meekly, her voice trembling.

'What is it, then?' I try to prise the problem out of her.

'The wedding,' she says as she bursts into tears.

I haven't heard her sound this upset in years.

'What's wrong with the wedding?' I ask as I stand up and walk towards the window.

'It's off, Dad.' She sobs. 'The wedding is off. It's not happening. I didn't want to disturb you, but I don't know what to do, and you . . .'

'It's all right, it's all right, I'm here,' I try to calm her down, struggling to understand her teary words. Ian looks at me, concerned.

'I've been trying to call you but you weren't picking up again.'

'I'm sorry, I don't know if my phone's on. I'm here now though. Just tell me what's happened.'

The signal cuts out for a couple of seconds and I can't hear her clearly. I walk around the room hoping it will help, but I'm not sure if it's at my end or due to the poor signal with Anna in the cottage. I pause under the sunlight which floods down from the dormer window.

'Sorry Anna, I can't really hear you, but I can come back today, darling?'

'Dad, you really don't need to do . . .'

'I said I shouldn't have left you with the B&B on top of everything. It's too much.'

'Honestly, it's OK.'

'Anna, I want to. I'm going to look now and see if I can get on a flight today. I can probably be back this afternoon,' I say as I look at my watch, trying to calculate how long it will take us to get to Bordeaux airport, and adding in the flight time back.

Ian looks at me even more concerned now.

'Are you sure?' Anna asks.

'Of course I am. We've scattered Raj's ashes which is what we came for so we can just come back a bit earlier than expected, that's fine.'

I look at Ian, checking if that's OK with him.

He nods, not knowing what is happening.

'I'm sorry,' Anna says, breathing heavily down the phone.

'Don't be sorry. You don't need to apologize for

anything. I promise everything's going to be OK. I'll go and look up the flights now, OK?

'Thank you,' she splutters between tears.

'Goodbye.'

I put the phone down, and immediately sink back on to the bed.

I knew I shouldn't have left her. I knew something was wrong.

As Ian tries to ask me what Anna said, all I can do is stare straight ahead, worried about Anna, worried about Ollie, worried about whatever's happened between the pair of them.

And then the thought creeps into my head again that maybe meeting Sylvie just isn't meant to be.

53

The shaving foam starts to drip off my face as I explain the predicament to Ian.

'There's a flight at 11 a.m., or one at 4 p.m.,' I say as I browse the easyJet website on Ian's phone. It takes me a while to navigate, as I fumble to remove the pop-ups warning me about cookies. 'It takes an hour to get to Bordeaux, and then probably another fifty minutes to get to the airport.'

'Hang on a second, we've come all this way. Are you really telling me you're not going to see Sylvie after all this? When I nodded to you, I thought Anna was ill or something. I'm sure flying back tomorrow would be fine?'

'Of course, I'd have loved to have seen Sylvie, but Anna needs me. She's distraught. I told you there was something the matter with her and Ollie. There's been tension between them for months.'

I wonder if Ian can truly know how it feels to have a daughter in distress.

'But you've been waiting for this for however many years, you have to do this for yourself.'

'It's just not meant to be.'

'Don't you dare start going on about signs again!

We're not going to make the earlier flight now anyway, so you can still see Sylvie, even if it's just briefly, before we head to the airport.'

I look at Ian, who is not giving up.

'But is it not going to be strange if I show up and say, "actually I've got to go now"? And my mind is going to be on Anna, and –'

'– You can make a million excuses if you want. But look, I ruined things for you last time with Sylvie, I'm not going to let you do it this time. Realistically, you can't sort anything until we're back in the UK and you've talked properly to Anna. Put it this way, would you rather –'

'We're not sixteen, Ian. One of your silly questions isn't going to help now,' I sigh, trying to weigh everything up.

'Just hear me out.'

'I'll go for the hundred-legged spider,' I say sarcastically.

'I said, hear me out.'

I exhale loudly.

'Would you rather see Sylvie briefly and find out if there is a connection in real life? Or sit in the airport terminal for an extra hour, and then go back to your cocoon in the B&B and spend the rest of your life wondering what might have been, again? I thought we promised to make the most of life?'

'Since when did you speak so much sense?'

'I've always been the one who speaks sense.'

I'd laugh if my sunburnt face didn't hurt so much.

'OK, so I'll book the tickets for 4 p.m., so that probably gives me an hour or so with Sylvie?'

As I pick up the mobile again, I accidentally open the other tab with the article about sunburn cures. I wrinkle up my face, reading it curiously.

'What's wrong? Are there no tickets for that flight?'

'It says menthol shaving foam, you idiot!'

'What?'

'You can help get rid of sunburn by applying menthol shaving foam,' I read aloud.

'Yes, and?'

'This isn't menthol shaving foam you've put on me!'

'Does it matter?'

'Yes, it's the menthol which would cool it. I've just been sitting here with shaving foam on for no reason.'

I grab some of the foam from my face, and throw it across the room at Ian.

An hour later, with new flights booked, we sit on the train to Bordeaux, eating punnets of pre-chopped mango.

54

The Grand Théâtre de Bordeaux, one of the most beautiful theatres in the world and an emblem of the city, stands proudly in the centre. The eighteenth-century, neo-classical, rectangular-shaped structure is sumptuous in its design, almost temple-like with its stone frontage of twelve Corinthian columns and a balustrade decorated with twelve statues of Greek influence.

I stand on the steps in front of it, looking out across the Place de la Comédie, scouring the crowd of people bustling through the city. Searching for Sylvie.

I look at my watch. It's ten to twelve. Ian, standing opposite on the other side of the square next to Gordon Ramsay's plush restaurant, waves enthusiastically. We agreed that he would leave me to meet Sylvie alone and we'd meet back here in an hour, but it looks like he is going to hang around until Sylvie arrives, albeit in secret.

I smile back, until a tram intercepts us and I lose sight of him. The trams come and go through the square, passing through the city centre like a model railway set.

I look across at a couple of twenty-somethings on the steps next to me. The man, English, and the girl,

French, chat away as if they've just been reunited. He's dressed in a light-blue Oxford shirt, sleeves rolled up, and beige shorts. She wears denim shorts, a striped t-shirt, and large sunglasses. Her nails are painted in different colours. From the man's awkwardness and inability to take his eyes off her, it's clear he likes her.

My attention is suddenly jolted as I'm brushed aside by a group of tourists entering the Opera House for a tour of the spectacular concert hall, and then I look back out across the square again, waiting, hoping for Sylvie to appear.

I wonder if I'll even recognize her. And will she even recognize me? Surely I look nothing like the photo of my sixteen-year-old self, especially with my sunburn and bandages. Maybe we should have let each other know what we are wearing.

A woman hiding under a sunhat approaches slowly, and for a second I think it could be her. She smiles at me, before turning around.

I start to worry that maybe she won't even turn up. I didn't give her much notice. Or my unannounced arrival and surprise message may have put her off. I breathe quickly, my hands are clammy, and my heart thuds through my chest, just like it did all those years ago when I knocked on her door. I just hope this time she's here.

The clock chimes twelve.

And then I see her. My heart, my gut, tells me it's her. She's right on time.

She walks across the square, looks up, unsure at first, before she catches my eye, and smiles. It's a smile which whisks me right back. Back to that black and white passport photo.

She's as pretty as she was as a teenager. Her long dark hair is now shorter, worn in a side-parted, fashionable bob. Her face is etched with wrinkles of happiness. She wears glasses now, like me. Her eyes, still as bright, still as glistening. Her smile, still gleaming.

We smile at each other as if we're close friends, not people who have never met.

I realize it is the first time I've seen her in colour.

Her red lipstick. Her gold earrings. Her blue eyes.

She walks across the square towards me, and I walk down the steps towards her.

I realize as we approach each other that all the teenage excitement and heartbreak, the planning, the cross-country trip, the upsetting my parents, the expulsion which in turn probably changed the whole course of my life, all of that has led to this moment.

The other people who sit on the steps of the Opera House, who walk past, who get on or off the tram, don't think of this moment as anything but a routine minute of their lives. But for us this moment is one we've waited decades for. The drama is not happening inside on the stage, but outside on the pavement.

'Hello Simon,' she says.

55

'Hello Sylvie,' I say warmly as we hug for the first time, and she kisses me on both cheeks.

As we let go and stand back, I can't help but continue admiring her, rather than the grand architecture behind her.

Neither of us knows what to say.

'Je n'en . . . crois pas . . . mes yeux,' I say, breaking the silence, smiling, hoping I've used her expression in the right way.

She laughs, hopefully at the sentiment, rather than my pronunciation.

'Very good. I mean it's not quite like Colin Firth in *Love, Actually*, but I'm pleased you've learnt one French phrase,' she smiles. 'I can't believe my eyes either. I can't believe we are finally meeting.'

Her English is polished, fluent, with only a trace of the French accent I remember.

'We took our time, didn't we?'

'We did.' Her eyes glint as she smiles.

'It's . . . it's lovely to see you, in person,' I muster, still dazed by the situation. 'I don't know where to even start.'

I laugh nervously. I may be sixty, but I suddenly feel sixteen again.

'Maybe with what you are doing here?' She looks me up and down, confused. 'Are you cycling somewhere?'

'So it's quite a long story.'

'It's a good thing I like long stories,' she smiles, and indicates the street ahead. 'Shall we walk and talk?'

As we leave the square together I fill her in on the memorial, reuniting with Ian, and the idea to cycle to Arcachon. I glimpse Ian still lurking, his face beaming. He puts two thumbs up, as we stroll across the tram tracks into a long shop-lined street. The Apple Store on our left, a shop selling the local sweet delicacy of canelés on the right.

'Where did you cycle from?'

'From England. From my cottage.'

'You're not serious?'

'Honestly, we did. Well, until La Rochelle at least, where as you can see I had a little accident.'

'I didn't want to mention that. What happened to you?' she asks, clearly too polite to mention my burnt face either.

'I didn't see the car coming! And falling off a bike at my age is quite painful. You don't just bounce back up any more. When I wrote to you about the last couple of days being crazy, it was because I've been in hospital.'

'Oh God. Are you OK, though? Should you be walking around?' She puts her hand on my shoulder.

'It's fine, thank you. Nothing too serious, thankfully. Although it did end our cycling. So we caught the train to Arcachon which, I'll be honest, was much easier.'

She pauses, seemingly more confused than before.

'Can I ask why did you choose Arcachon? I mean it's a very lovely place, but why there?'

I pause for a second, wondering whether I should say.

'So, this is the second time we've done this trip actually. We cycled here when we were at school, and we spent a night in Arcachon, and Raj loved it so we thought it was a fitting place,' I say coyly, knowing what her next question will be.

'Really? When was that?'

I look across at her.

'It's a bit awkward saying this now, but we actually came to see you.'

She stops in her tracks.

'What do you mean, you came to see me? When?'

'That summer after we'd been writing to each other, and we'd hoped to do the exchange . . .'

'Yes,' she nods.

'After our exams finished, we cycled to Bordeaux to see you.'

'No, you didn't.'

'Yes, we did,' I reply.

We now stand in the street, staring at each other, swarmed by tourists flooding out of McDonalds with paper cups and Big Macs.

'What happened?'

'You'd moved.'

It takes a couple of seconds and then Sylvie looks up at me as if everything has just clicked.

'We arrived at your house to find someone else there, and well, we had to turn around again.'

Her mouth hangs open as she tries to get her head around the revelation.

'You didn't know we moved?'

'No. No, I didn't. Apparently you'd only moved the day before.'

'I remember it was all so sudden, we were only renting that property, and Dad wanted to move. I definitely wrote to tell you . . . Oh God . . .' Sylvie looks completely bewildered, trying to process everything. 'You cycled all this way. I'm so sorry. I had no idea. Is that why you stopped writing? I don't blame you. You cycled all that way.'

'No, it wasn't like that at all. We . . . or actually, Raj and I, got caught when we got back and we were expelled from school. So I never got any of your letters. I never knew your new address. I had no way of contacting you.'

'But I wrote to Ian too?'

'So I've only just discovered! Your message the other day was the first I'd heard of it,' I roll my eyes.

'I always thought it was you who stopped writing, but you just didn't have my address. And of course, I moved that summer from what we call collège to lycée so you wouldn't have had my new school address either.'

'And I always thought it was you who stopped writing.'

'That's so bad. All those years. I can't believe it. If you'd got that letter with my address . . .'

'Or if we'd arrived a day earlier in Bordeaux.'

We pause again, looking at each other.

'I'm sorry to start with such a bombshell,' I joke as we slowly carry on walking.

'I know. I really don't know what to say after that. I am just trying to . . . I don't know . . . I just can't believe that you cycled to see me. That was . . . wow . . . so sweet of you.'

'With hindsight, it was probably more silly than sweet, not telling you about it though. The worst-planned surprise ever, I reckon.'

I smile at her as we carry on along the never-ending, paved shopping street in silence, just reflecting on everything.

'What did you do when you were here all those years ago?' Sylvie asks after a few moments.

'Nothing! Literally nothing. We cycled around the cathedral a few times, and then turned around and went all the way home.'

Sylvie covers her eyes with her hands again.

'I think I definitely owe you a tour then . . . if you'd like?'

'That's the other thing.'

As we reach another pretty paved square – where trees grow out of oversized terracotta plant pots, a mother chases her toddler, and a group of tourists surround a preserved Roman column – I explain the situation with Anna and the airport.

'So after all these years, we only have an hour together. Fortunately, I know just where to take you,' she smiles, and I immediately wish we had longer than an hour.

56

We've ventured down one of Bordeaux's many bustling alleyways where locals are sitting out at the street tables, drinking, eating and smoking. Restaurant chalkboards advertise their lunchtime specials, people flood out of the independent shops, and mopeds scoot in between families taking photos on their mobiles. The whole city looks different than I remember from our few hours here before. The buildings are cleaner – the layers of industrial pollution scrubbed off – and the city is clearly more geared up for visitors.

'Is that . . .?' I start to ask Sylvie, as we come to a stop and I look up at the mint green frontage of the shop in front of us. 'Is that the record shop that you always mentioned in your letters?' I shake my head, thinking I'm just being daft.

'You're right. It is. I told you I'd show it to you some-day,' Sylvie smiles.

I'm moved by the fact she remembered the details of our correspondence as well as I did.

'Wow, it's still here?'

'Yes, and seeing as we've got limited time, then this had to be the first place in Bordeaux that I took you to.'

'Of course.'

'Forget the famous landmarks . . .'

'I think we cycled in circles round them last time, so it's OK,' I smile.

I follow Sylvie off the street into the retro-looking record store. It is a music lover's heaven. Thousands of records are packed tightly on shelves, divided by red markers. Posters of French and British rock stars alike adorn the walls, The Rolling Stones play over the stereo system, and customers flick through the records at a rapid pace, their fingers trained over years of scouring. It is not just the usual music anoraks browsing though, noticeably there are a group of young, hipster-looking youths, who look way cooler than we were at their age.

'It's funny how vinyl has made a comeback,' I comment.

'I know, suddenly my sons are interested in my record collection, wanting to borrow them,' she says, using air quotes to emphasize the word 'borrow'. 'Apparently they look good on Instagram!'

'It's brilliant to finally see this shop.'

'Yes, I used to come here and spend all my pocket money. I still remember buying my first record here.'

We walk around the intimate shop, perusing each stack of records.

'Look what I've found. Did you ever get this album in the end?' Sylvie holds up the black cover of T. Rex's *Bolan's Zip Gun*.

I look at Sylvie, amazed that she remembers.

'This is the record you were always trying to save up for, wasn't it?'

'No . . . yes,' I slip over my words, with surprise and excitement. 'Sorry, yes, you're right that was the album I was saving up for, and no, I never ended up getting it. Raj taped some of the tracks off the radio for me, but I never bought the record.'

She hands it across to me, our fingers brushing together. The simple touch makes my heart flutter for the first time in years.

I study the back cover, reading the list of tracks, remembering how much I wanted this record. Remembering trying to save up for it for months.

I rub my fingers over its battered corners, and think about the life this record itself must have had since 1975, and how it has ended up here in Bordeaux.

I suddenly hear Sylvie's voice speaking quickly in French, talking to the man behind the counter.

He nods, and in turn points to the other side of the store.

I flick my head between them, trying to understand what they're saying.

It's the first time I've heard Sylvie speak in French. Her voice, her tone, different than in English.

'We can play the record over there if you'd like to listen to it,' she says to me.

'Really?'

I nod and smile to the shopkeeper, but he's already

340

looking down, sifting through a case of newly donated records.

We walk across to where the record player is, and remove The Rolling Stones record which is playing. I carefully take the T. Rex album out of its sleeve and place the needle on the outer edge of the record.

As the opening track, 'Light of Love', plays I can't help but beam, feeling like I've been transported back in time.

I look at Sylvie, a woman who I hadn't met until today, a woman who I haven't been in touch with for decades, but a woman who I feel I know so well.

'I'd like to get it for you,' she says as the first track comes to an end. 'Seeing as I've just learnt you cycled all the way to see me, it's the least I can do.'

'Are you sure?'

'Yes. It will make me feel slightly less guilty. And you spent all your pocket money sending me those letters, and probably on your trip, so I'm the reason you never bought it.'

'That's very kind of you, thank you. Are you getting anything?'

'No, my son will only take it for a photoshoot!'

As we head back out into the sunlight together, the record under my arm, it takes my eyes a while to readjust to the light.

'Is there anywhere else in particular you'd like to see, or are you happy just to keep on strolling?' Sylvie asks, deciding on which way to turn for the next stop on our overdue Bordeaux tour.

'Actually, I'd better keep an eye on the clock.' I look down at my watch, raising my eyebrows as I see the time. 'I said to Ian that I'd meet him back by the Opera House . . . well, five minutes ago actually. It's just our flight –'

'It's OK, I understand. Although there are so many other places I'd have liked to have shown you,' Sylvie says.

We stand there awkwardly, both feeling disappointed. I nod, feeling like I should say something more.

'I guess I'll have to come back again sometime,' I eventually muster, though it's not the emphatic declaration I meant.

'Yes, you must. Although please don't wait so long to come back!' She smiles. 'And you know you can fly now, you don't have to cycle.'

'Really? I didn't realize.' I laugh, as we continue gazing at each other, trying to take in everything in our limited time together.

I wish we had another hour. Even another five minutes.

'I hope everything with your daughter is OK, and the wedding goes ahead.'

'Thank you, I'll let you know . . . Oh, I nearly forgot,' I say as I reach into my bag. 'I brought this for you. Sorry it's slightly late.'

I hand over a cassette which she looks at, confused, turning it over in her hands.

'What is this?'

'The mixtape I owed you, of my favourite songs. Remember? The plan was to deliver it to you in person, but obviously I never got to see you. It's been in my attic for decades! Now we both have something to listen to.'

Sylvie looks down at my teenage artwork.

'I don't know what to say. Thank you,' she leans across and gives me a prolonged kiss on the cheek, looking rather emotional. 'This is so lovely.'

She turns the cassette over and starts reading the list of tracks.

'"You're My Best Friend" by Queen, "You're The First, The Last, My Everything" by Barry White, "She" by Charles Aznavour, "Let Me Be The One" . . .'

'I don't think I was being that subtle with my feelings,' I cut in before she can say anything. I realize I'm blushing as I say this, but maybe she can't see through my sunburn.

She laughs, then looks up and smiles, her eyes twinkling as they meet mine.

A beeping moped interrupts our moment, forcing me to step out of the road to avoid being run over.

'OK, I'd better hurry,' I say reluctantly, wishing that I didn't need to. 'It's just back along that street, right?'

'Yes, I can walk you back?'

'Which way were you going?'

'I'm this way,' she says pointing in the opposite direction. 'But I don't mind.'

343

'No, it's fine, thank you. I can remember.' I realize we're as awkward as we would have been had we met all those years ago.

'So, I guess this is goodbye. Or, au revoir, shall we say.'

Sylvie kisses me on both cheeks, her hair tingling against my skin.

'Au revoir.'

I turn around and head ruefully in the opposite direction, looking back at her walking into the distance.

57

'Oh, Dad, look at you,' Anna exclaims, as she greets us in the airport arrivals hall. 'Whoever said that exercise was good for you?'

I don't know if she is more shocked by my sunburn or by my bruises, but she is certainly less subtle than Sylvie.

'Don't worry about me, how are you?' I ask, as she wraps her arms tightly around me. I don't let on that the embrace is hurting and she holds me for a while.

'I thought you were meant to be looking after him?' she teases Ian as she eventually lets go, ignoring my question.

She looks tired, but she is more composed than she was on the phone. Her sore, bloodshot eyes are the only give-away that something is wrong. As she skirts around the issue of the wedding, I decide to wait until we're in the car, away from prying ears, to discuss it.

'Come on, let's get out of here!' I say, as we head outside to the car park. The French sunshine has been replaced by the wet and windy British weather, and I'm relieved that we don't have to cycle back to Dorset.

'I can't believe you managed to return without either of the bikes, after all that money you spent on them!'

Anna shakes her head as she quickly clears some space for our bags in the boot.

'Yes, that wasn't the shrewdest investment,' I say as Ian indicates for me to take the front seat.

I decide against putting the seat back as I watch Ian awkwardly shuffle across the back seats. He already looks squashed as it is, bending his neck so his head doesn't touch the roof of the car.

'So, tell me about your trip?' Anna asks, as she gets in and starts the ignition, wanting to leave the car park quickly before the fee becomes any more extortionate.

'It was –'

'We can talk about the trip later,' I interrupt Ian before he can get a word out. 'Let's talk about you, darling. Tell me everything that's happened. I couldn't really hear on the phone.'

'Erm . . .' She subtly nods towards Ian in the back. I realize he is the reason she is avoiding discussing it.

'Oh, don't worry about me if you want to have a, you know, father–daughter chat. Just pretend I'm not here,' Ian says as he looms through the middle seat, doing little to convince either of us of his discretion.

'OK, thanks,' Anna says unsurely, as she passes through the ticket barrier and starts driving out of the car park. 'Well, I feel a bit stupid for making you come back early. I'm sorry that you had to cut your trip short.'

'Don't be ridiculous. I told you I'd happily come back if there was a problem. Obviously you're always my priority. So what happened? Was it your choice to cancel the wedding? Or Ollie's?'

Anna looks up, baffled. 'It's nothing to do with either of us. It's the venue who cancelled, they contacted me first thing this morning. Apparently they'd double-booked the date. I honestly don't know how they managed to do that but they said there was no chance we could get married on that day and they didn't have another date for a couple of months. And then, talk about everything going wrong at once, the wedding band called up to say the singer is ill with laryngitis.' She pauses, realizing what I said before. 'You thought one of us had called off the wedding? Why would you think that?'

'I don't know, it's just when you called, the phone kept cutting out, and I presumed . . . So you still want to get married?'

'Of course, Dad. Of course, we want to get married. That's why I was so upset. I mean we couldn't help worrying that these were signs or something, that the wedding was jinxed but no, I can't believe you thought that.'

'It's just you've not been yourself recently. You've both been acting differently around each other. There's been a lot of tension between you two. I thought maybe that something might have happened.'

She pauses, and I decide to fill the silence.

'Look, I know I'm not your mum, but we can talk about these things too.'

'Dad, it's really not that.'

She stays silent for a few seconds more, as a car overtakes at a reckless pace, sending the puddles splashing into the air.

'I don't know how to say this.'

'You can tell me anything, Anna.'

She looks hesitant, opening her mouth but not speaking.

'Honestly, there really isn't anything the matter with me and Ollie. I'd tell you if there was . . . it's actually about you.'

'About me?'

'No, I don't mean I have a problem with you. Oh. It's just Ollie's been wanting me to tell you something for the last few months. And I haven't been sure of how to say it, or if it was the right thing to say or do. He just thought you should know, and he knew it was making me stressed, that's what the tension's been about, you see.'

'What did he want you to tell me?'

A series of scenarios rush through my head.

'OK.' She takes a deep breath. 'And, like, it's not because I didn't want to tell you, it's just . . .'

'Anna, please just tell me.'

'So, the last year or so, I've been thinking that I'd like to do something more. Like Ollie is doing great at work, and of course, don't get me wrong, I really love working with you, and I love the B&B, and we have fun, but I'm not sure it's really, like, what I always wanted to be

348

doing. And I realized it's been nearly ten years now since Mum . . .'

I nod along, wondering where this is going.

'And obviously, I always wanted to be an architect, but I kind of always thought that the time had gone, and it was too late for me. But at the end of last year, I don't know why, but I thought I'd have a look at universities and courses. And some of them take mature students. Apparently I now count as a mature student, which makes me sound really old . . .'

I try to interrupt but she continues rambling as she does when she's nervous.

'So the thing is I applied.'

'That's . . .'

'And I got a place.'

'Where?'

'New York,' she says quietly.

'Well, say something then.' Anna takes her eyes briefly off the road to look across at me, the windscreen wipers frantically moving back and forth.

I'm silent.

'Dad, are you crying? This . . . this is why I didn't want to tell you. I knew you'd be upset.'

I hadn't cried in years and now it's becoming an almost daily occurrence.

'I'm not upset . . . I'm . . . I'm so proud of you, Anna. Why on earth would I be upset?'

'That I'm leaving? That I'm moving to another

country? That you're going to struggle to run the business by yourself?'

'Don't get me wrong, obviously I'm upset because I will miss you enormously. But that's nothing compared to how happy I am for you. I know what this means. You should . . . you would have gone ten years ago to study.'

I pause to compose myself.

'I'm incredibly grateful that you've given up ten years of your life to stay back and help me. I don't want to hold you back any more. I don't want you to put off following your dreams any longer.'

'Dad, stop. You're going to make me cry again.'

'I think I'm going to cry too,' Ian pokes his head through.

'I thought you weren't listening,' I smile back at him as tears drip down my face.

'Oh, yes, sorry,' he ducks back again.

'I didn't know how to tell you. I wanted to. I've tried to bring it up a few times. I told Ollie I'd tell you when we got together for Eurovision, but then you mentioned your trip, and I didn't want to tell you before because I thought it might stop you going, or ruin it, or something.'

'I'm sorry you felt that way. I wish you felt like you could have told me. I want to know all about it.'

'It's so good, Dad. It's Architectural Design at the Parsons School of Design which is one of the best in the world.'

'The best in the world! That's amazing. I've always said how talented you are. And New York, too – you're going to have such a fantastic time. Hang on, didn't we walk past a design school when we went?'

'Yes, we did, it was the same place. And Mum joked that she was going to go in and tell them they should sign me up there and then.'

'She always was right.'

'And even better, they've given me a scholarship, too. They really liked my portfolio and my essay. I'll show you all the stuff when we get back.'

'Yes, please. I'd love to see it all. What about Ollie, though? What is he going to do?'

'He's had his application for a transfer approved. His company has offices in New York too, so that's all fine.'

'How exciting for both of you. I really am so happy. Although there is one condition . . .'

Anna looks across.

'As long as you come back for Eurovision every year!'

'Of course, Dad,' she smiles.

I sit and reflect for a few seconds, trying to process the news, thinking about Anna moving to the US. Thinking about how I feel about her leaving. Thinking about what my dad would have done in this position. Thinking how the last few weeks have changed my outlook. Thinking what it means for me.

It suddenly all clicks.

'Hang on, is this why you've been trying to get me

out of the cottage more? All that trying to set me up with online dating?'

She looks rather sheepish.

'I just didn't want to leave you on your own.'

'He's not on his own. He's got me now,' Ian shouts from the back.

'I thought you weren't listening,' I joke again, before smiling at Ian, grateful for the sentiment.

'Honestly, you mustn't worry about me. As sweet as it is, I don't want to stop you, or hold you back. You've grown into the most amazing woman. I don't know what I'd have done without you by my side. But you need to go out there and live your life now.'

'But what about the cottage? You can't run it on your own.'

'Maybe I'll promote Daisy!' I joke.

'Dad, can we be serious for a second?'

'Sorry,' I say. 'It was actually something we were talking about on the trip, something I've been thinking about.'

'The cottage?'

'Yes. What do you think about us selling the place? I don't mean selling it tomorrow. Just at some point, if we find the right buyer?'

Anna glances over to me.

'I didn't think you wanted to sell it.'

'I think I was worried that I'd be letting your mum down. That I had to keep it going for her. And I wasn't sure how you felt about it. I didn't want to kick you out of your job!'

'Of course, I know Mum loved the cottage. We all do. But there was so much more in her life than just that – we don't need to hold on to it forever. We have all the happy memories. They're not going anywhere.'

'That's very true,' I nod.

'Where would you live?'

'I haven't got that far yet, but I just think that –'

'– Maybe now is the time for a fresh start for both of us?'

'Exactly.'

'Isn't this sweet. I think I'm definitely going to cry now,' Ian chirps.

'I thought you weren't listening!' both Anna and I say at the same time, and we all start laughing.

'Look at you all grown up, getting married, moving to America . . .' I put my hand across on to Anna's lap.

'You're forgetting one thing though.'

'What's that?'

'We still don't actually have anywhere to get married. That's the problem!'

The car falls silent for a moment.

'I've got an idea,' I say smiling.

58

'Replanning a wedding, decorating the cottage and setting up a marquee in the gardens doesn't sound like no stress to me! I thought the doctor said you need to rest for at least two weeks?' Anna looks at me, bemused, as I hold the metal stairs to the attic.

'It's been almost two weeks now since the crash, and anyway, I'm only holding a staircase. I can handle this amount of stress . . . just!' I smile back.

The cottage with its beautiful gardens and views seemed the perfect place to hold the ceremony, and allow their wedding to still go ahead. We just need to get it ready for the big day. Fortunately we'd already booked rooms out for friends and family to come and stay.

While my bruising is fast fading, I'm still officially meant to be resting, so Anna won't let me climb up the stairs. Fortunately, Ollie is up there sifting through all the boxes, looking for suitable decorations. With the dreaded mice, I'd rather him than me anyway.

'We've got loads of nice decorations up here,' Ollie calls down.

'It's a good thing that I kept all that stuff in the attic after all.'

As he passes down box after box, I realize just how

much baggage I've been living with over my head – literally and metaphorically – for years.

'Yes. That will be lovely. We can use that outside. Ian, can you put these fairy lights up, you know, along the front of the cottage, by the windows?' Anna has turned into a master event organizer.

'Yes, ma'am,' Ian salutes her as he heads back down the stairs again to dangle fairy lights.

I smile to him as he goes, having got more than he bargained for after staying on to assist.

I'm touched that the whole village has clubbed together to help with the catering – a task beyond Mrs Cook – and even Daisy has shown up to help out. She seems to be a much more enthusiastic party planner than housekeeper.

'I don't know what's in that one, it's not marked.' Ollie passes down another box.

Anna looks at me as if I should know.

'Don't ask me, I did tell you most of the boxes are a mystery to me!'

She grabs it off Ollie and places it on the carpet, before scoring the Sellotape with her scissors.

'Oh look, it's more of Mum's stuff,' Anna says as she sifts through a variety of Caroline's possessions.

'I'm sorry that we've not sorted all her things out before. It just never seemed like the right time.'

'It's all right, Dad. I know. Look how nice these are. Aren't these . . . ?'

She holds a pair of pearl earrings up to me.

'They're Mum's old earrings.'

'Yeah, she used to love these ones. I always remember her wearing them on special occasions. She's wearing them in the photo of the meal for my eighteenth birthday.'

It's one of the last photos we have of the three of us together.

'If I remember correctly, I think that she may have been given them by her mother.'

Anna takes out the hoop earrings she has in, and replaces them with Caroline's pearl studs. She brushes her hair back so I can see them.

'They suit you,' I say, admiring her.

Anna walks across to the mirror at the top of the stairs and looks at her reflection, moving her head from side to side.

'You look beautiful, Anna.'

She smiles and pauses, clearly considering something.

'Do you think I could wear them for the wedding?'

'Of course! Mum would have loved you wearing them. There's your something old.'

As Anna continues staring at her reflection, Ollie pauses, loitering above with the next box, not wanting to interrupt the moment.

'I really wish she could have been here for my wedding,' Anna talks to me through her reflection.

'So do I. She'd be so proud of you. Not just with your wedding, or moving to New York, but because of the woman you've become.'

59

As the evening comes, Anna and I stand outside the cottage admiring everyone's hard work.

It looks truly beautiful. The garden furniture has been rearranged into rows of seats, creating an aisle through the middle, leading to the pergola which has been decorated with draped white cloth, flowers and fairy lights. The stunning background of the countryside, hill and sea are framed in the backdrop. The cottage has been decorated with lights, and there are many small touches like the specials chalkboard rewritten in calligraphy, now reading 'Welcome to the wedding of Anna and Ollie'.

'It's amazing what you can do with some old decorations,' Anna says delightedly, the misery of the venue cancellation now forgotten.

'And thanks to your expert design touch! It really does look wonderful.'

'Much better than the other venue!'

'Exactly. So once we've got the marquee delivered, is that everything sorted?' I look across to the bottom of the field where we've left space for the marquee, in which the evening meal and dancing will take place.

'I just need to re-do the seating plan for the millionth

time . . . and then the band. I still don't know what we're doing about music,' Anna sighs.

'Leave that one with me. I'll sort it.' I wrap my arm around her as the sea breeze floats in. 'How are you feeling now about it all?'

'Good. Excited. A bit nervous.'

'Don't worry, that's normal. I still can't believe you're getting married. It's crazy how quickly you've grown up. It only seems like yesterday that I'd give you a piggyback ride up that hill, or that you'd go swimming naked in the sea there.'

'Why did you let me swim naked?' Anna looks across, most concerned.

'You would always insist on taking your costume off because you didn't want to get it wet!'

'How old was I?'

'Oh, I don't know, about sixteen,' I joke.

'You'd better not mention that in your speech,' she rolls her eyes.

'There's a lot worse than that!'

She shakes her head.

'I'm sorry, Dad, that I didn't tell you before about New York.'

'No, I understand. It's just been the two of us for so long now. I hope you now know you can tell me anything.'

'What about you, then? I hear I'm not the only one who has been keeping secrets,' Anna jokingly tuts.

'What? Have you found something in the attic?'

'Is there something incriminating in the attic?!' she jokes, exuding mock horror. 'No, Ian told me.'

I look back at her, confused.

'He told me about Sylvie.'

'Oh.'

'Oh?'

'I told him not to tell you.'

'But why didn't you tell me, Dad?'

'I know you were the one pushing me to contact her, but I wasn't sure how you really felt about it all. I didn't know if it was a bit weird me getting in touch with someone who I knew before Mum.'

'I don't have a problem with it. Honestly. I'm pleased for you.'

'Thank you,' I smile. 'It's been nice writing to Sylvie again.'

'And Ian said that you two got on well when you met?'

'Yes, it was really nice to finally meet her after all these years, and we did have a lovely time in Bordeaux, but it was too short.'

'I know, I can't believe I interrupted your meeting. Obviously, I wouldn't have made you change your plans had I known. Why didn't you say anything?'

'Because you'll always come first, Anna. Wherever you are.'

As the seagulls bicker loudly in the sky, she takes my hand.

'If we're really doing this fresh start thing, I think we

should do it properly. It sounds like you might have a new friend in Sylvie, or possibly something more?'

'Hold your horses.'

'OK, well, I just wanted to say that's all that I want, and all Mum would have wanted, for you to be happy.'

'Do you reckon so?'

'I know so.'

We continue gazing out across the landscape as the sun sets. I look up to the bench on the hill and smile to myself.

'Why don't you invite her to the wedding?' Anna suddenly exclaims, excited by the idea.

'Sylvie?'

'Yes, of course, Sylvie.'

'I don't know. I think that's a bit much.'

'Dad, you cycled to France to see her, nothing is ever going to be a bit much compared to that.'

I chuckle, knowing she's right.

'But it's only in a few days. It's very short notice. I doubt she can just drop everything like that.'

'Surely you know better than anyone how important it is to act before it's too late. Look at Mum and Raj. Who knows, none of us might be here for as long as we think. If she can't come she can't come, but you could ask. Just please hurry up and ask her before I redo the seating plan!'

'I'll think about it, but thank you. I love you, Anna.'

'I love you too, Dad.'

As we turn to head back inside the cottage, to join

Ian and Ollie for an evening of board games, I admire Caroline's favourite sunflowers which have transformed from before our trip.

'Mum's flowers have just bloomed,' I comment, pointing to the golden yellow flowers which tower above the window sill.

'Yes they have! They are beautiful, aren't they? Did you know sunflowers represent new beginnings?' Anna smiles. 'Maybe it's a sign.'

'Maybe it is.'

From: Sylvie, To: Simon

Simon, I hope you had a safe flight back, and all is OK with Anna and the wedding? It was so nice, and unexpected, to see you. Do keep in touch, and let me know if you're ever back in France. Sylvie x

From: Simon, To: Sylvie

Hi Sylvie,

Thank you – yes, we made it back safely and the wedding is going ahead fortunately, but we're hosting it at our cottage instead.

Sorry for my delayed response, but as I'm sure you can imagine it's all been a bit manic here. It was lovely to see you too, and I'm just sorry I couldn't stay longer – especially after waiting so many years to see you.

I know this will sound quite out there, but I wondered if you fancied being my Plus One for the wedding on Friday? I appreciate it's very short notice, and obviously, I understand if you can't, or don't want to. But if you can get a flight you could stay in one of the rooms here at the B&B, and then I could show you around Dorset and Bristol afterwards.

Maybe we could finally do that exchange we wanted to do when we were teenagers?

I hope to hear back from you soon.

Simon x

60

It is a light, warm summer's evening; a gentle breeze flows in from the sea, and the sun which has shone all day slowly starts to make its descent. The cottage and gardens couldn't look more beautiful, decorated with all the old fairy lights that we found stuffed away in the attic. The day may not have gone totally to plan, but the important things did. Even my speech got a few laughs.

'How did you convince the band to perform? I thought they cancelled,' Anna leans across and asks excitedly as the tables in the marquee are cleared away to make room for the dance floor. I sit to her right, as Ollie sits the other side, still beaming with delight.

'It was only the singer who was sick, so I asked the band if they'd still be able to come, and well, I found you a new singer.'

'How did you manage that? Where did you find them?'

'Just an old friend,' I smile.

I point to Ian, who is dressed – for once – modestly in a smart black tuxedo. The weight we lost on the trip has benefitted both of our waistlines.

'Ian?!' Anna replies, looking shocked and unconvinced. She raises her left eyebrow.

'You're very privileged. It's the first time he's ever performed as himself. He's been rehearsing with the band all morning.'

'But is he actually any good though?'

'Do you think I'd let him perform at your wedding if he wasn't? I promise you he's fantastic,' I respond, realizing that I've probably never complimented him before.

'Good evening everyone,' Ian speaks into the microphone, testing if it is working. We turn to face the band, the marquee almost instantaneously transformed from restaurant to nightclub.

'My name is . . . my name is Ian Pratt,' he says proudly for the first time in his life, 'and this fabulous band behind me are the Dorset Dreamers. Now, without further ado, please can the bride and groom make their way to the front for their first dance.'

Everyone applauds, and whoops, and cheers, as they clear a path for Anna and Ollie to take to the dance floor.

Ian smirks as the band starts playing. After all these years of pretending to be Bowie, the first time he decides to perform as himself, and the song that Anna and Ollie have picked for their first dance is 'Heroes' by none other than David Bowie. At least he knows the lyrics perfectly to this one.

I look across at Ian smiling as he sings, and then at Anna and Ollie dancing together, and I'm not sure who I am most proud of.

I may be biased, but she looks beautiful in her modern, open-back ivory gown. Her brown hair is tied up, her make-up minimal showing her natural beauty. Caroline's earrings twinkling in the light. I can't stop smiling as I look at her and Ollie, happy together.

Anna was never into dancing in school, but clearly she and Ollie have been practising as they shimmy and sway together, before she beckons everyone else to join her as the chorus begins.

I laugh as Mrs Cook and Sue from the Post Office rush to be the first on to the dance floor. It seems that Ian finally has groupies of his own.

As everyone else celebrates joyously, I step back and out of the marquee, leaving Ian to revel in his new catalogue of songs. I carry on walking, slowly climbing up the hill to the castle ruins. Whilst I can still hear Ian's voice reverberating through the air, the countryside is as tranquil and peaceful as ever. I gaze across at the cows, who are wondering what all the fuss is about.

As I reach the top, I take a seat on the bench and reflect on all the changes of the last few months. I look down at the cottage differently now, smiling as I do so. Caroline's dream wasn't just to open a B&B, it was for us to create a happy family here. And that is just what we did.

I turn to stare at the sea, watching the rolling waves in the distance, wondering about the future.

'So this is where you got to.' The voice makes me jump.

I look down the path and see Sylvie. I was so distracted by my thoughts that I didn't notice her climbing up.

'How are you doing?' I say, standing up, walking down towards her, and extending my hand to help her up the last part of the incline.

'I don't think these shoes are the best for climbing hills! Wow, look at this view.' As we sit down on the bench, she looks around, admiring the panorama. 'This is nearly as nice as France!' She winks.

'Sorry I've not been able to spend much time with you today. I invite you all the way over here to the wedding, and then I'm busy chatting to everyone –'

'– No, there's no need to apologize. I completely understand. I've had a lovely time. Although some woman did seem to be asking me a lot of questions as if she was interviewing me!'

There's Shirley's lead story for the Gazette *this week.*

Sylvie smiles sweetly, finding her day most amusing.

'So you're happy you came?'

'Of course. You're the only man who has ever cycled six hundred miles to see me, not once but twice . . . I could hardly say no, now, could I?' She smiles. 'It wasn't what I was expecting to be doing this weekend, but that's a good thing. What about you? Have you been able to enjoy it?'

'Yes, it's been lovely. I just wish that Caroline could have been here to see it . . . sorry, is that weird me saying that to you?' I turn to face her, worrying I've said the wrong thing.

'No, not at all. You can talk about Caroline as much as you want to with me. I might not talk about my ex as much because he was an idiot, but there you go,' she smiles.

'Thank you,' I say.

'Honestly, you can talk to me about anything and everything.'

'Just like we used to.'

'Exactly.'

We both look down at the marquee, the flashing multicolour lights inside changing its appearance.

'I thought after everyone's gone home tomorrow, we could take a trip to Bristol so I can finally show you the city and my old school? Maybe we could see if we could have a look round inside, and I could show you where I used to write to you, and –'

'I'd love to,' she interrupts, smiling, placing her hand on top of mine.

'Good. We've just got to get rid of everyone first!' I joke.

'We'd better get back before they send a search party to look for you.'

As we walk back through the little white gate into the garden – the gate that Ian nearly broke a few weeks ago when he came back into my life – the band strikes up again.

I immediately recognize those first few notes.

'One for the oldies next. This is "Hot Love" by T. Rex, and it's dedicated to Simon, the father of the bride,' Ian announces over the microphone, winking at me as he sees us walk back into the marquee.

Anna looks across and smiles.

'I might have put in a request earlier with Ian,' Sylvie whispers into my ear. 'I think it's time we showed all these youngsters how it's done. Would you like to dance with me?'

'I'd love to.'

Acknowledgements

When I was on a writing course four years ago, aspiring to be a novelist, I could barely have dreamt that I would celebrate the publication of my debut novel with David Nicholls and Mike Gayle. Nor could I have imagined that the event would take place on Zoom, amidst a global pandemic.

Whilst *The Flip Side* may have been published in the strangest of times, and without some of the traditional highlights (no launch party, bookshops being shut, etc.), I have been overjoyed to find such a wonderful community in the world of publishing. As I've written this, the notoriously difficult second novel, from the confines of my studio flat, I've been so grateful for the camaraderie of other debut authors and the support of experienced writers.

I would also like to thank:

Stephen Burrough, whose real-life bike ride across France inspired this novel.

Florie Fournol for being my Bordeaux guide and go-to France expert.

Rebecca Hilsdon, Clare Bowron and everyone at Penguin Michael Joseph for their guidance and expertise, and for helping me to tell this story in the best possible way.

Hannah Ferguson and the whole team at Hardman & Swainson for their help, advice and encouragement.

My family and friends – here's to hoping that by time this book hits the shops we can celebrate properly!

And, of course, you. The readers. For picking up my book, for posting about it on social media, and for sending me lovely messages. Thank you enormously.

Enjoyed
THE WAY BACK TO YOU?
Then dive into . . .

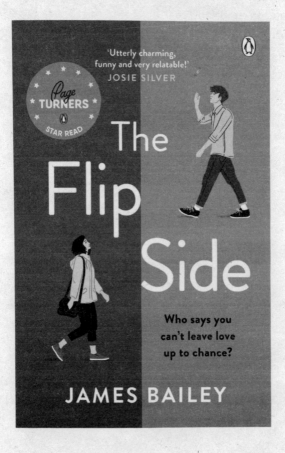

Available now

I

One hundred and thirty-five metres above London, with one of the most spectacular city views in the world as your backdrop, who could say no?

I now know who could say no.

Jade Toogood.

The girl I had called my girlfriend for four years. The woman who, until just a few moments earlier, I planned on spending the rest of my life with. The person who I am now trapped inside a glass capsule with, 443 feet above ground.

She could say no.

Rather, she had said no.

New Year's Eve. The London Eye. The girl of my dreams. A ring. A future together.

What could possibly go wrong?

I planned everything so meticulously. It was all meant to be perfect. The perfect end to the year, the perfect start to the next. I spent months secretly scouring websites, magazines and shops, looking at rings, thinking of ways to ask, waiting for the right moment. It was only when Jade mentioned how much she wanted to go on the London Eye that I settled on it for the chosen place. The venue for the story we would repeat over and over again to our friends, family and future grandchildren.

The glossy brochure advertising the 'Proposal Package' certainly sold it – if you ignore the exorbitant cost, what could be more romantic than hiring a private capsule? The pages were full of joyous couples smiling, laughing, kissing. It featured beautiful-looking people shedding tears of happiness. There were high-definition images of the magnificent view. The word 'magical' was emphatically printed in bold type. 'Special', it said. 'The perfect romantic setting'. There was no disclaimer declaring that it might not always be perfect. There was no small print proffering the warning she may say no. There was no money-back guarantee if she did. After all, as the tagline declared, who could say no?

We are not even high enough to witness the promised iconic skyline when it all starts to go wrong. We have only just boarded our capsule. Our private capsule which, for the next thirty minutes, is reserved for just us, a box of luxury chocolate truffles and a bottle of champagne. I don't even like champagne. But what with the nerves, and the pressure of the situation, I down a glass before we even set off.

I pop both the bottle and the question too early.

If there is a playbook for London Eye proposals then I imagine it would instruct you to get down on one knee as you reach the highest point of the rotation, when you have the maximum impact of the spectacular 360-degree view. Not before you even leave the ground.

But I don't wait.

Maybe she would have said yes if she had been faced

with the wondrous sights of Big Ben, Wren's baroque architecture and the modern metropolis of the City. Instead, as I utter the fateful words 'Will you marry me?', we are face-to-face with the London Dungeon. The question scares her more than the blood-soaked billboards.

'No, Josh, no.' Jade stares straight into my eyes. A horribly blank expression. She looks at me like I'm a stranger she's never met, rather than the man she lives with. The man she is meant to love.

We met while working together in Bristol, the city in which I grew up and where we live. I took what was intended to be a temporary job at a hotel after studying History at King's College London, simply as a way to tide myself over until I decided what I wanted to do in life. Jade started a few years later, after her father, the owner, found her a job as a receptionist. It wasn't quite love at first sight, but just as we both fell into the career, we soon fell into a relationship. Four years later, after we'd been a couple for three and lived together for two, did she not think that I would ask soon?

'Marriage, Josh? Really? What are you thinking? I said I wanted you to take me on the London Eye, not for you to propose to me on it.'

It can't have come as too much of a surprise. Does she think you get champagne, truffles and a private capsule all for your standard £24 ticket?

'OK, I'm sorry. Obviously I've got the timing wrong. But why would you not even consider it? Why are you so adamant we're not ready? You know how much I love you, right? We want to spend our lives together? Isn't this the next step?'

'You can stand up now,' she says bluntly, ignoring my questions, as I realize I am still on one knee, ring in hand. For someone who is usually so touchy-feely, she moves as far away from me as is possible.

I get back on my feet and look out of the capsule in disbelief. Just as the perfect moment is annihilated, so too are all the happy times I have spent around this area. Forever ruined in my mind. The childhood memories of family trips to the capital, when everything seemed bigger and brighter and generally more impressive, to the student days and nights spent catching an art-house film at the BFI, pretentiously perusing the stalls of the booksellers underneath Waterloo Bridge, or getting a last-minute discounted ticket to a play at the National, which I wouldn't understand but I'd pretend to enjoy.

The South Bank has always been my favourite place in London. The paved street snaking alongside the river, encompassing so many of the city's sights, full of tourists pulling suitcases and mums pushing prams, joggers navigating flocks of schoolkids, skaters weaving in and out of pigeons, couples holding hands, cameras and coffee cups. I know the area well. So well that I could tell you that the roof of the National Theatre is home to around 60,000 bees, or that the Shell Mex House opposite has the largest clock face in the UK. I could tell you all these things but I couldn't have told you that my girlfriend doesn't love me the way I love her. I couldn't have told you she would say no. And that is now all I can think of. I now never want to see this place again. Most of all, I don't want to be here right now. I want to be somewhere else.

Except I can't. I can't be anywhere else, not for another twenty-eight minutes at least.

He just wanted a decent book to read ...

Not too much to ask, is it? It was in 1935 when Allen Lane, Managing Director of Bodley Head Publishers, stood on a platform at Exeter railway station looking for something good to read on his journey back to London. His choice was limited to popular magazines and poor-quality paperbacks – the same choice faced every day by the vast majority of readers, few of whom could afford hardbacks. Lane's disappointment and subsequent anger at the range of books generally available led him to found a company – and change the world.

'We believed in the existence in this country of a vast reading public for intelligent books at a low price, and staked everything on it'
Sir Allen Lane, 1902–1970, founder of Penguin Books

The quality paperback had arrived – and not just in bookshops. Lane was adamant that his Penguins should appear in chain stores and tobacconists, and should cost no more than a packet of cigarettes.

Reading habits (and cigarette prices) have changed since 1935, but Penguin still believes in publishing the best books for everybody to enjoy. We still believe that good design costs no more than bad design, and we still believe that quality books published passionately and responsibly make the world a better place.

So wherever you see the little bird – whether it's on a piece of prize-winning literary fiction or a celebrity autobiography, political tour de force or historical masterpiece, a serial-killer thriller, reference book, world classic or a piece of pure escapism – you can bet that it represents the very best that the genre has to offer.

Whatever you like to read – trust Penguin.